Happily Ever After *Collection*

New York Times Bestselling Author
Melanie Moreland

D1319191

Dear Reader,

Thank you for selecting my collection of Happily Ever Afters. You may recognize a few of these titles as they were featured in a charity anthologies. Although donating my words to raise funds for these worthy causes, I am sad to see my characters gone after a short time.

These short stories have all been expanded to contain new content from their original published version.

Be sure to sign up for my newsletter for up to date information on new releases, exclusive content and sales.
Or visit https://bit.ly/MMorelandNewsletter

Always fun - never spam!

xoxo,
Melanie

Happily Ever After Collection by Melanie Moreland
The Taste of You Copyright © #1159265
Stitches Copyright © #1172039
Love Under Construction Copyright © #1172037
House Arrest Copyright © #1159265

ISBN Ebook 978-1-988610-41-2
Paperback 978-1-988610-40-5
All rights reserved

MORELAND

BOOKS INC.

Edited by
Lisa Hollett—Silently Correcting Your Grammar
Copyediting by Deb Beck

Cover design by Karen Hulseman
Feed Your Dreams Designs

DEDICATION

For my readers
Summer and love—what better combination?

But given that this is 2020, and summer has effectively been cancelled,
here are some short stories to keep you entertained and safe.

Because no matter what is happening out there, we all need love.

So—enjoy.

Matthew - always and forever.

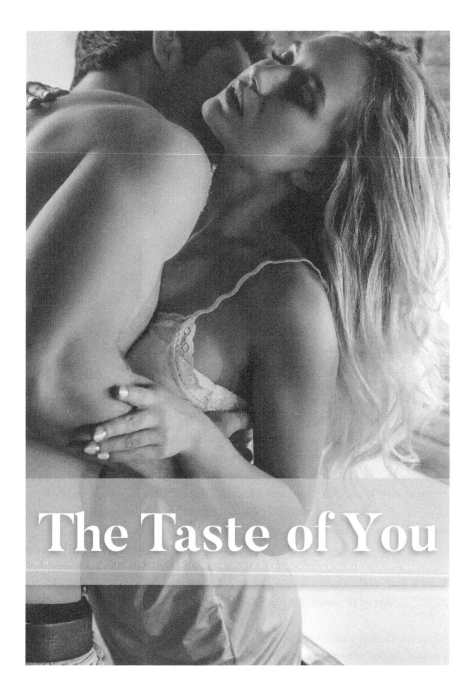

The Taste of You

called out of town and I had to bring you here, of all places, on my anniversary."

I frowned. "I still don't understand why you just didn't cancel?"

"Julia, Julia, Julia. Don't you read the paper? Keep up with the local news?"

I sipped my water. "Rather busy here, Melinda. Between school, midterms, and two jobs, I barely have time to sleep, never mind read the paper. What does that have to do with this place anyway?"

She sighed. "This *place*, as you so charmingly call it, is booked solid for the next six months. Mark had to call in a personal favor to get us in here tonight. Creations is the hottest restaurant in town and so unique. The head chef and owner is brilliant. Mark went to school with him years ago, and they're still friends. He arranged this for us."

"Oh."

I looked around. I had to admit, as far as fancy restaurants went, it was lovely. The rooms were warm and inviting without being pretentious. And the menu had been different. There were only four set items to choose from, and the rest changed daily. Whatever was local and fresh was what was featured that day. Our meals weren't even listed on the menu—they were created especially for us, Gerard, our waiter, had informed us.

"The entire meal has been prepared only for you." He poured us some wine. "I assure you, you will enjoy it."

The food was lost on me. All of it was. Admittedly, this was the kind of place I never went to. My idea of dinner out usually consisted of something that came in a box or a plastic container that I could eat while running from one of my jobs, to school, or the library. It was rare when I actually sat down for a meal.

I took in all the people enjoying their dinners and the warm ambiance. I looked across at Melinda, noticing how comfortable she was in this gracious setting, and once again, I glanced down at my simple yellow dress and sighed. I didn't belong in a place like this—it was apparent now more than ever.

"Excuse me."

I started at the sudden appearance of a tall, dark-haired man in an immaculate white chef's coat standing beside our table. He didn't look happy.

"Byron!" Melinda smiled and held out her hand. I watched as his long fingers encompassed her tiny ones, and he bent down and brushed a light kiss on her cheek.

"Melinda," he murmured. "Lovely to see you again. Happy anniversary." He glanced my way, confused. "Where is Mark?"

"This is my friend, Julia Nichols. Mark was called away this afternoon on an emergency, and she agreed to have dinner with me tonight in his place. I didn't want to give up the chance to come here after all the trouble you went to for us."

He held out his hand to me. "Julia."

Wordlessly, I placed my hand in his, feeling the warmth of his fingers as they squeezed mine. He seemed to freeze for a moment before his grip tightened around my fingers again, and then he withdrew his hand.

He turned to Melinda. "Perhaps it was a good night for him not to dine here. I understand your meal was not satisfactory?"

She shook her head quickly. "No, Byron, it was divine."

His brow furrowed. "Your plate came back virtually untouched."

"Um, that was mine," I advised him.

His eyes snapped back to me, his bright-blue gaze holding my own. "You didn't enjoy your dinner, Julia?"

"No, it was, ah, fine. Really."

He arched one eyebrow, turning to face me fully, his vivid gaze piercing. His voice was low when he spoke. I felt myself shrink into my seat under his stare.

"*Fine?* I believe Gerard said you described it as passable. I will not accept that any dish which came from my kitchen was simply *passable*. Allow me to make something else for you."

I could feel Melinda's glare across the table, and I scrambled to assure him. "I used the wrong word. Really, it was great. Really…*really*…great."

His expression turned to utter disbelief, and he leaned down closer to me. "So *great* you didn't even want to take it home with you?"

I swallowed, my throat suddenly dry. "I don't have a fridge to keep it fresh," I whispered, feeling sheepish.

He stood straight, his eyes locked on me. "Let me prepare you something else. I insist." He drew in a deep breath. "Please, allow me to do that."

I shook my head. "I had a late lunch. Really, I'm fine."

"Byron."

He turned to Melinda.

"She never eats very much," she assured him quietly. "She meant no disrespect. The meals were amazing. Truly."

He stood silently for a minute, his hands clenched at his sides, his brow furrowed. With a sharp dip of his chin, he spoke. "As you wish. Enjoy your dessert, ladies. I hope it proves to be more than *passable*." Abruptly, he turned and strode toward the kitchen. I watched as he stopped and said something to our waiter, before disappearing through the kitchen door.

I turned to Melinda. "Wow. He's intense. He and Mark are friends?" I found that hard to believe. Mark was the most laid-back person I had ever met.

She nodded. "They went to high school and university together. When Byron left to go to culinary school, they stayed in touch. Mark was thrilled when he decided to move back to Toronto and open this restaurant."

We were quiet as Gerard placed our dessert and coffee in front of us. When he left, I leaned forward. "I didn't mean to insult him or his food, Melinda. Really, I didn't."

She smiled. "I know that. Byron *is* very intense. He has very high standards and is incredibly picky about his restaurant. Which is why it has been such a success, I think." She chuckled. "I doubt many plates get sent back uneaten." She mock-glared at me. "Did you eat at McDonald's again today?"

I nodded. "I had just ordered when you called."

She gaped. "And you still ate it? Knowing we were coming here?"

I shrugged. "I know what I'm getting at McDonald's, Melinda. I wasn't sure about this place."

She chuckled as she stirred the cream into her coffee and added some chocolate shavings and whipped cream that came with it. It was a lovely touch.

"Good thing Byron didn't know that piece of information. The fact that you would eat at Rotten Ronnie's and barely touch his cuisine might send him over the edge. I pity the chefs in the kitchen if that happened."

I made a horrified face at her, then grinned. "Our little secret."

She indicated my plate. "Eat your dessert please, Julia. I don't think I could take another visit from the kitchen."

I agreed. The way Byron Lord looked at me? I didn't want another visit either.

～

I watched Melinda drive away and sighed, grateful dinner was over. I shook my head as I made my way to my car where I had parked at the edge of the lot. My car was older and run-down, but all I could afford. It had been as out of place in the parking lot as I was in the restaurant.

No bill had been offered at the end of our meal, and Gerard refused any sort of tip, saying the meal in its entirety had been looked after by Chef Lord, with his compliments. No doubt he was just anxious to get the troublemaker out of his restaurant. I hoped I hadn't caused a problem for Mark with his friend.

"So, you find my cuisine stuffy, do you, Julia?"

Startled, I spun around to find Byron Lord leaning against the hood of a car, looking irate. His chef's jacket hung loosely from his shoulders, and he was smoking a cigar in short, angry puffs. I swallowed the sudden lump in my throat. Melinda and I had one of the last reservations of the night and we had lingered over dessert, so the lot was now almost vacant and I was alone with Byron.

"Do you wait for all your customers in the parking lot?" I managed to gasp out.

He shook his head. "Only the dissatisfied ones. So, you would be the first."

"I apologize, Mr. Lord. Obviously, I've insulted you, and that was not my intention."

"Chef."

"Pardon me?"

"At my restaurant, I am addressed as Chef Lord."

I bit my lip. He *was* angry. He was a friend of Mark's, who was very dear to me, so I needed to fix this.

I drew in a deep breath and used the politest tone I could muster. "Chef Lord, I apologize." I offered contritely. "I'm a simple girl. Your food is wonderful, I'm sure, but it's just lost on someone like me."

He pushed off the car and stepped toward me. "Someone like you? I don't understand."

I shrugged and waved my hand toward the restaurant. "I never went out to dinner as a child or even as a teenager. Meals in my house came from a can or a box." I chuckled. "I never learned to cook, so they still do. Food is just a necessity for me." I looked at him, the strangest feeling welling up inside me. I wanted him to know I wasn't insulting him. I didn't want him upset. "I know for someone like you, food is your life. No doubt you live it twenty-four hours a day." I shrugged again. "If it weren't for the fact that I had to eat to keep going, I wouldn't bother. It's just fuel for me."

His eyes widened. "You don't like to eat?"

I thought about it. "It's not that I don't like to eat. I just don't really get any enjoyment out of it. I don't think I have very good taste buds. Everything basically tastes the same to me."

For a minute, he was quiet. When he spoke, his voice was softer and without the trace of anger it had held previously.

"That is a shame. You're missing so much."

I shook my head. "I think that, like someone born without one of their senses, I never know to miss it. It's just the way of it for me."

He edged closer. "Food is a vital part of life, yes. But it is meant to be savored. Enjoyed. I love spending time, selecting the right ingredients, blending them together so they are perfect. Mixing, measuring, *tasting* as I create a dish is critical. The experience is incredible. I spend hours perfecting a recipe, making it flawless. One ingredient can change the flavor, the composition of an entire dish." He paused his fervent speech and sighed quietly. "Watching people eat a meal I have cooked and seeing their reaction is…almost orgasmic at times."

I blinked at him. He was mesmerizing in his passion. His face came alive, his hands gestured in the air, and his voice was rich and vibrant.

"I wish I could feel that way about it, but I don't. I can't understand your passion," I whispered. "I'm not sure I feel that way about anything in life, to be perfectly honest."

He studied me intently. "What did you have for lunch today?" he demanded suddenly.

My eyes widened. I shook my head, remembering Melinda's words.

"What? Tell me."

I straightened my shoulders. I didn't have to defend myself to this man. "A cheeseburger."

"From a box or a package?"

"Um, McDonald's."

His expression was filled with revulsion. "*McDonald's?* And that filled you up so much you couldn't eat the entree I made for you?"

I shook my head. "I-I didn't know you had made it yourself."

He nodded. "I made your dinner. I thought it was for Mark and Melinda, so I made sure I looked after that ticket. I wanted it to be perfect for them. It was perfect. But you barely touched it…because your *cheeseburger* had filled you up and left you so satisfied you couldn't eat *my cuisine*."

I felt my face flush. "I had fries, too…" I mumbled. "And I like the food at McDonald's," I added.

The look on his face was pure horror. "*That* is not food. It is overprocessed, unknown ingredients, kept warm on the heating rack for a couple of hours, *garbage*! You shouldn't be eating that!"

I snorted. Didn't he watch TV? All their commercials gave you the information. "It's 100% beef, Byron. And I order it with extra pickles, so they make it fresh," I huffed at him.

His head fell forward, and I was sure I heard a whimper escape his throat. "Oh my God," he muttered.

He stepped closer and thrust out his hand. "Julia, I need you to come with me."

I stared at his hand. "What?"

He moved his hand impatiently. "I need you to come with me. Now." His face gentled as he saw my confusion. "Please, I won't bite. I just want to hold your hand."

Tentatively, I placed my hand in his, finding an odd sense of comfort as his fingers closed around mine, his large palm encompassing mine easily. Wordlessly, he tugged me beside him, and I followed him into the back door of the restaurant. The kitchen was being cleaned, and Byron continued to lead me through the building, up the stairs, and into a private office.

Gently, he removed the jacket from my shoulders and indicated a chair for me to sit in. He excused himself and told me to make myself comfortable before exiting the room. As I waited, I wandered and looked around, noticing the many diplomas and awards he had scattered on shelves and hanging on the wall. There were various pictures of him in the kitchen, standing outside Creations, smiling, looking totally different from the serious man I had seen this evening. He looked so open and warm; his grin caused my heart to clench a little. His brown hair was slightly curly, shorter in the front, and longer in the back. His shoulders were broad, his suits obviously custom tailored for him. There was a dimple on his left cheek just above his full lips, and his rich blue eyes sparkled with life in the pictures. He was very attractive.

Music played softly from hidden speakers, the dulcet tones of the Beatles making me smile. I thought of how he had said, "I just want to hold your hand." Had he been quoting a song? Or had he been making sure I didn't run away from him? Sitting down, I shook my head. What was I doing here? What did he want with me? I stood to leave as he walked back in, carrying a tray.

"Going somewhere?"

"Look, Byron, I'm sorry. I didn't mean to insult you…" I trailed off as he set down the tray and covered my mouth with one finger.

"You didn't insult me. But I can't let you go on like this anymore."

"Excuse me?"

"I'm going to teach you to love food."

I stared at him. "What?"

He grinned, and for the first time since meeting him, I saw the man in the photos. I also realized he had removed his chef's jacket and was wearing a simple gray T-shirt that clung to his sculpted chest and arms. He held up his hands in supplication.

"All right, maybe saying I will teach you to love food is a rather large goal. But I can teach you to enjoy it, savor it." He paused and shuddered. "To stay away from McDonald's."

I laughed. "I can afford McDonald's, Byron. I don't think I can afford to eat here every day." I shook my head. "I don't think I can afford to eat here once a year. This is really a wasted effort on your part."

His face changed and became serious. Lightly, he pushed on my shoulders, so I sat back down in the chair, and he sat across from me. He smiled as he leaned forward and brushed the hair away from my cheek. "If I have my way, you'll be able to eat here or anywhere I am and not have to worry about the cost. Trust me."

I stared at him as he busied himself with the tray.

What did he mean by that? And why did I want so badly to please him? To be with him in this room?

Suddenly, I was even more nervous than before.

He turned to me, smiling. "Now, we begin."

CHAPTER 2

BYRON

The nervous look on her face was priceless. Her strawberry-blond hair shone under the lights, the curls falling over her shoulders. Her green eyes were wide and anxious.

"Relax, Julia, this isn't going to hurt."

She eyed the contents of the tray in front of me suspiciously. "What is all that?"

I grinned at her. "Just some tidbits. I want to see if I can find out your reactions to different flavors and textures."

She made a face.

"What?"

"I don't like...textures."

She didn't like textures, yet she ate the crap they called food at McDonald's. All that consisted of was texture held together with fat and salt. I chuckled, already enjoying this. "I'll remember that."

Leaning forward, I picked up a small piece of Brie cheese and lifted it to her lips. "Open up," I instructed. For a second, I thought she would refuse, but then she shut her eyes and allowed me to feed her the small morsel. "Chew it slowly. Tell me what you taste. What it feels like on your tongue." I sat back, watching her, already moving ahead in my mind to what I would feed her next.

"Well?" I prompted after she had chewed and swallowed.

She opened her eyes and looked at me sheepishly. "It was cheese?"

11

"Yes. How did it taste?"

"Um, okay?"

I shook my head, reminding myself to be patient. If she had replied it was buttery, rich, and creamy in her mouth, we wouldn't be sitting here.

"Nothing else?"

"Soft?"

I nodded. At least she got that right. I offered her a piece of apple to clear her palate and watched as she nibbled on it.

"Aren't you having any?" she asked.

Smiling, I obliged and picked up a piece of the juicy apple, enjoying its crisp texture. That seemed to make her more comfortable, and I saw her relax a little.

Next, I fed her a small piece of Swiss cheese, secretly enjoying the fact that I had neglected to bring anything to feed her with other than my fingers. A fact that I noticed she hadn't objected to.

She chewed, and a slight frown appeared on her face.

"Well?"

"That was cheese again, right?"

"Yes."

"It was harder than the other one."

"Anything else?"

"It was dry?"

I fought back a groan. "You didn't find it slightly nutty or sharp on your tongue? Whereas the first bite was smooth and rich?"

She looked at me as if I had two heads. "Neither one tasted like the cheese I get on my burger."

I couldn't help the groan that escaped my mouth this time.

She began to stand. "This is a waste of your time, Byron."

My hand shot out, grasping hers, and I stopped her from leaving her chair. "No. It's not. We're just getting started. Trust me, Julia."

She looked at me quizzically. "Why is this so important to you?"

For a minute, I was silent. I had no idea what to tell her, except that from the second I had seen her sitting there, looking so lovely with her uniquely colored hair swept away from her face and her pretty yellow dress, a vivid contrast to the black leather chair she sat in, she had captivated me. Her large green eyes darted around the room, and she looked uncomfortable and almost vulnerable in my dining room. I had felt drawn to her—she seemed lost, and I didn't like that. When I had left the kitchen to find out why Melinda had not enjoyed her dinner, I was so focused on the full plate that came back, I hadn't even noticed it wasn't Mark sitting across from Melinda, but rather this appealing woman, until she had spoken.

Earlier, I had arranged for my maître d', Gerard, to be the one looking after the table and that I was preparing their meal myself. Mark had told me he wanted the evening to be very special, and I was pleased to be able to help my friend, even planning a different dish for them. The fact that the dish was deemed passable and came back barely touched had shocked me, and I had immediately gone to find out why. Faced with Julia's wide-eyed reaction instead of Mark's calm gaze, I had been momentarily stunned. That he was called away was unfortunate. Although, right now I couldn't find it in myself to really care, since I was sitting across from Julia, alone in my office. I shook my head as I realized she was now gazing at me warily, wondering why I wasn't answering her question.

Looking at her, I knew the answer. Somehow, I knew she was going to be important to me, and I wanted to share this part of my life with her. I had a strange desire to feed her and look after her, but if I told her that, I had a feeling she would be out of the chair and gone before I could even blink, so I simply shrugged. "I enjoy a challenge."

She shook her head sadly. "Some challenges are insurmountable, Byron."

I realized I was still holding her hand, and I squeezed it softly before letting it go. Leaning forward, I picked up a small piece of melon. I wanted to see how she reacted to something slightly sweeter. "Not this. Open up."

~

TWO WEEKS LATER

"Well?"

"It looks good, Byron. But if you gave me a garlic stick to dip in the sauce, I would probably like it more."

I shook my head. "It's fresh marinara, Julia." Quickly, I rolled some homemade penne in the sauce and lifted the fork to her mouth. "Taste."

She chewed slowly, and her expressive face brightened. "Hey, I like that!"

I smiled at my small victory. It hadn't taken me long to figure out Julia's palate was so used to bland, overprocessed, oversalted food that her taste buds didn't know how to handle other flavors. For the past two weeks, every chance I was able to tempt her away from her busy schedule, I had her in my office or perched up on the counter beside me in the kitchen, getting her to taste things I would make for her. I kept the herbs and spices subtle, using layers of ingredients I would combine to see how she would react to them. So far, I knew without a doubt, she enjoyed pasta, chicken, and vegetables, as long as they were simply prepared. Anything too over-spiced or rich sent her taste buds into overdrive. I also discovered she disliked salmon intensely, tolerated milder fish, and she had a sweet tooth.

I speared more penne and fed it to her. I loved watching her eat when she actually was enjoying it. Her expression was one of surprise and delight. It thrilled me to be the one to put that look on her face. I found myself looking forward to these little experiments more every day, thinking of things to tempt her with. Not only did I enjoy discovering what she liked and disliked, I enjoyed discovering things about her. She was highly intelligent and witty, and our conversations left me smiling and wanting more. More conversations, more time with her, more *of* her.

"You listen to the Beatles a lot," she mused one night. We were alone in the kitchen, the staff having left. She'd had a late class, and I had been waiting for her, preparing her meal and listening to music.

"Yes. One of my favorites. There is a song of theirs named 'Julia'—do you know it?"

"No."

"John Lennon wrote it for his mother, although he later admitted it made him think of his feelings for Yoko as well. It's very pretty." I paused, spearing the roasted asparagus I made for her. "Like you."

Her flushed cheeks made me grin. I loved her reactions to my food—and my words.

For the first time in many years, my concentration was not solely on the restaurant or my career. I found myself distracted by the thoughts of a lovely strawberry-blond-haired girl several times a day.

I lifted another forkful, but she shook her head. "Your turn."

I grinned as I added more penne and took a much larger bite. She refused to be the only one to eat whatever I had made, saying it made her too self-conscious. The first time she had insisted, I informed her I only had the one fork, and she had snorted, took the fork from my hand, speared a piece of the beef and grinned at me.

"Open up."

When I looked at her, she rolled her eyes.

"I think we're past not being able to share a fork, Byron. We share. Everything. It's the rule."

And from then on, we did.

I sliced off some grilled chicken, watching as her eyes lit up again. "That is delicious!"

After a positive reaction from the chicken, I was disappointed to see her frown as she chewed on an herb-roasted potato. "Too much?"

She shook her head. "No, it needs something."

I was shocked. She *wanted* more flavor? Curious, I picked up a piece and tasted it. The flavors of rosemary, pepper, and thyme blended with the olive oil were subtle but pleasing. Not too much, not too little, just right for her.

"What does it need?" I asked encouragingly.

She paused as if thinking and then grinned innocently. "Ketchup."

I gaped at her. *No.*

She winked and began laughing, her beautiful eyes dancing with mischievousness.

Unable to stop myself, I joined in. She had a way of making me laugh when I least expected.

"Gotcha," she giggled.

I nodded. "You did, you little tease. You didn't like it?"

She shrugged. "I liked the pasta better."

"Excellent."

"Why?"

"You showed a preference for something. That's progress." I drew in a deep breath. "What are your plans tomorrow afternoon?" Tomorrow was Sunday and the restaurant was closed, which meant I was free all day, and I was hoping her schedule was the same.

"I have a day off—a whole day!" She threw her arms in the air in celebration. Her enthusiasm was contagious, and I chuckled. I loved seeing her happy.

"Okay. Are you up for a challenge?"

She bit her lip. She hadn't liked the last challenge I'd given her. "Okay?"

Leaning forward, I pulled on the soft flesh of her lip, my fingers lingering a moment longer than needed. "Relax. It's an easy one."

"All right."

"I can't believe I'm saying this, but I want you to go to McDonald's."

Her eyes widened. "What? But you made me go all week without going there. You made me promise!"

I had. And every day, when she got to her car in the morning, I had been waiting with a little cooler containing lunch and a snack for her. She rented a small room and bath in a private house and the landlady was not pleased with her having an early morning visitor, so I waited tolerantly each day for her to come out to me. Normally not a patient person, I had found a wealth of it for her. The mornings had quickly become my favorite part of the day. I would hold out my hand, and she would slide her palm against mine, letting me hold her fingers for a few moments. Her sweet kiss on my cheek, thanking me every morning, made my day complete.

I nodded. "I know. I want you to bring your three favorite, um…*items* —since I just can't call them food—with you."

"You want me to bring them *here*? To your restaurant?"

I nodded painfully. I never thought I would see the day I would voluntarily let those items cross my threshold. "I assume they're the cheeseburger, the fish sandwich…"

"For Fridays," she interrupted.

"Yes, of course," I snorted, "Because you're such a good Catholic girl. You don't even like fish very much."

"I know, but my friend is, and I eat the fish thing to support her. The sauce is good, and they put cheese on it too. It adds something to the overall dish," she teased.

I shook my head. "Yes, Julia. Because melted fake plastic on top of an unknown fish by-product makes it extra delicious."

She nodded happily. "It does."

I glared at her. "And the third thing?" I couldn't even bring myself to say it.

She sighed longingly. "The McNuggets. With sweet-and-sour sauce."

I grimaced. "Right. Can't forget the sauce."

"It makes it better, Byron," she retorted, her tone haughty.

I barked out a laugh. "Nothing makes any of that better, except a garbage bin."

"Why am I bringing it, then?"

"To show you something."

A sly look crossed her face. "Do I get to eat it?"

I nodded. "Unfortunately, yes. At least a taste."

She grinned. "Okay. Eleven? It's all fresh then."

I shuddered as I pressed some money into her hand, daring her with my eyes to argue with me. "Yes, let's get it while it's *fresh*. Eleven is good."

She frowned but tucked the money into her coat pocket before standing to leave. I always hated this part of our time together, not wanting her to walk away from me, but I escorted her down to the restaurant, depositing the tray in the kitchen. When we got to her car, she turned and looked up at me. Her face in the shadowy moonlight was alight with mischief.

"What are you up to?" I asked quietly, unable to stop drifting my fingers down her soft cheek.

Slowly, our touches had increased over the past two weeks. The brush of a finger, the gentle graze of her lips on my cheek when she said goodnight, the warmth of her pressed against me as I hugged her. She leaned up closer, and my heart began to beat faster. The longing I had to sweep her into my arms and kiss her senseless tore through me. I felt her lips at my ear, and I shivered.

"Looking forward to tomorrow, Byron. Especially the rule." She stepped back, grinning.

I looked at her stupidly. "The rule?"

She nodded. "We share. Everything."

I stared at her, confused. She brushed her lips across my cheek, then climbed in the car. I watched her reverse before she rolled down the window. "You are gonna love the nuggets!" She laughed and drove off, leaving me gaping after her.

I forgot about the fucking rule.

We share. Everything.

Nuggets.

I shuddered.

CHAPTER 3

BYRON

I stood back, satisfied with what I had prepared, hoping my plan would work. A gentle rap on the back door had a smile lighting up my face, and I hurried over to let Julia inside. She entered with her own smile and her usual quiet hello, and unable to help myself, I leaned down and kissed her forehead as I returned her greeting. I grimaced when I saw the bag and large cup in her hand.

"Added a Coke, did you?"

She smirked at me. "I got the combo with one of them. You get fries that way, you know."

I shook my head. "Yippee. How *delicious*."

She chuckled as she set down the bag. "Okay, what are we doing?"

Smiling, I lifted her up onto the counter, loving the small squeak she made as I did so.

"I'm about to prove my theory." I tapped the end of her nose. "Or at least, I hope to."

She watched as I unpacked the bag she had brought, grimacing as I smelled the grease and salt wafting up from the contents. I watched in amusement as her hand snuck over, stole a French fry, and popped it into her mouth. She closed her eyes as she chewed. "Mmm…crispy and salty."

I smirked as I moved the container out of reach. "Enough, minx."

She giggled and winked at me. I couldn't resist returning her smile with one of my own and adding another gentle kiss, to her cheek this time.

"Aren't you going to have one?" she teased.

I shook my head. "No, we're not sharing yet, thank God. You ready?"

She straightened her shoulders and nodded.

Grimacing, I picked up the cheeseburger and unwrapped it. "Have a bite."

Grinning, she took the burger and took a bite. I watched closely as she chewed and swallowed. A strange look crossed her face, but otherwise, she didn't react.

Silently, she offered it to me, and I held her gaze as I took my own bite, instantly scowling at the burst of salt in my mouth. I picked up the bottle of water and drank deeply.

"Do you want me to describe it?" she asked quietly.

"No. Not yet." I lifted the cover on the dish beside me and picked up the small cheeseburger from the plate. "I want you to taste this, and then tell me the difference between the two."

Julia took the burger from my hand and took a little bite. She chewed silently before swallowing, and she sat, not saying a word for a minute.

"Can I have another bite?"

Disappointed, I picked up the McDonald's burger and offered it to her. She shook her head. "No, I mean of this one."

I beamed widely at her. "Yes."

She took two more bites, chewing slowly. After a minute, she held up my sandwich. "I like this one. It had…*flavor?* I could taste more than one thing, but I liked it."

"What could you taste?" I asked eagerly.

"Garlic, um, herbs, and the meat was very fresh."

I nodded encouragingly. "And the other?"

She shook her head sadly. "It tasted like salt. Just salt."

Without thinking, I grasped her face and kissed her lips. "Clever girl." I praised her.

Her eyes widened at my impulsive gesture, but she smiled, her cheeks turning a lovely shade of pink.

The same thing happened when she took a bite of the fish sandwich. She chewed both thoughtfully and informed me the one from McDonald's was greasy and…blah.

I couldn't have been happier with that description. I even grinned as she insisted on "cleansing her palate" with a sip of Coke.

Finally, I offered her a nugget. I opened her beloved sauce and held it out to her. She looked at both with a grimace. "Could I taste yours first?"

Pleased, I lifted the lid on my offering. I had prepared small chunks of chicken, dredged them in flour and herbs, baking them in a garlic-ginger sauce that was slightly sweet, yet tangy. Something flavorful that gave her some of the salt she loved, but that she wouldn't find overwhelming. Anxiously, I watched as she speared a piece and tasted it. Slowly, a delighted look came over her features, and she gazed at me. "Byron, this is the most delicious thing I've ever tasted!"

My smile was brilliant. I picked up one of her nuggets and offered it to her, but she shook her head. "I can't eat that once I've had this. Knock yourself out. They're all yours."

I threw back my head, laughing. Leaning forward, I kissed her warmly again. "Congratulations, Ms. Nichols. You have just graduated from no taste buds into the flavor academy."

She shook her head. "How did you do this?"

"You needed to give yourself a break from the overload of crap you kept eating. All I did was help you discover what real food tasted like. That there was something out there other than processed garbage. If you keep trying new things, your taste buds will develop. I promise."

Her happiness faded a little. "So, I'm done?"

I shook my head. "No, I have a reward for you." I pulled a small pot off the stove and lifted the lid, taking out a bowl and setting it on the counter.

Her eyes widened as I poured out the contents. "Is that chocolate?"

Grinning, I reached over and picked up a piece of angel food cake and dipped it in the warm, molten richness. Slowly, I raised it to her lips. "Open up," I whispered.

I placed the morsel in her mouth and stifled a groan as her lips closed around my fingers. I felt her tongue gently flick against the tips as she removed all traces of the chocolate from my skin. She closed her eyes, and a low moan escaped her lips after I withdrew my fingers, the skin tingling where her tongue had touched them.

I stood in front of her, immobilized, watching her. Her tongue peeked out, licking her lips.

"I was wrong, Byron."

"Wrong?"

"Your chicken isn't the best thing I've ever tasted."

I blinked. "You like the chocolate?"

"Not just the chocolate.

"The angel food cake?"

She shook her head as color flooded her cheeks again. She leaned closer, her voice low and husky.

"You, Byron. I like how *you* taste. It's…addictive."

There was no thought. Just reaction. One second, I was standing in front of her; the next, I had her crushed up against me, my lips on hers, my tongue deep in her warm, delectable mouth. I yanked her against me tightly as I explored her sweetness. I vaguely registered the flavor of the chocolate, but I found her own essence far more appealing. I couldn't get her close enough as our tongues met and danced together, stroking, caressing, never ceasing their movements. She wound her arms around my neck, and I groaned as her hands found their way into my hair, tugging softly and teasing me. Regretfully, I pulled away, my breath coming out in short gasps as I rested my forehead against hers.

"I've wanted to do that for so long," I confessed quietly.

"I've wanted you to." She gently touched my face.

I pulled her closer. "Good."

"Are you done with me? Is this over?"

I pulled back in shock. "No!" I cupped her face in my hands. "I've enjoyed every second of our experiments, Julia. But I ceased to care if you ever got past your love for…*that*." I indicated the bag sitting beside us. "All I wanted was more time with you." I lowered my voice. "To get to know you. To be able to do this…" My mouth closed on hers once again, and for several moments, the world outside the softness of her lips ceased to exist.

She pulled back and looked at me, her chest moving rapidly, her lips swollen. "I'm never going to be like you, Byron. I don't think I'll ever love food the way you do."

I shook my head. "I don't need you to. I'm thrilled you understand it a little more now, though. And that maybe I can help you keep moving forward." I drew in a deep breath. "And that perhaps you'd still see me for me. I want to get to know all about you, and for you to know me. But I still want to cook for you…and take care of you that way. If you'll let me."

"I'd like that." She smiled shyly. "I don't think I can go back to eating that." She pointed at the McDonald's leftovers.

Grinning, I swept the contents from the bag into the garbage bin that was sitting beside us. "Then my work is done."

"I love watching you cook, you know. And I love how passionate you are about it."

21

Beaming, I leaned forward. "I'd be happy to show you something else I'm passionate about," I murmured against her lips.

I wasn't expecting the sharp tug as she wrapped her arms back around me and I stumbled forward, bracing my hands on the countertop, only to knock one into the bowl of melted chocolate. I gasped and stood back, watching the chocolate drip from my fingers. I heard a small whimper, and my gaze flew to Julia, who was watching me with hooded eyes, her teeth pressing down into her bottom lip. Holding her gaze, I raised my hand to my mouth and licked the chocolate off one finger. Another whimper escaped her lips. "I suppose I should go and wash this off." I grinned playfully.

She shook her head furiously. "No."

"No?" I whispered, my voice raspy. "What should I do, then? How will I ever get it cleaned off?"

Her hand moved and wrapped around my wrist, bringing the chocolate-covered skin close to her face. She grinned up at me, and her tongue came out and licked its way across my palm, swirling and teasing as she gathered up the sweet goodness. I hissed as she moved onto my fingers, my other hand closing over the top of her leg as she worked her tongue on my skin.

"Julia," I warned softly.

She drew back. "Rich, dark, and molten, Byron. Not like any chocolate I've tasted before."

I groaned, even as I smiled at her description. I saw her hand move, and then her finger lifted, dripping with the dark, sweet liquid. Slowly, she rubbed it on her lips as she leaned forward, her voice low and pleading. "The rule, Byron. Remember the rule. We share…everything. You have to taste this." She paused. "It's amazing. The *chef* who made it is amazing."

I leaned forward and tenderly stroked her lips with my tongue, enjoying the bittersweet of the chocolate mixed with the velvet of her lips. Her low moan spurred me on, and I covered her mouth with mine, kissing her deeply.

She was right.

It was amazing.

Her, her mouth, her rule, her adorable ways.

The taste of her.

They were all amazing.

And now…they were part of my life.

CHAPTER 4

JULIA

A MONTH LATER

"All right, do you have everything you need for tomorrow?" Gerard smiled gently at me.

I furrowed my brow in thought. "I hope so. I want to make this special —and surprise Byron."

"Follow the instructions, watch your timing, and everything will be fine. He'll be thrilled you went to all this trouble for him." He paused, winking at me. "Of course, his best birthday gift will be spending the weekend with you."

On cue, my cheeks grew warm, the color flooding right down my neck. "I'm not sure how much of a gift that is."

He chuckled. "Julia, I have been his maître d', business partner, and friend since he opened his first restaurant. I have never known him to take a weekend off—ever. You're good for him—you help him remember there is life outside the walls of his kitchen."

I glanced around the spotless kitchen I was standing in. Gerard had been sweet enough to try to teach me how to make Byron a dinner as a surprise for his birthday. It would be the first meal I had ever attempted to cook. I was delighted and thrilled to find out when not cooking and creating, Byron kept his meals fairly simple. Pasta, chicken, and salad were his favorites. Byron explained to me with all the tasting and rich foods he ate all the time, when not in "chef-mode," he liked simple fare more.

Except dessert.

His favorite was an amaretto crème brûlée, served with fresh fruit he spiced and sweetened and the thinnest wafer biscuits I had ever seen.

His own recipes, of course.

Gerard was endlessly patient with his lessons, even accommodating my weird hours, using his own kitchen and trying not to alert Byron that anything out of the ordinary was happening.

I thought I had everything under control.

Dinner would include a simple marinara with fresh pasta, although not homemade—Byron would have to make allowances for that minor technicality.

Salad, I could handle, and even though Gerard rolled his hazel eyes, I insisted on garlic bread. There were some habits not even Byron could break.

Dessert worried me the most, but while Gerard offered to make it himself, I insisted on doing it. I wanted to make all of it for Byron. I knew he preferred it made and served the same day, so it was important to me to follow his pattern.

He constantly cooked for me—lunches, dinners, and on occasion, breakfast. He hated the thought of me hungry or eating anything he hadn't made for me. Every time I walked into the restaurant, I was swept into the kitchen or his office, and once he kissed me thoroughly to say hello, he would instantly inquire if I was hungry. It only took one look of total disappointment when I answered no for me to understand that was how he showed his love for me. After that, the answer was always yes. Seeing the delight on his face when I praised whatever dish he would slide in front of me, I knew I would never say no again.

To anything he asked me.

God, I loved him. We hadn't said the words to each other yet, but we both felt the emotion. I wanted to tell him this weekend, and that was why I wanted to make *him* a meal.

As simple as my offering would be, he would know the effort I'd made and understand its significance. He would feel cared for. Loved.

Gerard's voice interrupted my musings. "You have your lists?"

I held up the stack of papers.

"Your timelines?"

"Yes. Dessert first. Then I'll make the sauce and salad, set the table, and when Byron calls to say he's almost there, I'll cook the pasta and heat the bread."

"And?" he prompted.

"Garnish the brûlée!"

"Excellent. Don't melt the sugar on the brûlée too early, or it will get soft. Forty-five minutes will chill it again the way Byron likes it. Don't garnish it with the fruit until you're ready to serve." He pointed to two small containers. "I did make you some of Byron's wafers and the spiced fruit. He loves them with the brûlée, and they take practice to get right."

"Not too early. Right. And thank you, Gerard."

He waved away my thanks. "Are you sure you're okay to use the torch? The broiler will work as well." He frowned. "I don't want you to burn yourself."

"Nope. I've been practicing with you. I think I have it under control." I had eaten a lot of brûlée lately during our experiments.

"Okay. Good. It's a simple menu, and you have all day. It'll be perfect, and Byron will be thrilled."

I felt a small flutter of nerves in my stomach. "I hope so."

Gerard snickered. "If things go badly, text me. I'll send dinner over from the restaurant. As long as you're there, Byron will be happy."

I nodded gratefully. It was good to have a backup plan, although I hoped I wouldn't need it.

He glanced at his watch. "You'd better go. Your class starts soon, and I know Byron is looking forward to seeing you later." He grinned with relief. "It'll be good not to have to pretend I haven't just seen you after tomorrow. I'm afraid neither of us are good liars."

I had to laugh with him; he was correct on that. Both of us had slipped a couple times, but luckily Byron hadn't become suspicious.

I kissed Gerard's cheek. "Thank you again."

He smiled warmly. "My pleasure."

I slipped through the back door of the restaurant, glancing around the still-busy kitchen. Business was better than ever, the waiting list long, and dinner service was packed every evening. Still, all the chefs and kitchen staff waved and called out hellos, used to my appearance by now. Gerard was talking to one of the chefs and came over, looking concerned.

"Are you all right, Julia? You're late this evening. Byron was getting quite worried."

I nodded wearily. My professor had been on a tear and kept us all late. When I dropped by my rooming house to pick up my bag, my cranky landlady had been upset over something and yelled at me. She informed me she'd decided no longer to rent to students and I would have to find another place to live at the end of the month, which meant I had to be out before the term was even done. I had tried reasoning with her, but she said she was giving me a month's notice and that was more than fair. She was always grumpy and rigid, but this time, she wouldn't listen to me. Never mind that with the school year now partway through, the chances of me finding a place as reasonable were slim, or the fact that I had been an excellent tenant for two years. She was, apparently, "done with housing irresponsible people." I had no idea what set her off, as I wasn't irresponsible, but it had been an unexpected, unwelcome ending to my day.

I had to put those thoughts aside, though. I would deal with them after this weekend. I didn't want anything to spoil Byron's birthday.

"Long class. Is he upstairs?"

"Yes."

"Okay. I'll go up."

I paused outside the door to Byron's office. I could hear his muffled voice through the door, and he didn't sound pleased. I was unsure if he was alone or if I should interrupt him, but Gerard said Byron was concerned. I gently rapped on the heavy wood, stepping back when it was flung open almost immediately by Byron himself. The phone was pressed to his ear, and he looked upset, his facial expression changing when he saw it was me.

"Never mind," he muttered into the phone and tossed it behind him. Reaching out, he dragged me into the office and kicked the door shut. He wrapped his arms around me, his mouth on mine immediately. He kissed me deeply, his tongue delving and possessive. Unsure what was causing his reaction, I clung to him, kissing him back and groaning as he lifted me, trapping me against the door. Finally, his head dropped to my shoulder with a heavy sigh as he set me back on my feet.

"What was that for?" I whispered.

His warm blue eyes were troubled. "You were two hours late, Julia. *Two hours*. You're never late. I called your cell phone, and it went straight to voice mail. I called the rooming house, and that cranky landlady of yours told me you weren't there and to stop bothering her—she was no help at all. Melinda hadn't heard from you—I couldn't find you." He pressed his forehead to mine. "I was so worried, my girl."

I slipped my fingers into his hair, massaging his scalp. "I'm so sorry. My class ran late, and then the professor kept me back about my last assignment. He doesn't let us have our cell phones on…and I forgot to turn it back on when I went to get my stuff…" I rambled until he laid his finger on my lips.

"Okay, it's okay now. You're here." He glanced at the bag I had dropped when he picked me up. "I have you the rest of the weekend, right?"

"Yes. You'll be sick of me by Sunday."

"Impossible." He wrapped his arms back around me. "Nothing can happen to you. I need you too much."

He still sounded so stressed. Wanting him to relax, I grinned up at him. "Admit it, Byron. You were just afraid I went back to the dark side and I was sitting at McDonald's stuffing myself on McNuggets."

His lips quirked. "With sauce, of course."

"What are nuggets without sauce?"

"What, indeed?" He smirked. He pulled back, straightening his shoulders and once again becoming Chef Lord. Cool, in charge, controlled— except for the passionate look in his eyes as he gazed at me. He held out his hand. "You've had a long day. You must be hungry."

I slipped my hand into his, loving how it felt as he folded his much larger one around mine. "Yes."

"Good. I'll make you dinner."

I kissed his cheek, the stubble on his skin rough under my lips. "Thank you. You look after me so well."

He pulled me into his side. "I like looking after you." He pressed his lips against my temple. "It's my favorite thing to do."

I pulled on my hair in frustration. The day had passed by in a flurry of preparation, hours of phone calls, and pounding the keyboard looking for a place to live. Places that were available, I couldn't afford unless I got another job, which I didn't have time for. The ones I could afford made the small room and grumpy landlady I'd been dealing with seem like the Taj Mahal. I shut my eyes, taking in a deep, somewhat calming breath. I had lined up two places to see on Monday. I already knew I would hate both of them, but I reminded myself it would only be for a few months. Once school was done and students were moving out, I could find a better place. Maybe Byron or Gerard would know someone looking to rent out a room. I could stay with Melinda for a couple weeks if I had to, but their condo was small. Also, Mark often worked from home, using the second bedroom as an office, so it would be a huge imposition for them; although I knew they would make me welcome. I hated putting anyone out. Byron would no doubt let me stay, but I hated asking. He was so busy all the time and such a private man. I wasn't sure he'd want me camping out in his guest room.

I stayed with him the occasional night and had even spent the odd weekend when I was studying hard, but our relationship hadn't moved to the next level. We still hadn't had sex—Byron insisted he wanted the time to be right and not to rush into anything. I slept in his bed, curled into him, but aside from some heavy make-out sessions, he hadn't let things progress past that point yet. I did enjoy staying here, though—the house was peaceful and so comfortable. The added bonus was Byron coming home at the end of the day, but still, I hesitated. It had only been six weeks, so I didn't want to ask and put him on the spot. I would go and see the places on Monday, and then tell him what was going on. He hated where I lived—for some reason, my landlady disliked him intensely and was always rude. Byron was unfailingly polite when he would see her, but she never once returned the favor. She constantly muttered about chefs being untrustworthy and wasting my life. I gave up trying to convince her Byron wasn't like that and made sure she saw him as little as possible.

Deciding to call her, I picked up my phone, hoping maybe, after a good night's sleep and thinking about it, she would have changed her mind and allowed me to stay. Ten minutes later, I hung up, defeated. Not only had she not changed her mind, she was threatening to dump my stuff in the street before the end of the month for "pestering" her. I still had no idea what set her off, but no amount of pleading on my part softened her hard demeanor. Finally, I got her to agree to give me to the end of the month as she had promised the day before, assuring her I wouldn't bother her again.

Wearily, I checked the screen of my phone, seeing a voice mail had come in. My eyes widened in panic at Byron's cheerful voice, telling me he was coming home early and would arrive in the next thirty minutes. He sounded so pleased at the thought he would have an extra couple of hours for our evening, which he thought would entail him cooking, then us going to a movie.

I stood, looking around wildly. He was early, and I had been so busy on the computer, I wasn't ready. I raced around the kitchen, turning up the marinara to warm, filling the pot with water for the pasta, and getting the bread ready. Luckily, the salad and dessert were done, and the table in the dining room was set. I had used his favorite china and candles, even remembering to get some flowers to make the table nice when I was out doing my errands this morning. Gerard had told me Byron's favorite flowers were lilies, showing me how they arranged them at the restaurant in small vases, and I imitated the style, pleased with how good it looked.

I glanced at the clock—I had ten minutes before he arrived. I yanked open the fridge door to grab the salad and stopped dead. I had made the brûlée earlier—but I hadn't melted the sugar on top and rechilled it. Byron loved his brûlée cold. Cursing, I grabbed four of the ramekins, leaving two, and placed them on the counter, deciding I could improvise. I could still melt the sugar topping and be on schedule. Maybe Byron wouldn't want dessert right away, then they would have a longer chance to cool. I sprinkled the sugar on the way Gerard showed me and glanced over at the stove.

The water wasn't even steaming yet, and I realized I had turned on the wrong burner. I dropped the sugar and moved the pot to the burner that was already warm. I stirred the sauce and popped the bread in the oven, congratulating myself on still having things under control. Byron was going to be so proud. I wanted everything ready to go when he got here so he could have a shower while the pasta cooked, then enjoy his dinner. Tasting the sauce, I pursed my lips—it was nowhere near as good as Byron's, but I thought it was still passable. I looked over at the bowl on the counter and groaned. I hadn't added the chopped fresh basil. Grabbing it, I dumped the herb in and stirred, my nerves starting to kick in. Sauce splashed over the edge, and I grabbed a dish towel, wiped the side of the pot, and flung the towel over my shoulder to the counter.

I looked over and cussed again. I still hadn't finished the damn sugar. Dropping the spoon into the sauce, I turned up the heat to make sure it would be hot and picked up the torch. I tucked my hair behind my ears and leaned over to brown the sugar. Biting my lips in concentration, I got the first one done and smiled proudly. The second one went well, but as I started on the next one, a funny noise caught my attention as well as the smell of something burning, and I looked over, gasping. The sauce was boiling rapidly—tomato puree and basil splashing everywhere. I had turned up the heat too high. Smoke was leaking through the top vent of the stove and I could smell bread burning. I stared dumbfounded, until the screech of the smoke alarm startled me. And with heart-pounding horror, I realized while staring at the mess that was supposed to be dinner, I had lit the dish towel I'd flung on the counter on fire with the torch and it was now in flames.

I had officially burned dinner and set Byron's kitchen on fire.

I looked around frantically, a hysterical laugh escaping my throat.

What the hell else could happen?

In wild desperation, I grabbed another dish towel and tried to smack at the flames in front of me. The second towel caught fire and, without thinking, I tried slapping the flames with my hands. I caught the edge of the platter I had brought from the dining room to put the bread on—Byron's favorite platter he had bought in Italy—and watched with horror as it tumbled over the edge of the counter, shattering into millions of shards as it hit the ceramic tiles.

The door from the garage was flung open, and Byron rushed in, stopping dead at the sight of me standing, flabbergasted, one burning dishtowel in my hand, while the other smoked away on the countertop. The sauce was still spitting everywhere, and rancid smoke now poured from the oven as the smoke detector screeched away.

"What the fuck?"

He moved fast. In three strides, he was across the kitchen, grabbing the fire extinguisher, and pushing me out of the way. He tore the smoking dish towel from my hands and tossed it into the sink. He flicked off all the burners, slammed the lid on the boiling sauce, and swept everything on the countertop into the sink—brûlées and all—and doused the flames with the fire extinguisher he'd snatched from the counter. He grabbed the oven mitt and pulled open the oven door, seized the burning bread, and tossed it out the back door, before returning and staring at me, wide-eyed and confused.

"What on earth?"

I surveyed the damage I had done. *Everything* was ruined. Burned or destroyed. I barely felt him grab my wrists as he inspected my hands. "Are you hurt? Did you burn yourself? Julia?" He cupped my face, forcing me to look at him. "Julia, my love? Are you hurt?"

I blinked at him, dazed.

"I made you dinner. Happy birthday, Byron."

Then I burst into tears.

CHAPTER 5

JULIA

Byron's arms were locked around me, holding me close, as he murmured small hushing noises. Over and over, he kept repeating everything was fine, as long as I wasn't hurt, the rest didn't matter. I kept crying. Finally, he drew back, cupping my face again and holding it tight.

"Yes, dinner is burned. We'll throw it out and start again. The smoke is already disappearing. We'll light a few candles, I'll turn on the fan, open some windows, and the smell will be gone soon. It *doesn't* matter, my love. As long as you're okay, *it doesn't matter.*"

"Your kitchen," I hiccupped. "I burned your kitchen."

"The cupboards will wipe down, and the counter is granite. It's not damaged. It's all fine, my girl. Look at me, please."

His low voice and anxious tone made me look up. His eyes held nothing but tenderness and worry. He wasn't angry.

"I broke your platter. Your favorite one."

He kissed the end of my nose, wiping the tears from under my eyes with his thumbs. "I'll call Giuseppe and ask him to send me another one."

"I ruined dinner."

"We can order pizza."

Byron wasn't big on pizza—at least, not the kind you could get for delivery.

"Gerard's on standby," I offered.

His eyebrow quirked. "Gerard knows about this?"

31

I sniffed. "He's been teaching me. I wanted to make you dinner. Surprise you. I thought it was all under control—and then it wasn't."

Byron's lips twitched. "Well, you certainly got the surprise part right."

My eyes filled again. "I'm…so sorry."

"Hush. No more crying. It was so sweet of you to try to make me dinner. I'm touched by your efforts." He glanced toward the stove. "Maybe we can salvage something."

"There are still two desserts in the fridge. They need the topping, though."

"I think I'll handle that part," he stated dryly. "No more torches for you."

"I have salad, and there's bread I didn't, ah, cut or burn."

He hugged me. "See, that's a good start. We can have that, and I'll call Gerard. He'll send some other things over, and we'll be right back on track."

I tried to pull out of his arms. "The mess—"

He didn't let go. "There is glass everywhere. Your feet will get cut. I'll sweep it up, and the rest will wait until things have cooled down."

"But—"

He covered my lips with his finger. "No buts. I won't risk you being hurt." I gasped as he swept me into his arms and carried me upstairs to his huge bathroom. Setting me on my feet, he leaned over and turned on the tap. "You have a warm bath and calm down. I'll sweep up the glass and organize dinner."

"But it's your birthday. You aren't supposed—"

"It's good. It's all good. You're with me. That is all I wanted today. Just you."

"I wanted to do something special. Make you dinner so you knew how important you are to me."

His lips were gentle as he kissed me. "I do, my love. Now, please, for me. Soak in the tub and come downstairs when you're ready."

My smile was shaky, but I nodded. He leaned down and pressed his lips to mine again. "Thank you for trying."

"I failed big-time."

"I don't care. You tried."

"Good thing Gerard talked me out of coq au vin. Imagine what damage I could have caused then—flambéing something that big."

His eyes crinkled as he laughed, hugging me hard. "Imagine."

Forty minutes later, I came downstairs, feeling calmer—no longer covered in tomato sauce or smelling of smoke. The kitchen looked pristine, no sign of the events from earlier. There was still a faint trace of burned something in the air, but Byron had the windows open, scented candles burning, and I knew it soon would be gone. One of his favorite Beatles recordings was playing in the background. He smiled as he held out his hand. "Feel better?"

I nodded. "You cleaned."

He shrugged. "The kitchen is sort of my area, you know. I work fast." He tugged me into the dining room, where dinner was waiting. My salad and sliced bread were there, but it was the two domed plates that caught my attention.

"How?" I gasped.

Byron wrapped his arms around my waist, pulling me back against him. "Gerard. I called and told him what happened, and here we are." He kissed my neck, his touch gentle as he tasted my skin with his tongue. "They arrived a couple of minutes ago. Helps to own the place, you know."

I sighed. "This is so much better than I could have done."

Byron laughed, a low rumble in his chest as he led me to the table, lifting the lids. "Tomorrow, we'll work together and make your dinner the way you planned it. Tonight, we can enjoy what my chefs have sent us. Deal?"

I inhaled the marvelous aroma coming from our plates. "Deal." Settling beside him, I lifted my glass. "Happy birthday, Byron."

His eyes were warm as he touched the rim of his glass to mine. "Thank you, my love."

The food was, of course, magnificent. Unpretentious, but delicious. I knew Gerard would've made sure to keep things simple for my benefit. Byron was sweet and praised my garden salad, even making sure I knew he had noticed the bread I picked was from his favorite bakery.

"How hard did Gerard laugh?" I asked between bites.

Byron shook his head. "Gerard is always a gentleman. He didn't laugh."

I pursed my lips at him, shaking my head in disbelief, and Byron smirked. "Okay, he may have tittered a little."

My lips quirked. "Tittered?"

Byron laughed. "A guffaw or two may have happened," he admitted. "But he was glad you weren't hurt, and that I called him. He, ah, apparently was organized, just in case."

I paused, my fork midway to my mouth. "He had it ready to go, didn't he?"

Byron refused to answer me directly. "Gerard is always prepared," he said simply. "He sent the food over right away. I told him we didn't need dessert." He paused. "Eat, please, my love. You might not have made it, but it's still special because you're with me."

I smiled at him, fighting my watery eyes.

"And your table is beautiful. I would be proud to have it in my restaurant." He lifted my hand and kissed the palm. "Almost as beautiful as you."

With a wink, he started to eat again, and I lifted my fork, determined to make the best of the evening. It wasn't what I planned, but he was right. We were still together.

My appetite wasn't great, but I did manage to eat a little, especially when he would lean forward and press a morsel against my mouth, quietly asking me to try it. I never could resist him. I held my breath as he tasted his brûlée, almost giddy when he declared it delicious. At least that part I got right—even if he did finish it.

"Tomorrow," he announced, "we'll go to my favorite market, buy some things, and make dinner together—okay? But we're not leaving the house again after that. I want you all to myself."

My chest warmed at his words. I liked the sound of that.

"I could make pancakes tomorrow," I offered.

His gaze flew to the kitchen. I could see the worry on his face.

"I used to make really good ones," I teased. "Hardly burned any of them. Bisquick and I were a good team."

He snorted, his spoon dropping from his hand to cover his mouth. I had to laugh with him.

"Okay, maybe it would be best if I didn't try to cook again this weekend without supervision. I could set the table again?"

He dragged my chair over and kissed me. "That sounds like a plan." He grinned. "At least until I get a new fire extinguisher…a big one."

When we were done, I tugged him into the living room. I'd messed up dinner, but I still had a few surprises.

"*Julia.*" He frowned as he took in the little pile of gifts.

"They're just small. Honest. I didn't spend much. Dinner was supposed to be your big gift." I pushed the long, flat box with my finger. "Well, and this one."

"I'll save that one to last, then."

His smile grew wider with every gift. There was so little I could buy him, but I knew the things he said he constantly needed. Thick, gray T-shirts to go under his chef's coat, double-layered socks to keep his feet comfortable during long hours of standing. Luckily, the brands he preferred were ones I could afford. The bag of his favorite coffee beans had been extravagant, but as usual, he was correct; it was the best. His coffee spoiled me for any other kind.

For each gift he opened, I got a deep, lingering, thank-you kiss. I berated myself for not wrapping each T-shirt and pair of socks separately. I liked his thank-yous.

He picked up the last box and shook it. "Light," he mused. "But very well wrapped." He quirked his eyebrow at me, and I had to laugh— compared to the others I had clumsily wrapped, it was a work of art.

"The store did it."

I watched with growing nerves as he slowly opened the paper and lifted the lid. He parted the filmy tissue paper with his long fingers, and a strange expression came over his face. I could feel my cheeks growing redder every passing second as he stared into the box. Maybe it had been a bad idea. I never should have listened to Melinda when I told her what I wanted to give him for his birthday.

Me.

I was about to speak when he lifted his head and gazed at me, his eyes suddenly dark and heavy-lidded, a smirk playing on his lips. "I've never really thought pink was my color, Julia."

"I—"

He pulled the lacy pink camisole out of the box, holding it up against his chest. "You don't think this cut might make me look a little hippy? The lace is gonna fall *right there*. And this bow at the front? Not sure how it will go with my chest hair. It hurts like a bitch if they get pulled."

I started to giggle as he dropped the camisole and held up the very tiny scrap of lace that constituted underwear. "And this...this is *not* gonna hold the package I've got for you in return, my girl." He grinned and winked at me. "Not even remotely."

"It's...it's for me to wear for *you*, Byron."

"Ah. That makes so much more sense." He paused. "Are you sure?"

I didn't hesitate. "Yes."

He waggled his eyebrows at me and handed me the box. "I'd like to see my gift, then." He drew in a deep breath, his voice dropping. "Now."

"Are *you* sure?"

Bending forward, he pulled me between his widely spread knees, his hands running up the backs of my legs. Up and down they went, higher every pass—touching, caressing, teasing. I stared down at him, my breathing becoming faster as he slipped his fingers under the waistband of my yoga pants and cupped my ass, kneading it lightly. "I. Want. My. Gift. *Now.*" He pulled me closer, tight against his thighs. I could feel his hunger now, straining against the material of his trousers, pushing against my leg. "You have ten minutes."

My voice was trembling in anticipation. "Okay."

Clutching the box, I backed out of the room and fled upstairs.

I waited with bated breath for the shower to shut off, then a few minutes later, Byron appeared, a towel draped around his hips. He smirked at me as he rubbed his damp hair. "That doesn't look like my gift," he drawled, indicating his robe I was wearing. "Mine was far prettier." His eyes glinted as he tossed aside the towel he'd used on his hair. "And far less concealing."

He stepped closer until he was a foot away.

"You enjoyed unwrapping it so much, I thought you'd like to do it again," I whispered, my voice husky with desire.

"Is that so?"

I nodded, my eyes widening as he pulled on the towel at his waist and it fell to the floor.

His erection sprang free, long and heavy. He stroked himself twice, his eyes on me the whole time. "I'd like *you* to unwrap it."

I drew in a long breath. Byron smiled. "You know they say you eat with your eyes before your mouth, Julia? *Feed me.* Slowly."

I stood taller, my body shaking with the want I had for this man. I opened the belt and pulled on the sleeves, so they rested on the edge of my shoulders. With a deep breath and a flex of my arms, the robe fell, joining Byron's towel on the floor. From his sharp intake of breath and the way his cock twitched, I knew he liked what he saw. Feeling braver, I tossed back my hair. "You like?"

Without a word, he twirled his finger midair, and with a grin, I spun on my feet, internally praying I could do so without falling. When we were once again face-to-face, he narrowed his eyes. He reached out his long forefinger, slowly trailing down the thin strap on my shoulder, across my collarbone, and traced the small bow that held the camisole together.

"Where did you get this again?"

"Victoria's Secret."

"Were there more of them?"

I frowned. "Yes."

He nodded. "Good." He raised his eyes, meeting mine. They were so filled with passion that my throat went dry. "Because this one isn't going to last the night."

And then he crushed me against him.

His mouth was hard. Possessive. Talented. His tongue slid and caressed, claiming me, making me his. Byron's hands trailed along my arms, cupped my head, stroked my back, and pulled me up against him, his cock pressed between us.

My fingers pushed into the taut flesh of his back, holding him close. His firm chest cemented to mine, the coarse hairs rubbing into my skin. Every part of me was on fire. I couldn't get close enough to him. I wanted to feel every inch of his body. I wanted to touch—and to taste him.

All of him.

I eased away, pushing on his chest. He groaned as our lips pulled apart, his low *"no"* bringing a smile to my mouth. Without a word, I dropped to my knees, wrapping my hand around his thick cock. "God, Julia," he rasped. "You don't have   "

The rest of his words were lost; he threw his head back with a curse as I took him in my mouth. I teased and licked, his weight hot and heavy on my tongue. He buried his fingers in my hair, the tips caressing my scalp. Our eyes locked as I moved over him, my mouth, hands, and tongue working in tandem. He groaned and hissed, my name falling from his mouth as he rocked, sliding in and out, deeper and faster, his hand tightening in my hair. His chest rose and fell rapidly, his breaths becoming pants. He was beautiful above me, losing himself in the passion I had stirred within him.

"Julia," he pleaded. "You need—baby, *fuck*, you need—"

I took him in deeper with one long suck, and he fell. I swallowed around him as he shuddered and cursed, roaring my name before he stilled, his head dropping to his chest, hands falling away from my hair. For a minute, there was no sound in the room as he stood trembling in front of me. Gently, I rubbed his legs, feeling the small shudders that ran through him. He remained quiet, his eyes closed. But then…

He opened his eyes, the blue of them brilliant and alive. Pulling me to my feet, he lifted me up, crashing his mouth to mine as he carried me to the bed.

"My turn."

I'd had sex before I met Byron. But I'd never experienced sex the way I did *with* Byron. It wasn't just sex. It was so much more—so profound. He was sin incarnate, and he let go completely; cool, controlled Chef Lord was nowhere to be found. He was frantic and wild in his passion. His mouth possessed me—every part of my body was touched by his full lips. His warm tongue tormented and licked; his sharp teeth nibbled and bit. His long, talented fingers teased, stroked, and touched me. Everywhere. He brought me to orgasm with his fingers first, his mouth next, and finally, his thick cock. He took me powerfully, his thrusts demanding and hard, his body pinning me to the mattress, our bodies slick with sweat. The sheets pulled from the bed and wrapped around us, the bed frame creaked and bent with his aggression, and the top of the nightstand was cleared when Byron's arm swept out as he looked for a place to brace himself as he pounded into me. None of it mattered. All that mattered was the look in his eyes, the dark timbre of his voice as he chanted my name, and the way we felt joined together in the most intimate of dances. His body demanded my complete surrender to his, and I gave it to him until I collapsed, exhausted and spent, sinking into the mattress with a long, shuddering exhale of air.

Byron hovered above me, the passion in his eyes turning to tenderness as our gazes locked. He rolled, pulling me with him. His lips grazed mine gently, his breath warm as it ghosted over my skin. "My beautiful girl," he whispered, his hands trailing up and down my back in featherlight touches. "Mine."

I nuzzled into his chest, too tired to talk.

"Bath?"

I managed to shake my head.

"Food?"

"No," I mumbled incoherently.

His laugh was low and reverberated in my ear. "Sleep?"

I grunted in contentment and burrowed farther into his warmth. I felt so safe with him.

He tightened his arms, his lips against my hair. "Sleep, my love. I have you."

CHAPTER 6

JULIA

I woke up early the next morning, alone. Frowning, I sat up, wondering where Byron was. Usually if I spent the night, he was beside me in the morning, his warm body curled around mine. After our lovemaking last night, I expected to find him with me—especially given the fact that he had woken me in the night, making me his again. That time, it had been slow, sweet, and erotic, the dark of the room making it seem so intimate as our hands and mouths pleasured each other.

Slipping on his robe, I padded downstairs. He was standing at the back window, staring outside, sipping a steaming cup of coffee. I took a minute to ogle the way his T-shirt stretched taut across his broad shoulders, narrowing into a tight waist and slim hips. I knew the powerful muscles that piece of material hid from my eyes. His sleep pants were resting low on his hips, and a small sliver of bare skin was revealed every time he lifted his cup to his mouth. My chest warmed, remembering how my hands had clutched the skin of his back as he thrust into me last night, groaning my name. Walking over, I slid my arms around his waist, pressing my lips to his back. His hand covered mine and he squeezed, but he didn't say anything.

"You were gone."

"I woke up and thought I'd best make those pancakes before you got any bright ideas about breakfast in bed—Bisquick-style." He shuddered. "I rather like my griddle."

I giggled and pressed another kiss to his back, slightly surprised he hadn't turned around and pulled me into his arms yet. He was always very affectionate in the mornings if I was here. It was far more enjoyable than waking up alone in the small room I rented.

"I made coffee."

"It smells amazing."

He moved away. "I'll get you a cup. Sit down, and I'll get the pancakes too. You get the cream."

I tried not to pout that he still hadn't kissed me, but I failed miserably. With a small smile, he leaned down and pressed his lips to mine—far too briefly and lightly for my liking. I watched him go to the cupboard and grab a mug for me. I got the cream and put it on the table, eyeing the coffee with appreciation as he handed it to me. The plate he slid out of the oven was stacked high with pancakes, and the syrup he poured into a jug was warm. As usual, everything looked and smelled incredible. But Byron's movements were stiff, and he was far too quiet. He sat down, but instead of pulling his chair closer to mine like normal, he stayed on the other side of the table from me. Something was off. A small flutter of nerves rippled down my spine. Did he regret last night? Was he trying to find a way to tell me?

"Are you okay?" I asked cautiously.

He smiled, but it was tight and didn't reach his eyes. "Yes. I'm fine."

I glanced around, feeling strange. Something was wrong. "Are we still going to the market?"

"If you have time."

I frowned. "Time?"

"Do you have something you need to tell me, Julia?"

I shook my head. "No."

He lifted one eyebrow in disbelief. "I used your laptop to look up the hours of the market."

I was bewildered. "Okay, that's fine."

"You had a lot of windows open."

I nodded. I'd been using my laptop all afternoon looking for a place to live. In my panic at his early arrival, I hadn't shut anything down.

Oh.

Oh.

"And your phone has been beeping constantly. I plugged it in so your battery wouldn't die, and the screen lit up. Your crabby landlady has been

41

trying to get hold of you. She is as equally rude and insulting to you as she is to me, I see."

I laid down my fork. He sounded so angry.

"I can explain."

"A month? She is giving you a month to find a new place? In the middle of term?"

"A month less three days. She told me I hadn't been around enough to tell me." I indicated the laptop. "I was searching for places yesterday."

"Do you have a lease?"

I shook my head. "It's always been month-to-month. But I've been there for two years and never had any trouble, aside from how grumpy she was all the time. But suddenly—" I shrugged "—I'm a huge issue."

"The places you're looking at are unacceptable."

"They're what I can afford, Byron," I explained quietly. "I don't have any extra funds for anything more. It's only until I can find more time to look for something better."

"Why didn't you come to me with this problem?" He narrowed his eyes. "Were you even going to tell me? Or did you not think I should be informed of this important detail?"

"Of course I was." I gasped. "I didn't want to spoil your birthday weekend! I was going to arrange to look at a few places next week. I got so caught up in trying to find something halfway decent, I lost track of time yesterday and then…destroyed dinner. I didn't want the fact that I need a place to live to taint the rest of the weekend as well. I only wanted it to be about you. About us."

He stared at me, the muscles in his jaw tight. He was really angry.

I threw my napkin down on the table and stood. "But apparently, I ruined the weekend anyway."

I hurried from the kitchen, trying not to cry. All I'd wanted was to give Byron a nice weekend. And I had screwed up almost every part of it. I'd wrecked dinner, almost burned down his kitchen, and broken his favorite platter. Giving myself to him last night was now tarnished by the fact that he thought I was hiding something from him—as if I didn't trust him enough. I shared my body with him, but not my problems. I should have known better—he was so protective of me; he would want to know and help me any way he could. I had planned on telling him when the weekend was over, but now it was too late.

I hesitated as I looked around his room, unsure what to do. It was his house. Should I leave? Give him some time, then go downstairs and apologize again? I picked up my travel bag from beside the dresser and sat down on the edge of the bed. I had no idea what to do. I didn't even know what would happen when I showed back up at the rooming house. My lip began to tremble, and I bit down, trying to stop the tears, but they rolled down my cheeks, splashing onto my hand that gripped my little overnight bag.

"Stop, my love." Byron appeared in front of me, gently pulling the handle from my fingers and tossing the bag to the side. He sat beside me on the bed, drawing me into his arms. "Hush. I didn't mean to make you cry. I was just so angry." He pulled back, brushing away my tears and dropping gentle kisses onto my damp skin. "But not at you, Julia. I'm not angry with you."

"Who are you angry at?" I hiccupped.

"That stupid cow landlady of yours. She's been a thorn in my side from the day I first met her. She won't let me into the house. She won't let you keep snacks in your room. You can't use the kitchen, but she refuses to allow you a small fridge in your room. You can't use her laundry machines. She's rude on the rare occasion I speak to her and is consistently nasty to you." He dropped another kiss on my cheek. "You don't deserve that— you're far too wonderful. Now, she is kicking you out? Without reason? I swear she's doing it to piss me off."

"She doesn't like you."

He grimaced. "No kidding. That was obvious the first day I met her. After she saw me in my chef's attire, it got worse. She looked at me like I was a bug she wanted to squash under her foot."

"I told you once, her ex-husband ran off with a chef. It would seem she hates anyone who wields a spatula."

Despite the seriousness of the moment, he snorted. "First off, working at Burger King does not make you a chef. I'm not even sure it qualifies as a cook." He narrowed his eyes. "Is that why she's doing this? Because of me?"

I sniffed. "I have no idea why she's doing it. But I was going to tell you, Byron. I swear I was. I wanted your birthday weekend to be perfect." My eyes filled with fresh tears. "And it's been anything but. I fucked it all up!"

He widened his eyes at my curse. I rarely ever swore, unless it was at the height of passion, and even then, I was pretty tame. Byron cursed like a trucker at times. He could swear in nine languages, he'd once told me proudly. It was important to be able to swear at the various chefs he hired in their own language, he had informed me in a serious tone.

"It always gets their attention."

43

For a minute, I was taken aback, but then he winked.

"You fucked up nothing. I hate to think of you worrying about this all by yourself." He ran his hands through my hair, gently moving the long length over my shoulder. "I want to be the one to help you with anything that is upsetting you. Always—birthday or not. You should have told me right away."

"I didn't want you to think—"

"Think what?"

"We've only been together a little while. I didn't want you to feel pressured or think—"

I shook my head, unable to explain.

His voice was tense. "Is this about money? You're afraid, if you ask, I'll think you want my money?"

"Maybe a little."

His irritation seemed to dissolve away, his shoulders loosening and his face becoming smooth. His gaze was warm and tender as he looked at me. He cupped my cheek, his thumb stroking my skin tenderly.

"Julia, my love, I could buy you a condo, pay off your student loans and any other future tuition you incur and not even make a dent in my savings account. I would give it freely and without another thought. The fact that I know you would refuse any and all offers to do so is one of the many reasons I love you."

"You love me?"

He huffed a sigh. "Not the way I planned on telling you, but yes. I love you. So very much."

I looked at him but said nothing.

"I do," he said, his voice lower now. "I love how stubborn, feisty, and funny you are. I love your independent streak. How loving you are to your friends. I adore the fact that you let me teach you about food. Even after you almost burned down my kitchen, I love the fact that you can't cook to save your life, but you still tried to. And I adore, absolutely adore, that if I make you something to eat, even if you're not the least bit hungry, you eat it, because you know how much I want to take care of you." He picked up my hand and kissed the palm softly, then pressed it to his cheek. "But the thing I love the most about you is how you make me feel."

"How?" I whispered.

"Loved. Cared for. And only for me. You make me feel like I matter."

I drew in a deep breath. "You are." I pressed my hand firmly against his rough cheek. "You do."

"Yeah?"

"I love you, Byron. With all my heart."

His mouth covered mine, our lips fusing together. He pulled me up his chest, holding me tight and showing me with his caresses how true his words were. When he leaned back, he tucked me under his chin, holding me in place.

"I want something. Something that would make my whole birthday weekend perfect. And only you can give it to me."

"Tell me," I pleaded.

"Move in here—with me."

"What?"

"It's perfect. I have this whole house to myself, and the only time it feels right is when you're here with me. I want more than the occasional weekend or sleepover. I have for a while now. After last night, I want it even more. You need a place, and I need you."

"I can't afford—"

He covered my mouth with a gentle finger. "I don't need your money. I need more of you. The thought of coming home every night and knowing you'll be here waiting for me? That I can wake up with you every day and spend more time with you? Make love to you anytime I want to? That's what I want."

"I can't live here for free."

"Fine. Then you can pay me what you pay now. On one condition."

"Which is?"

He rubbed his nose against mine affectionately. "You don't cook alone in the house for a while."

A small giggle burst from my mouth.

"And that," he stated. "I want that."

"What?"

"Your giggle. Your laughter. The way you look at me. I want to hear them, see them every day." He gathered up my hands in his. "Please."

I looked around, imagining living here with him. Waking up with him. Making love with him. Every day.

He sweetened the pot. "I'll add an extra desk in the office for you." He leaned forward. "Think of all those books in the library you could read, while you sit on a comfy couch with a snack and a cold drink you can refill anytime." He arched his eyebrow.

I gazed up at him. "I like all those things, but I don't need any of that."

"What do you need?"

"Just you."

"Julia—" His breath caught. "Is that a yes?"

"Yes."

His lips hovered over mine. "Today? Can we go today and get your things?"

"I have to go to the bank." I didn't meet his eyes. "She never asked for first and last, so I will have to pay this month's rent whether I'm there or not."

He slipped his fingers under my chin, making me meet his gaze. "I'll pay the old hag, and you never have to go back there."

"You really want that?"

"Yes. It would be the best present I've ever received. And then I can tell that bitch off."

"Byron—"

"I'll do it in Hungarian. Or French. Or maybe even Portuguese. She'll never know what hit her."

I laughed at his expression. "Be good."

"Just one good cuss. She deserves it. Consider it part of my present."

"Just one."

"I love you."

"I love you too. Happy birthday, Byron."

"Best one, my love, by far," he whispered, pressing his lips to mine.

His kiss was full of promises—of a life together filled with cussing, laughter, and great meals.

And the main ingredient—the one I'd been missing all my life—love.

So much love.

CHAPTER 7

BYRON

Julia glanced over at me, her green eyes anxious. She'd been quiet on the drive over, unlike her usual cheerful, talkative self. I pulled into the driveway of the house where she had been living.

"Why don't I just go in and get my things? You can go to the market, and by the time you come back, I'll be done and we can go."

I shook my head. "Nope."

"Byron, really, it's not necessary."

"Oh, but it is."

She sighed, her hands fidgeting on her lap. I frowned at the two small burn marks from her disastrous attempts to make dinner last night. She insisted they didn't hurt, and I had made sure they were covered in salve last night and this morning, as well as kissing them several times, assuring Julia that kisses promoted healing faster. She had rolled her eyes but didn't stop me.

As I remembered last night, my frown became a smile. Hearing the smoke alarm blaring when I pulled up in the garage, I had rushed in, not at all prepared for the sight that met my shocked gaze. Julia standing frozen but looking utterly panicked, holding a burning dish towel as smoke poured from the stove and tomato sauce splattered all over the walls. She'd been so upset even though I assured her it all looked and smelled worse than it was. I had cleaned it all up while she recovered in the bath, and after that—well, the evening got infinitely better.

Her sweet and thoughtful gifts had warmed my heart. Usually my birthday passed with the minimum of fuss. Gerard always found a special bottle of wine or liquor to mark the occasion, and the kitchen would echo with birthday wishes, but that was about it. Julia's offerings had shown how well she knew me and how, in her own way, she wanted to care for me, the same way I wanted to care for her.

And when she gave me the gift I'd been longing for the most—the gift of her and her love—the day, the year, my entire future was bright.

Finally making her mine, holding her close and feeling her warmth wrapped around me in the most intimate of ways had been nothing but perfect.

When I saw the problem she'd obviously been trying to solve on her own, my anger raged. Her landlady was, without a doubt, the biggest bitch I'd ever met. Whatever life had done to her, Julia didn't deserve her attitude or to be kicked out of her small room. She bent over backward to follow every rule the cow put in place, constantly polite and never once complaining. I had never even seen her room, as I wasn't allowed to enter the house.

Until now.

"Really, it's fine. I don't have much," she insisted.

"Good. It won't take us long, and we can be done."

She made a small distressed sound in her throat. "Maybe you could just wait in the car."

I chuckled as I shook my head. "Nope. You promised. It's my birthday."

"Byron, it's fine."

Leaning over the console, I dragged Julia close and kissed her hard. "She kicked you out. In the middle of term, for no reason. It's *not* fine."

"But now I'm going to live with you. So, it's a good thing in the end. Just leave it. I'll get my things, and you come back in about an hour."

I ran my finger down her soft cheek. "I'll bring in the totes and help you pack. I'm not leaving you alone with her so she can berate you more, my love. Not happening."

"Will you be polite?"

"Not a chance."

"But—"

"What's she going to do? She already kicked you out. As soon as she opens her mouth, I'm going to let her have it. She deserves it."

Ignoring her groan, I glanced past Julia to the nondescript house.

Today would be the last day she had to worry about stepping over an imaginary line or upsetting the old hag. I had a check in my pocket and some totes we had stopped and picked up at the restaurant. I was going in with her, no matter what her landlady said.

I opened my door, sliding out, and went around to her side of the car. I tugged Julia out of her seat, dropping a kiss onto her hand. "Come on. Let's go get your stuff, and then we can get out of here."

She stood, not moving. "I can do it alone."

"I know you can, but you don't have to. So, why?"

"She's going to be upset."

I laughed. "So? What else can she do?"

She bit her lip, worrying the plump flesh. "What if…" She trailed off.

"What if what?"

She peeked up, her wide eyes filled with worry. "What if I need to use her as a reference at some point? If I…if I needed a place to live one day."

"Oh, Julia." I wrapped my arms around her, pressing her into the side of the car. "My love, do you really think once I get you under my roof, I'm ever going to let you go? I love you. I want a life with you."

"I might burn the kitchen once too often."

I chuckled as I traced my lips over her sweet mouth. "There is nothing you can do that would make me not want you with me. Nothing."

"Promise?"

"Yes."

She drew in a deep breath. "Okay."

I noticed the curtain move in the window behind us and saw the flash of brassy blond hair. The cow was home and watching us. She told Julia once she didn't want any PDA on her front lawn. She strictly forbade it.

With a grin, I lifted Julia, pressing her farther into the metal of the door and covering her mouth with mine, kissing her passionately. She whimpered, wrapping her arms around my neck and holding me tight.

Time to start breaking the rules.

We were both panting by the time I lowered her back to her feet. I leaned my forehead against hers, nuzzling the supple skin. "We may have to skip the market, my love."

She giggled breathlessly. "Okay."

The crunch of tires behind us made me grin. My sidekick was here.

"Byron, why is Gerard here?"

"The totes won't fit in the car once they're full. His SUV will hold them."

She glared up at me. "Byron."

I grinned. "Gerard is even more fluent than I am in foreign cussing. He wanted in on the action."

She rolled her eyes, pushing me back and glaring at the both of us.

"The two of you need to behave."

We shook our heads.

With a groan, she pushed past me. Gerard and I shared a smirk as we reached in and grabbed the totes, following close behind.

The door flew open, Mrs. Gertrude Newcombe standing in the space, blocking our way. "What is going on? You aren't allowed visitors. Certainly not men—and especially *not them!*" she screeched, her arms flailing.

Gerard chuckled dryly, taking in her overdone appearance. "You weren't kidding, Byron. What is the hag's problem?" he muttered in Italian.

"I have no idea. Probably that Julia is getting some. Grumpy old bat," I replied in the same language.

"What? What did they say?"

Julia's cheeks darkened. "They said you look nice today. Mrs. Newcombe. I'm only here to get my things, and then I'll be out of your hair."

Mrs. Newcombe's face under the layers of makeup turned a strange shade of puce. She poked Julia's chest with her finger, jabbing the skin as she yelled. "What? You think you can come move out and not pay your rent? What are you trying to pull?"

I grabbed her hand. "Touch her again, you *peasant*, and I'll break your fucking fingers," I swore in German.

"Why isn't he speaking English? What is he saying?"

Julia laid her hand on my arm. "It's, ah…Gerard. He doesn't understand English. Byron said he is only here to help."

I pulled the check out of my pocket. "She isn't doing anything. Here is your money. We'll take her things and be done."

Mrs. Newcombe grabbed the check and scowled at us. "You can't have her things until this clears. It might bounce, and then I'm screwed. I wouldn't put it past you."

Gerard let out a string of profanities anyone would recognize, no matter the language they were uttered in.

I glared at her. "You are the most obnoxious woman I have ever met. I'm glad Julia doesn't have to deal with you anymore," I spat out, lapsing into French.

Mrs. Newcombe's eyes narrowed. Julia's nervous voice piped up. "He says he'd never do that. Gerard said your dress is very pretty—very bright and flowery."

I snorted. It looked like a paint store had exploded on it. It matched the overprocessed hair piled up on the top of her head like a helmet.

"I'll pay you cash," I hissed between gritted teeth.

Julia looked at me, aghast. "It's five hundred dollars, Byron."

I reached over and grabbed back the check. "Fine. Once we have your things. And I want a receipt."

"No men."

I shook my head. "We're coming in and doing this. If you want your money, you'll let us in, you…"

"Byron," Julia pleaded.

"…awful excuse for a human being," I finished in Spanish.

"I think I want to accidentally run her over, thirty or forty times," Gerard announced cheerfully, the r's rolling off his tongue in his perfect French.

"Not sure if even that would kill her."

"But what fun I would have trying."

That made me chuckle. Mrs. Newcombe continued to glare at me, and I grinned widely in her direction.

"Do you want the money or not?" I asked in English.

I could see her wavering. She wanted the cash. And she wanted rid of Julia.

"If we help, she will be done in thirty minutes, and we'll be out of your hair. Otherwise, it could be hours, and Gerard and I will stand here on your doorstep the whole time," I stated.

"Naked," Gerard added with a smirk, in Hungarian.

Mrs. Newcombe began to protest when I threw out my ace in the hole. "Or I contact my lawyer, who is waiting for my call. He'll start proceedings against you for keeping Julia from collecting her things, and he'll be making inquiries to the Canadian Revenue Agency about the cash payments you insist on from her monthly. Just to be sure that all the income is, indeed, being claimed."

She went pale beneath her layers of makeup. But she shut up and huffed out an exaggerated breath. "You have thirty minutes. And I'll be watching."

"Trust me, Madame, so will we," Gerard stated dryly.

She frowned. "Wait, I thought he couldn't speak English?"

Julia waved her hands. "He can speak it. He just can't understand it."

I glanced at her, trying not to laugh. That made no sense.

But the woman bought it.

"Oh."

"Ignorant cow," I muttered in Spanish as I pushed past her. I wanted Julia out of here as fast as possible.

I was horrified at how Julia had been living. The room was small. A bed and dresser, an old, small desk with a battered lamp, and a bookcase was all the room held. Her bathroom had a stand-up shower, sink, and toilet, all of which had seen better days. Everything was neat, orderly, and totally depressing. The walls were beige, the cover on the bed a dull yellow, and the only picture was a ghastly oil painting you would find at a garage sale.

"This is it?"

"I have two boxes in the cupboard."

I handed Julia an empty tote. "You get your clothes. Gerard and I will do the desk and bookcase."

Not meeting my eyes, she nodded. Gerard pulled open the closet door and lifted the two boxes from the floor.

"I'll take these down."

I knew he was giving us a moment. I stepped forward, tugging Julia close. "Hey."

She looked up at me, her gaze nervous. "I know it's ugly. She wouldn't let me do anything. I knew it wasn't forever, and at least it was clean."

I had to give her that. The entire house smelled of bleach and cleaning products. How she lived with the smell burning her nose, I had no idea. But she had no reason to be nervous or ashamed. I was in awe of her—she was strong and positive, never complaining.

"I'm not judging. I just want to get you out of here and home with me." I dropped a kiss on her head. "That is your forever place—with me."

She smiled, and it was like the sun coming out from behind the clouds. "Yes."

"Hey! That's enough! You are supposed to be packing. I didn't let you in here so you could defile my house!" Mrs. Newcombe thumped on the door for good measure.

"If I thought that bed could take it, I'd throw you on it and fuck you just to listen to her scream and run," I growled. Then just to piss off the old cow, I lowered my head and covered Julia's mouth with mine, kissing her hard.

The screech I heard was so worth it. I pulled back, grinning.

"Okay, my love, let's get you packed."

Twenty of the longest minutes of my life later, Julia was packed, the totes in the cars, and I handed Mrs. Newcombe the five hundred dollars, refusing to leave until I had a receipt in my hand. I still planned to make that call to the CRA. She held out the slip of paper, the look on her face telling me exactly what she thought of me.

I stepped forward, keeping my voice low.

"You are, without a doubt, the nastiest piece of work I have ever met. The way you treated that lovely young woman, you should be ashamed of yourself."

"I don't have to take that from the likes of you," she sneered. "I know your type. You'll use her until something better comes your way."

"There *is* nothing better." I eyed her up and down. "If you treated your husband half as badly as you treated her, no wonder he left you."

She gasped, raising her hand. I arched my eyebrow. "Go ahead and try, lady. Give me an excuse to return the favor."

I never would hit a woman, but she didn't know that. She stepped back, clutching her frilly collar. "I hate cooks."

I laughed. "Good thing I'm not a cook. I am a chef. A fucking great one. Not that your opinion matters in the least. And I doubt you would know good cuisine if it bit you in the ass."

I walked down the steps, opening the door and waiting until Julia slid in. Leaning forward, I tipped up her face, kissing her until I heard the door of the house slam so hard the windows rattled. With a chuckle, I drew back.

"You ready to go home, my love?"

"Yes."

"Then let's go."

I got behind the wheel and pulled out of the driveway, resisting the urge to swing wide and drive over her grass and crush the ugly gnomes gracing the edge of her property. They looked very much like her.

Julia slipped her hand in mine, and I smiled at her, then hit the gas, taking her away from the depressing house and home with me.

Where she belonged.

CHAPTER 8

JULIA

A FEW MONTHS LATER

"My hand is tired."

Byron's voice was amused. "Switch hands, then."

I looked down. "Are you sure it's not stiff enough?"

He chuckled. "Trust me, it's nowhere near stiff enough—it still needs work. Move your hand faster."

I groaned and tried again. "I can't, Byron. I have no idea how you do this every day."

"I don't do it every day. In fact, I'm probably out of practice since you moved in."

I snorted. "I don't ask for it that often."

"Often enough. You've been cheating—I'm trying to teach you the right way of doing this. Faster, Julia. Do it faster. It won't work otherwise, and you'll have nothing."

I worked my hand as quick as I could. Over and over, I repeated the pattern, but nothing.

He held me back against his chest, his arms coming around my front. His lips grazed my ear. "Do you want me to do it?"

"Yes."

I felt his smirk. "You want to watch me?"

"Yes."

With an exaggerated sigh, he lifted me to the counter. "Watch my hand."

Two minutes later, he stopped. "*Voilà!* Stiff as can be. Perfect."

I leaned forward and peeked in the bowl. He was right.

Perfect whipped cream.

With a grin, I dragged my finger through the white clouds and lifted it to my mouth. Before I could take a lick, Byron grabbed my finger and pulled it between his lips, his tongue sliding over my skin. I shuddered at the sensation, giggling when he gently bit down, tugging on the end of my finger.

"I wanted a taste." I pouted at him. "I got it started for you."

With a laugh, he dipped his finger in and held it up to me. I leaned forward, gasping when he grinned and covered the end of my nose with the cream, then kissed it off. "Hey!"

His smile was wide. So wide, his eyes crinkled and he laughed. Relenting, he slipped his finger into my mouth so I could have a taste.

"Mmm. Good." I grinned at him. "But really, Byron. That's what mixers are for."

"Mixers are shortcuts. I was taught to beat the cream by hand." He frowned at me. "What if there was an electrical failure? How would you beat the cream then, hmm?"

I giggled. "If there was an electrical failure, Byron, I probably caused it while burning dinner. I doubt I'd be worried about whipping cream for dessert."

He laughed again and rewarded me with another of his kisses. "Point taken."

My cooking hadn't improved much in the months I'd been living with Byron. I could now make pancakes from scratch, but I still got distracted easily. Byron's griddle had been replaced twice. So now, the past couple Sundays, he made the pancakes, and I sliced the strawberries and whipped the cream. The first time I pulled out the store-bought can of whipped cream from the refrigerator, he almost passed out with fright. I was forced to listen to his lecture on the dangers of what was in the can, not to mention the poor quality of the product. I didn't dare tell him about the Cool Whip in the freezer. I simply disposed of it the next day on my way to school. The next week, I bought a carton of the right cream, and he watched, amused, as I pulled up instructions for how to whip it using the expensive mixer he had in his high-tech kitchen. This week, he informed me he was teaching me how to do it properly—he even put a copper bowl and whisk in the freezer to get them cold.

Sundays were officially my favorite day of the week. I made sure to have all my schoolwork done and the house tidy. I had given up my part-time jobs, except for being a TA, and since Byron refused to accept much money for me living here, I liked to keep it clean. He knew I had to feel as if I was contributing, and I liked doing things in an effort to look after him. He said we made a great team. He did the cooking; I did the cleaning.

We stayed up late on Saturday nights after Byron came home from the restaurant, slept in on Sundays, and spent the day together. We rarely left the house; in fact, some Sundays, we rarely left the bedroom, except to get something to eat. Even then, Byron would carry me downstairs on his back and sit me on the counter while he prepared some delicious dish. He let me do the basics and was always surprisingly patient with me. I had heard the way he carried on at times in the kitchen at the restaurant, but he never lost his temper with me, even when I burned something or destroyed one of his expensive pots. I had to admit, the day I snapped his knife in half trying to get a drawer open I had overstuffed, his face had frightened me. Then he calmly removed the handle from my hand and suggested perhaps next time I use a screwdriver instead of a seven-hundred-dollar kitchen implement to unstick something. I had gasped at the price, but he shrugged and grinned, then told me he'd had his eye on a newly designed one anyway, and now he had the perfect excuse to buy it. I hadn't touched it to this day.

He had almost laughed himself sick when he found a small set of knives I'd bought at the dollar store in the drawer. I'd seen them advertised on TV years ago—they were supposed to be the sharpest knives around. I decided they were good enough for me, so if I broke them, it was only a dollar to buy another set. But once again, he surprised me, only smirking when I would pull one out of the drawer to slice strawberries or whatever other chore he would assign me.

"Are the pancakes ready?"

He shook his head, still leaning on the counter, watching me.

"Oh."

I peeked over his shoulder. "Byron, you forgot to put the griddle on."

"I didn't forget."

I frowned. "Do you want me to cook them?"

"No. I want you to sit right there."

"Okay. I'm kinda hungry, though."

"Are you?"

I grinned up at him. "You've kept me busy since we woke up."

He pressed closer. "Is that right?" He ran his nose up my neck, his lips on the lobe of my ear, tugging gently. "Busy doing what?"

I whimpered as he ran his hands ran up and down my bare thighs, his fingers tracing my skin, while his lips and tongue were moving on my neck. "Well…um…we made love." I gasped as his teeth bit down at the juncture of my neck.

"Twice," he agreed, his voice low and husky. "What else?"

"The…the whipping cream," I mumbled, having trouble concentrating on forming any words as he slipped his hands under the shirt I had on, pushing my legs apart and standing between them.

"This cream?" he asked huskily, gathering a large mound of the sweet substance on his fingers and smearing it across my collarbone.

"Yes!" I moaned as he drew his tongue over my skin, swirling and licking.

"Hmmm…so good," he replied. "But I know how it would taste better."

Cold air hit my skin as he grasped the two sides of the shirt I was wearing and pulled. Small white disks hit the floor, scattering and rolling in every direction as the buttons met the ceramic tile. Byron growled as he tugged the shirt off my shoulders, leaving it hanging from my arms. "You look so fucking hot in my clothes, Julia, but you look especially good when they're off."

He pushed me back so I was leaning on my elbows, and he grinned, arching an eyebrow at me. "No panties in the kitchen?" He shook his head. "I don't think I can let that infraction slip."

My chest heaved at his words, my breath coming out in sharp exhales.

He arched one eyebrow. "I think maybe you need to be punished."

He was sin incarnate when it came to sex. Cool, calm, in control Chef Lord became hot, sexy, foul-mouthed, dirty-talking, I'm-gonna-fuck-you-hard Byron.

And then he fed me later. It was the best of both worlds.

Never breaking eye contact, he smirked. A long, lazy, up-to-no-good smirk. He traced his fingers over my torso, barely grazing my hardened nipples. Once, twice, and again. I groaned—each time his fingers dipped lower, touched harder, lingered longer. But it still wasn't enough. I whimpered and he grinned, his eyes darkening to the point they were almost black. I shut my own, tilting back my head as I arched into his touch.

"Please," I breathed. "I've been bad, Byron."

He chuckled, a low, deep sound in his throat. "Yes, you have. I think a tongue-lashing is in order."

I felt the flow of smooth cream trail across my breasts, gasping at the cold followed by the heat of Byron's mouth lapping at the whipped cream swirling over my nipples and down my stomach. I cried out as he dropped a huge mound of cream over the top of my pussy, letting his tongue gather it up. "Now that—" he groaned "—that is the best creation I've ever made. Julia a la mode." He nudged my legs farther apart, opening me up more to his sexy ministrations. The cream was ice-cold when it landed on my aching center, and I moaned at the mind-blowing sensations of the cold and the heat of Byron's tongue.

Byron was like a man possessed—swirling his tongue, licking and nibbling as he cursed, moaned, and hissed. He nipped and lapped. Teased and stroked. He used his fingers like his cock, filling me, thrusting hard as his tongue slid sensuously, pressing and touching until I came. Hard. Screaming his name, bucking under his fingers as I exploded and my body shook, my muscles gripping his fingers tightly. He didn't even give me time to take in a deep breath before he slammed into me, pinning me down, his hands locked on my hips as he took me. Deep, powerful thrusts that made my eyes roll back in my head as I clung to his arms and tried to keep up. He growled and hissed as he threw my legs over his shoulders, burying himself deeper and taking me even harder. One shudder after another racked my body as I began to feel the coil tighten again, deep in my stomach. I gasped his name as he cursed, clutching at my shoulders, our bodies slippery and wet. Sweat dripped down his cheeks, his chest glistening in the light as his head fell back and he roared my name, just as another orgasm tore through me.

"Fuck...*fuck*...fuck...*Ju*...*lia*...fuck... *Yes!*"

He collapsed onto my chest, breathing loudly. It took every bit of energy I had left to lift my hand and run it through his hair in a lazy motion.

I felt his grin against my skin, followed by the gentle nuzzle of his lips.

"Kitchen sex. So much better than pancakes," he murmured.

I giggled. "Messier."

"A hot bath will fix that up."

"I think it's like Chinese food, though," I mused.

He was already laughing as he lifted his head from my chest, his eyes dancing, once again blue and happy-looking. "This, I have to hear. Why is kitchen sex like Chinese food?"

I smirked. "An hour from now, I'll be ready for more."

His mouth curved into his crooked grin, and his eyes gleamed wickedly. "Not a problem, Julia. I promise I'll fill you up again before an hour passes."

Oh.

Oh.

He stood, taking me with him, our chests meshed together. I wrapped my legs around his hips, burying my face into his neck, flicking my tongue out to taste the saltiness of his skin. He grabbed the bowl of whipped cream, holding me against him with one hand. He was chuckling as he climbed the stairs. "In case you need to, ah, eat something before the hour is up."

I tugged on his ear with my teeth. "Oh, I know exactly where I want that whipped cream, Byron. And I guarantee it'll be stiff by the time I'm done with it."

"I think you have that wrong," He smirked as he deposited me on the bathroom counter. "I'm pretty sure by the time you're done with it—it'll be anything but stiff." He winked. "But I'm happy to let you try."

I grinned.

Yep. I loved Sundays.

❧

I shifted nervously in my seat, waiting for my new professor to arrive. A sudden windfall had enabled my professor to retire, and his replacement arrived today. I was meeting with her to discuss my staying on as her TA. I rolled my shoulders and stretched my back. Both were still a little sore from the kitchen sex yesterday, even though Byron had treated me to a lovely warm bath and massage afterward.

Not to mention the pancakes. Light, fluffy pancakes we ate with syrup, since all the whipped cream had been consumed in more resourceful ways. Byron had thoroughly enjoyed my ingenious use of the whipped cream, burying his hands in my hair as I teased him with my tongue, swirling the cool cream around and licking it off his length until the bowl was empty and he had come with a low, sexy moan that echoed off the walls around us.

A hot, soapy shower was needed for both of us.

The shutting of the door behind me startled me out of my thoughts. I sat up straighter as the whirlwind that was Lila Peters blew into the room. Her arms were full, an iPad tucked under her arm, a McDonald's bag clutched in her teeth, and a cup of coffee clasped in her hand. Dark hair was swept off her neck in a braid, and she had large brown eyes that glittered in the light.

With a grunt, she opened her arms, dumping the files and briefcase onto her desk. She opened her mouth and let the bag fall on top of the pile and set her coffee down on the corner, then grimaced and moved it closer to the center.

"That—" she grinned "—is a disaster waiting to happen." Then she stuck out her hand. "Dr. Lila Peters. You, I hope, are Julia, and if you're not, then I'm in the wrong office."

Without giving me a chance to reply, she sat down with a huff, reaching for the bag. "Please tell me I'm in the right office. I'm starving, and this chair is pretty comfy."

I gaped at her as she unwrapped a McMuffin and took a bite, closing her eyes with a satisfied smirk. "Damn, that's good." She reached into the bag and held out a second sandwich. "Hungry?"

I bit my lip. No matter what Byron had done, no matter how many mouth-watering, delicious breakfast sandwiches he made me, this one still tempted me as my guilty pleasure. Every so often, I gave in and had one, and every time he laughed and shook his head. He'd kiss my temple and shudder, mumbling that if I had to succumb on occasion, at least I did it with the least offensive thing on the menu.

With a nod and a mumbled, "Thank you," I reached out, took the proffered sandwich and bit into it with a satisfied hum. It might not contain an egg gently coddled with tarragon and aged cheese, or topped with hardwood-smoked bacon Byron drizzled maple syrup on while cooking, but it was damned good.

In between bites and sips, Lila and I talked. She was fascinating. Well-traveled and read, she had a whole new approach to teaching, and by the time the meeting was done, I was beyond excited about being her TA. She explained how she had agreed to the position, even though she had to finish out the year using the current structure and curriculum, but said she could infuse more interesting aspects into it. I was also thrilled to discover she taught another higher-level course I would be taking in the new school year. I knew I was going to learn a great deal from her. We talked about some of the reading material she wanted me to be familiar with. I had a few of the books, but there was one I didn't.

"I'll pick it up later."

She waved her hand. "I have several copies. I'll drop one off to you this evening. You live on campus?"

I shook my head. "No. I, ah, live with my boyfriend."

She nodded. "Good idea. Off campus is so much quieter. What year is he in?"

"Oh, he isn't a student."

"Already working, then?"

"Yes, he's a chef."

"Excellent. You'll have to tell me where he works. I love to cook—maybe we can share recipes." She laughed.

Before I could explain anything else, she stood. "I have another meeting. Leave me your address, and I'll drop off the book. I have to run around and find some things later, if that works for you."

I stood as well, nodding. "I'll be home tonight."

Tonight was Monday—my second favorite night of the week. Gerard and I shared a love of old movies. *Casablanca, The Maltese Falcon, An Affair to Remember*—we loved them all. Every couple of weeks, he came over, and we watched a movie after he made dinner. Byron joined us on occasion, but he didn't like to be out of the restaurant if Gerard wasn't covering. If things were quiet, Byron would come home early and join us for the second feature; although often he'd fall asleep with his head in my lap. He worked too hard, even though he'd cut back a little since I'd come into his life. Gerard told me that before I was around, Byron worked seven days a week—even when the restaurant was closed. Now we had Sundays, the occasional Monday when he'd let Gerard handle everything, and when he could, he left early and came home. It wasn't often, but I loved it when he did.

Tonight, we were watching *Roman Holiday*. Byron promised to try to come home early. They were both pleased with one of the chefs and the way he was actively taking on additional responsibilities. He was ecstatic when Byron showed enough faith in him to leave early, entrusting the kitchen and restaurant to him. It was only for a couple hours, but for Byron, it was huge—especially since Gerard wasn't there either.

I was curled up in the corner of the sofa, the movie ready to play. Gerard was stretched out in the chair beside me. Tonight, he had created a spread of finger food to snack on while we watched the film. He was a brilliant chef, but severe early onset arthritis in his joints prevented him from being in the kitchen for long periods. Instead, he became Byron's right-hand man, his essential maître d, and business partner. There was no one Byron relied on, trusted, or respected more. Gerard and Byron developed the menus, shared recipes, and both admitted to never wanting to have a restaurant without the other. Their teamwork was what made them such a success.

I adored Gerard, not only for how he treated Byron, but for how wonderful a person he was—kind, thoughtful, sweet. I'd never seen him lose his temper or even appear upset—he seemed unflappable. I was surprised he wasn't married, but as he explained to me one day, he had never allowed himself the time to find the right person when he was younger—far too busy becoming a chef and opening his own place, he let time slip past. I scoffed at him, reminding him he was only forty, which was hardly in his dotage. He only shook his head, telling me he had a good life, was happy and settled, and that was all he wanted. He did, however, admit he was thrilled Byron had found me and wouldn't be alone the way he was. Byron, he said with a gentle smile, had so much to give.

He only shook his head when I replied I felt that he, *Gerard*, did as well.

Byron and I tried to include him in as much of our life as we could. Dinners, movie night, whenever we could, we made sure he was part of it. He wasn't much older than Byron, yet I knew Byron thought of him as a father figure. To me, he was a favorite older brother.

Gerard laughed loudly as I described my new professor and the fact that we shared a love of McMuffins. Although he wasn't as vehement in his dislike of fast food as Byron, he preferred to cook himself. He was pleased at how excited I was about the direction Lila seemed to be heading in since he loved to hear about school and what I was learning.

A knock at the door startled me; it was then I remembered Lila was dropping off a book.

"That's her now." I grinned. "You can meet her yourself."

"I'll get another plate."

I nodded. "She'll love that!"

Lila breezed in, chatting about everything she'd done that day and laughing over some things she'd seen on campus. She admired the house, and when Gerard appeared, she was rendered speechless for a moment before shaking his hand and accepting the offer to stay and enjoy the movie with us, tempted, no doubt, by the delicious repast he had prepared. She sat down, accepting not only the plate but a glass of wine. Gerard started the movie then proceeded to ignore the screen, as did Lila. The two of them started talking about different places they'd both visited, books they'd read, and she praised his cooking, asking questions about ingredients as she sampled various tidbits.

"Is this tarragon with the chicken?"

"Yes, it is, Lila." Gerard beamed at her.

"Do I detect a hint of saffron?"

"You do!"

I sat in the chair, watching them, also ignoring the movie. What was happening in front of me was far more entertaining. Gerard was effusive, happy, his hands gesturing as he spoke, sometimes so quick his words ran together. There was something different about him. Then it dawned on me —he was nervous. Unflappable Gerard was nervous. I watched them closer. Lila had two bright spots of color on her cheeks, and her dark eyes never left his face as he spoke.

They liked each other. A lot.

I hugged myself. Until that very second I'd never thought about it, but they were perfect for each other. Polar opposites in some ways, they complemented each other. Her flightiness was the perfect contrast to his steady countenance. Her very presence made him lighter. Byron often said the same thing about me in relation to him.

Gerard stood. "We need more wine."

Lila's gaze followed him across the room, then her eyes met mine, widening in panic. I smirked, about to tease her, when she suddenly leaped to her feet.

"I have to go."

I frowned. "But—"

She shook her head, almost running for the door. "I'm so sorry!"

I didn't even make it to my feet when the door slammed shut behind her. I gaped at the door in shock.

What the hell just happened?

Gerard came into the room, a fresh bottle of wine in his hand. He looked around, confused. "Where's Lila?"

I pointed to the door. "She suddenly said she had to leave."

"Just like that?"

I nodded.

The squeal of tires backing out the driveway made us both swivel our heads in the direction of the street.

"Did you say something to upset her?" he cried.

"No." I shook my head frantically. "She just…bolted!"

He sat down heavily. "Well, *fuck*."

I sat beside him. "You like her, Gerard?"

He frowned. "She seemed wonderful."

I nodded. "She is."

A few minutes later, the front door opened and Byron strode in, muttering, his face dark.

"What's wrong?"

"Some woman almost ran me off the road. She was going like a bat out of hell down the street—crazy driver!"

I giggle-snorted. "Was it an old Mustang?"

Byron nodded as Gerard groaned. "She drives an old Mustang?"

Byron looked confused. "Who?"

"My new professor. She came by to drop off a book. One minute, she was flirting with Gerard, then the next, she took off. We're not sure why."

Byron sat down and picked up a small puffed morsel, chewing it slowly. "Maybe these chicken bundles. A little heavy-handed on the tarragon, Gerard."

He groaned. "I know. I thought so too."

I burst out laughing—they tasted great to me. "I doubt it was your bundles, Gerard. Something else happened."

"What?"

"I don't know, but I'll find out," I promised.

Byron leaned back. "Are we watching this movie or not?"

Gerard nodded and picked up the remote, starting it over from the beginning. "Might as well."

He sounded so sad. I met Byron's gaze and shrugged. I'd go see Lila first thing the next morning and get to the bottom of her abrupt departure.

Lila avoided me for three days. She was busy or in meetings. She didn't return my calls. Finally, I decided to show up unannounced and meet her face-to-face. Byron said Gerard hadn't been himself since Monday, and I was determined to find out why she ran, when they were so obviously attracted to each other.

I squared my shoulders and knocked on her door, entering when I heard her call out, "Come in!" To say she looked surprised to see me would be an understatement. Her face went pale, but she invited me in anyway.

I sat across from her, noticing she looked tired and anxious. "Are you okay, Lila?"

She drew in a deep breath. "I'm fine."

"You worried us, leaving so fast."

"I'm sorry—that was rude of me. I remembered a previous engagement."

"I see. We were very concerned—especially Gerard."

"Please tell him I'm fine, and he doesn't have to worry."

"Maybe you should tell him yourself."

She frowned at me. "That's not a good idea."

"Why?"

She stood up pacing. "Julia, I can't see Gerard again. In fact, I think it would be a good idea if, after this course is done, I find you another TA job."

I gasped. "Why?"

She sat across from me. "Do you want me to be completely honest?"

"Yes."

"I liked Gerard."

"He liked you too."

"No, I mean I *liked*, liked him."

I waved my hand. "I understand that. I don't see the problem."

"You don't *see* the problem?" she asked shrilly.

"No."

She looked aghast. "He's your *boyfriend*. You don't see the problem with the fact that I found him sexy and wanted to lick off the little bit of pastry he had stuck on the side of his mouth with my tongue? That isn't a problem to you?"

I blinked at her for a moment, then started to laugh.

"What's so funny?"

I hadn't even thought of that. I told Lila I lived with my boyfriend and he was a chef. I introduced her to Gerard, not *as* my boyfriend, but since he was there, had cooked the food she was eating, and seemed at home, of course she thought he was my boyfriend. My boyfriend she was now lusting after hard.

"He's not my boyfriend," I gasped between gales of laughter.

"He's not?"

"No, I think you…you almost ran my boyfriend off the road in your haste to get away from us."

"Oh." She frowned. "The black BMW?"

I nodded, wiping tears off my face. Byron was going to laugh himself sick over this.

I calmly explained it all to her. I showed her Byron's picture and clarified who Gerard was to both of us. Told her about our Monday movie nights. Then I winked at her and said Gerard probably would have liked it if she had, indeed, licked his face.

She buried her face in her hands. "Now, I'm even more embarrassed," she groaned. "I can never face him."

"You have to. He really liked you," I informed her.

She blushed, looking hopeful. "He did?"

I nodded. "Very much so."

"He must think I'm crazy for running out."

"He'd be thrilled to see you again."

She sighed, looking uncertain.

"Do you have plans tonight?"

She shook her head.

"How about dinner?"

"Will Gerard be there?"

"Yes. It'll be somewhere you can interact, but no pressure. I promise you one of the greatest meals you've ever eaten."

"Gerard and great food? I'm in."

I scribbled down the address. "Meet me here at nine."

Her eyes widened. "Your boyfriend works at Creations? I've heard people talking about it. I read a write-up on it in the weekend paper. The critic raved about it."

I smiled proudly at her. "My boyfriend *is* Creations."

"Wow."

Then I leaned forward. "So is Gerard."

"Oh my."

Byron laughed when I spoke with him later and told him the whole story. In fact, he dropped the phone, he laughed so hard. Once he stopped guffawing, he agreed my plan was a good one.

"You're sure you want the kitchen spot, my love?" he asked.

"Yes."

Byron had a special table in the kitchen, tucked into its own alcove. It was set up so you could see what all the chefs were doing. He sat there on occasion to observe if he felt something wasn't working properly. At times, the chefs sat at it on their break, and every now and then, it was used to host special guests—people who paid big money to a charity to watch Byron cook a special meal for them. They were waited on by only Byron and Gerard and catered to for a night. Sometimes, Byron would grant them access and even allow them to do some simple task, so they could brag and say they had cooked with him.

He preferred when it was used as "Julia's spot," as he called it. I would sit, surrounded by schoolwork, interrupted only when Byron would slide some snack in front of me, nuzzling my head or dropping a heavy kiss on my lips and murmuring I was working too hard and needed to eat. He would sit with me when he could and talk quietly about his day or our plans for the next Sunday. Even after I came to live with him, he liked me there, saying he never saw me enough. I liked looking up and watching him in his element. Listening to him issue orders, commanding the flow of the kitchen, and keeping it running seamlessly. He looked so sexy in his chef's attire, as he created, led, and tested, making sure each dish that left the kitchen was perfect. He would catch my eye and wink when he'd given someone hell about something, never raising his voice, only changing the tone. It was enough to bring them all to attention. Me included.

I had asked about bringing Lila and he told me it wasn't booked, so he would have it prepared for me. "Gerard will be thrilled," he assured me. "Once he gets over the surprise anyway."

"I hope so."

"Are you sure you can do this?"

I sighed. "I can carry dishes, Byron."

"Okay. Just checking."

"You'll be okay out front?"

"I'll make sure."

"Byron?"

"Yes, my love?"

"I need you on top of your game tonight."

He snorted. "Aren't I always?"

"For me."

He lowered his voice. "Do I get to be on top of you later, then?"

"Yes."

"Done. We'll give Gerard and Lila a night they'll never forget."

~

Lila's eyes were huge when I met her in the parking lot. "Julia," she called, hurrying toward me. "How did you manage to get a reservation—even if you know the owner? I was told it's booked up for months!"

I hooked my arm through hers and walked toward the back of the restaurant. "We have a special table."

I opened the door, and we stepped in. She looked around, taking in the busy kitchen and inhaling the delicious aromas. I smiled at her as I saw Byron approaching.

"There's someone I'd like you to meet."

Byron leaned down, kissing my cheek gently. He extended his hand. "Hello, I'm Byron Lord. Julia's official boyfriend. Welcome to my restaurant."

Lila's cheeks colored, and she tossed back her dark hair, then shook his hand. "Lila Peters. Dr. Lila Peters."

"Pleased to meet you. May I take your coat?"

She slid it off her shoulders, and it was all I could do not to clap my hands. From the moment I met her, she reminded me of a movie star from the era Gerard and I loved so much. Tonight, with her dark hair down around her shoulders and an elegant dinner dress on, she looked the part. Gerard wouldn't know what hit him.

Byron draped her coat over his arm and escorted us to the table. She sat down, glancing around nervously. I knew she was looking for Gerard. Byron winked at me, and I stood beside the table, chatting to Lila.

"Aren't you going to sit down?" she asked, eyeing me suspiciously.

I saw Byron return, Gerard in tow. I stepped back, and he froze when he saw Lila. Then the warmest smile broke out on his face and his hazel eyes lit up. Glancing at her, I saw the same warmth being returned, her dark eyes glowing. He stepped forward, and I indicated with my hand he should sit. I beamed at them, while Byron stood beside me. He cleared his throat.

"Welcome to Creations. Tonight, you'll both be my guests as I prepare you a special dinner. Julia—" he lifted my hand and kissed it "—has arranged for this special evening for you, and she'll be acting as your server."

Gerard chuckled, and I fought the urge to kick him. Instead, I glared, and he ducked his head. Byron kept talking. "Do you have any dietary concerns I should know of?"

They both shook their heads "no," and Gerard spoke up. "Byron—"

"Everything is looked after, Gerard," he assured him.

"Of course it is. I was thinking perhaps, though, I might take care of the wine myself. I have a special bottle in mind."

Byron tilted his head. "By all means." He held out his hand. "Come, my Julia. I need your help."

I stood beside him, almost bouncing with excitement as I looked over at the table. They were already laughing, and I had no doubt Lila had told him the whole I-thought-you-were-her-boyfriend-story.

"Do you really need my help?"

Byron chuckled. "You can carry the food to the table."

"I could chop stuff."

"Ah, we don't have any dollar store knives here." He held up his shiny, lethal blade. "I don't think our guests want blood in their food, either."

I sighed. "Carrying plates. Yeah, I can do that."

Byron bent close to my ear, indicating the table with a subtle tilt on his head. "Besides, you can watch the show from here."

I peeked over his shoulder and giggled. Lila's and Gerard's foreheads were practically molded together, and whatever they were discussing was obviously intense. They were totally focused on each other.

"I have a good feeling about this," I observed with a huge smile on my face.

Byron brushed his lips over my forehead. "I have a good feeling about you. Now, move or become part of the dinner!"

I rolled my eyes.

"Yes, Master…I mean, Chef Lord."

Two hours later, I was exhausted. Byron slipped his arms around me. "Go upstairs. I'll finish up."

I leaned back against him. "How can they possibly still be talking?"

He chuckled. "They took breaks to eat."

I shook my head. "I don't think so. They both talked with their mouths full."

"Go. I'll get Tom to clear the dessert. I'll just make sure everything is done, and Gerard will close up when they're finished." He snickered into my ear. "I have a feeling they may be here for a while yet."

After I gave a small wave to Lila and Gerard, I slipped out of the kitchen and trudged upstairs to Byron's private office. I sank onto the sofa and kicked off my shoes. I had no idea how anyone stood on their feet for hours on end or carried plates of food all night. I only had to go from the counter to the table a few times, fill up their water glasses, and make sure they were happy. Most of the time, Gerard simply waved me away, taking the plates right from my hands and serving Lila himself. He obviously didn't want me to interrupt the flow of their endless conversation.

It made me happy, seeing how much they were enjoying themselves. I curled into the corner of the sofa, wondering how long it would be before Byron joined me. I was glad tomorrow was Friday. It was going to be a long day, but my classes started later. My last class was Lila's, and I would meet her in the afternoon before it started to go through anything she wanted to discuss. I yawned and shut my eyes. I would just rest them until Byron came upstairs.

Warm lips brushing my cheek and his low voice in my ear woke me. "Sit up, my love. I brought us dinner." Sleepily, I allowed myself to be lifted into the sitting position and obediently opened my mouth when Byron pressed the fork on my lower lip. I chewed the pasta slowly, blinking in the light.

"How long was I asleep?"

He smiled gently at me as he chewed his pasta. "Not long." He lifted up another mouthful for me. "You're tired, my girl."

"I'm not used to being a waitress. It's a lot of work—and I know I had it easy tonight." I wiggled my toes. "My feet hurt."

He nodded. "Working in a restaurant is a lot of work for everyone— from the busboys to the waitstaff and the chefs."

I shook my head when he tried to give me more pasta. "I'm too tired."

"I'll make you a good breakfast before you go tomorrow," he promised, not forcing the issue. He finished off the pasta and set down the bowl beside him. He grinned at me as he scooped me up in his arms. "I can't have you stopping back at McDonald's again. One McMuffin this week was enough."

I rolled my eyes at him. I never should have mentioned it.

"I can walk," I protested weakly, even as I snuggled into his chest. I loved it when he carried me—I always felt so safe and loved when he cradled me protectively.

"Be good, and I'll give you a foot massage when we get home. Maybe even a back rub."

"I thought you were gonna get on top of me?" I breathed into his neck, letting my tongue flick his warm skin.

He growled low in his throat, his chest rumbling against me. "Since you'll no doubt sleep all the way home in the car, we'll be doing *that* in the morning, Julia."

I sighed and snuggled in deeper as the cool night air hit me. I realized he had bypassed the kitchen totally, giving Gerard and Lila their privacy. "I'm looking forward to the morning, then."

He lowered me into the passenger seat, cupping my face. He kissed me until I was breathless.

"Me too."

I knocked on Lila's door, stifling another yawn. It had been a long day. Byron had been right, and I'd slept in the car all the way home. I was barely awake to walk into the house. He was sweet enough to give me the promised foot and back rubs—although I did fall asleep while he was working on my back. This morning, he let me sleep as long as possible before waking me up and driving me back to the restaurant to get my car. Just as Byron parked the car, Gerard pulled in behind us. He got out of his car, beaming. The sun couldn't compete with the brilliance of his smile.

I giggled at the look of happiness on his face and smiled widely when he handed me a small bag.

"You've already been cooking?"

"I was hungry in the night, so I got up and did some cooking," he stated. "I made you a snack for later today—I know it's a long one."

I opened my backpack and slipped it inside, chuckling. Byron had already made me breakfast, packed me a lunch, and now Gerard looked after dinner for later. Between the two of them, I would never starve.

Gerard clapped Byron on the shoulder and walked over to the back of the restaurant, entering through the door. He whistled the whole time. Byron smirked as he watched him and turned to me. "Ten to one, he's tapping that before the weekend is out. If he hasn't already."

"Byron!"

"What? He has that same blitzed-out expression on his face I did after we made

love the first time. And after the meal I made them—he was hungry in the night? He must have worked up an appetite somehow!"

I shook my head. "They were probably up late talking. And you know how Gerard is… When he's excited over something, he has trouble sleeping."

Byron waggled his eyebrows at me. "He was excited, all right."

I slapped his arm and walked over to my car, yanking the door open and muttering about men and thinking only one thing. I gasped when Byron's arms wrapped around me, pulling me against his chest. He nudged my hair out of the way and ran his lips over my neck.

"All I'm saying is, I think your plan worked, my little matchmaker."

"I didn't plan on them…" I groaned. "I think you're wrong anyway. He's just happy."

"Care to make a little wager?"

I turned in his arms. "And how are you gonna find out? You can't just ask him."

"I'll figure it out. You want that bet?"

"What's the wager?"

"Winner gets whatever they want…anything…for a week."

I frowned. I didn't have a lot of money to spend. "Anything? Like what anything?"

"Food, massages, foot rubs—" he lowered his mouth to my ear "—anything sexually…"

I swallowed, the words popping out of my mouth before I could stop them. "Could I tie you up?"

His eyebrows shot up high, and his eyes darkened. "If that's what you want." He brushed his lips over mine. "Maybe I'll tie you up."

Heat tore through me.

His tongue traced my bottom lip. "Maybe, even if I win, I'll let you tie me up. Like a freebie. Or maybe that will be my prize."

"Oh."

His mouth covered mine in a long, passionate kiss. Vaguely, I was aware other cars had pulled into the lot and his staff were walking past us, but I didn't care. They were used to his displays of affection.

He stepped back, his eyes hooded and his chest heaving.

"This is gonna be a great week."

"You haven't won yet."

He winked. "I already have."

After another long, passionate kiss and my promises of making up for falling asleep last night, he sent me off to school. His warm eyes were gentle as he leaned into my window, and I whispered I loved him. He still liked hearing me say it.

"I'll see you at home, my love."

~

Lila's voice bade me to enter, so I stepped inside, clutching my backpack of books and the snack from Gerard. She looked up from the mess that was her desk and grinned at me.

Beamed, more like it. The same wide, bright smile Gerard wore this morning. She looked…blissful.

Oh God—was Byron right?

Sitting on the only neat spot on her desk was a huge vase of flowers. Roses, carnations, and orchids overflowed the vase, their fragrance filling the office.

I leaned forward and smelled them. "They're beautiful!"

Lila giggled, sounding like a young girl. "I know. He's too much."

I set down my bag. "You had a good time?" I asked cautiously. I was still getting to know her, and I didn't want to cross any lines.

"Wonderful! My God, can your Byron cook!"

I nodded proudly. "He's amazing."

"And Gerard," she gushed. "He is just so…so…yummy!"

I laughed. "I saw him this morning when Byron drove me to get my car. I think he feels the same way about you."

"It was such a great night. Thank you."

I shrugged. "The two of you hit it off so well—I thought you'd be perfect for each other."

She nodded. "Almost."

"Almost?"

She waved her hand around. "He's such a neat freak. I'm afraid when he sees what chaos I surround myself in, he might run. His place is immaculate."

My throat became dry. *She'd seen his place?* Was she there all night? I couldn't ask her that question. It was too personal.

Her voice interrupted my thoughts. "Okay, we need to go over some notes. Did you need to get something to eat?"

I shook my head. "No, I have something."

"Me too!"

I leaned over and pulled my bag from my backpack, freezing when I saw Lila open the same sort of bag. When she pulled out the exact same container as mine and opened it, I knew without looking, it would contain chicken and asparagus roll-ups. Freshly made and packed by Gerard.

Her eyes widened when she saw my container. "Gerard dropped this off after he made it at the restaurant earlier," she murmured, the tips of her ears turning red.

"He gave me mine this morning. He said he made it at home." I paused. "In the *night*—when he was hungry."

For a minute, she said nothing, then she started to laugh. "Busted."

I gaped at her. "Lila!"

She giggled as she lifted a roll from the container. "What can I say? The man has moves." She heaved a huge, shuddering sigh. "So many, many moves."

She took a bite out of her sandwich and winked. "And then he fed me. It was the perfect night, Julia. I look forward to many more."

My mouth opened and closed, no words coming out.

Those were my thoughts—about Byron.

She now had the same thing I did. A great guy…great sex…great food.

Knowing Gerard, he was the same as Byron. If they had already progressed to that step…he was all-in.

Byron was right. I'd never live it down. And now I was at his mercy for an entire week.

God only knew what he'd think up.

Deciding to get it over with, I picked up my phone and texted him.

Julia: *You won.*

My phone chirped a few seconds later.

Byron: *I know. He was far too smug all day. I finally got it out of him.*

I shook my head.

Julia: *Lila spilled in about five seconds. All she said was: Busted.*

Byron: *LOL. Guess you're busted now. Seven days, my love. All mine.*

I sighed.

Julia: *I guess so. Be gentle.*

My phone rang, and I accepted the call. Byron's voice was low and warm in my ear. "Julia, I love you."

I glanced up at Lila, but she seemed to be busy eating and typing on her own phone. "I love you, too," I whispered, mystified at his greeting.

"You're not really worried, are you?"

I giggled. "No."

"Good. Have a good evening, and I'll see you at home."

"Okay."

"And, Julia?"

"Yeah?"

"I ordered extra whipping cream today. I'll bring it home for Sunday." He drew in a deep breath. "And I'm going to let you have that freebie."

Then he hung up.

Remembering the last experience with whipped cream, I grinned.

Losing was going to be okay. I was looking forward to my freebie.

And I had a good feeling I was going to enjoy the next seven days.

Immensely.

~

FIVE YEARS LATER

I woke up slowly, my eyes blinking in the late morning light. I glanced at the clock, surprised to see it already past nine. Byron had let me sleep in. I slipped from our bed, got ready, and headed downstairs.

I heard them before I saw them. Byron's warm voice and the excited giggle of our goddaughter, Nikki. I rounded the corner and bit back my laughter. There was flour on the floor, the table, and all over them, and Byron's kitchen was a mess. But he wore a wide smile, and his voice was patient as he taught his favorite tiny human how to make cookies.

"Like this, Nikki. Roll it in your hand gently." He paused. "A bit gentler, little one. We want balls, not pancakes."

She stared up at him, her hazel eyes wide and hopeful. "You make pancakes, Unca By?"

I already knew the answer before he responded. He couldn't say no to her. Ever.

"Yes."

I chuckled, and he glanced up, already smiling. "Hello, my beautiful wife."

I still got a thrill when he called me that. We had gotten married two years ago, right after I graduated, in a simple ceremony in the back

76

garden. Lila and Gerard had married not long after they met, and Nicola had been born a year later. We adored her and enjoyed having her stay overnight. She and Byron always got up early and had "fun" in the kitchen. His patience with her was endless, and she loved spending time with him.

I moved forward, kissing a tiny flour-covered cheek, then lifting on my toes to press a kiss to Byron's mouth. He smiled against my lips. "You look better. You were so tired last night."

"I am," I assured him.

"I made coffee."

"In a while."

He frowned but didn't say anything. I sat with Nikki, and together, we rolled out balls as Byron made pancakes. We tidied up the table and had just sat down when Gerard and Lila arrived, prompting a round of happy squeals from Nikki. They sat having coffee, Nikki on her daddy's knee as he sipped from his mug and let his daughter feed him drippy pancakes, his eyes filled with adoration. She had Lila's dark hair and tiny stature, but Gerard's hazel eyes and his wide smile.

Gerard was a changed man, much the same way Byron's attitude in life was different. They hired the right people, took time for themselves and family, and still maintained incredibly high standards at the restaurants they owned. As Lila stated, they had learned balance.

Gerard shook his head as Byron placed a plate of still-warm cookies on the table.

"Pancakes and cookies, Byron?"

Byron lifted one shoulder. "Your daughter helped make them. I thought you'd like to sample one."

I chuckled at Nikki's abandonment of her pancakes in order to feed her daddy a cookie. "I made dis one," she informed him. "It's special."

He ate it, looking at her tenderly. He adored his girls.

They left not long after, and Byron cleaned the kitchen while I had a shower. When I came out of the bathroom, he was lounging on the bed. He patted the mattress. "Come here, my love."

I curled up beside him with a sigh. Close to Byron was still my favorite place in the world.

"You've been quiet the last few days."

"Hmm," I replied.

"And tired. Are you unwell?"

"No."

"You didn't drink any coffee this morning. That's a first."

I sighed and sat up. I met his worried gaze and smiled in reassurance. "I'm fine, Byron. But there is something I want to talk to you about."

His frown deepened. "You can talk to me about anything. You know that."

I ducked my head, trying not to let him see my excitement. I traced my finger along his hand that was holding mine.

"What if I told you I didn't want to work anymore?"

I had only been able to secure part-time teaching since graduation and was doing a lot of substitute work. It kept me busy, but it wasn't what I had planned for after school. And now, my plans were changing yet again.

He lifted my chin. "Then don't. I have told you time and again, you don't have to work."

"There is something else I want to do."

"Good. That's good. Tell me," he said encouragingly.

I slipped my hand under my pillow and handed him a tiny whisk. "This."

He looked startled. "Ah, Julia, my love, I don't think cooking is your forte."

I giggled. "But Byron, I think you're wrong. I already have a bun in the oven, and from all I've been told, it looks perfect."

He blinked. Looked at the whisk, caught on to what I was saying, and then his gaze flew to mine. His eyes flared with understanding.

"You're pregnant?"

"Six weeks."

I was in his arms in an instant, and his mouth was on mine. "Julia, my darling wife. My girl. *A baby*. We're having a baby!"

"Yes."

He kissed me again, dropping his hand to my stomach and spreading his fingers wide. "Our baby is right here. Right now."

Tears filled my eyes. "Yes."

He wrapped me close. "Thank you," he breathed. "You have made my entire world even better. I didn't think that was possible."

I snuggled close. "I love you."

He kissed my head. "Love doesn't even begin to cover it. I need a far bigger word for you, Julia."

We sat, letting the joy of the moment sink in.

"Quit the teaching. I want you home. You can do things you enjoy. Help Lila. Come to the restaurant and spend time with me. We need to decorate the nursery. I get to come to the appointments, right?" He paused to take a breath. "I have to tell Gerard—he'll be thrilled. I need to borrow his books. I need to buy a bigger car. One we can put a baby seat in like his."

I reached up and covered his mouth. "One thing at a time, Daddy."

He melted. That was the only way to describe his reaction to being called Daddy.

"A baby," he whispered. "Our baby. We'll be a family."

"Yes."

"Can we have more?"

I laughed. "Can we get through one first?"

He laughed at his own eagerness. "I suppose. But I have a feeling we're going to need a bigger house, Julia. Because I want lots of babies with you. I'll teach them to cook, you can teach them how to read and love books the way you do. Together, we'll teach them everything else. Especially about love. We'll make sure they know how much they are loved." He ran a finger down my cheek. "Just like their mother."

I smiled through my tears. "Sounds like a plan."

He wrapped me in his arms again.

"Yes, my love, it does."

Stitches

CHAPTER 1

IAN

I signed the last of the forms, checked all my patients had been discharged or sent on to other doctors, then stood with a tired grimace. I handed off the final charts to the head nurse.

"I'm out of here, Gail."

She smiled, glancing at her watch. "Only three hours past shift change," she stated dryly. "Hot date somewhere?"

I laughed as I slung my messenger bag over my shoulder. "Yep. Me and my pillow. I'm planning a hot make-out session with it for the rest of the day."

She shook her head. "You need a life."

I pushed up on the counter separating us and planted a kiss on her plump cheek. "Still waiting for you, Gail. When you're ready to leave Marv for some hot action, I'm your guy."

"I'll meet you at sundown," she quipped.

"Done."

Her laughter followed me from the ER. Gail was old enough to be my grandmother, and I had a soft spot for her. She doted on her husband, and I loved teasing her about running away with me. She was a good sport and gave as good as she got, even making me blush with her innuendos. I often thought she was the closest thing I ever got to foreplay anymore. There was simply no time in my life for a girlfriend or even a non-serious relationship. No woman in her right mind would want to take me on. Between

83

my shifts at the hospital, my volunteer work, and my irregular sleeping patterns, I was far too much effort. So, aside from my slightly inappropriate teasing with Gail and the occasional disastrous date, I was firmly single—my only constant companion in the romance department, my hand.

Cool, fresh spring air hit me as I walked out the doors. I stood breathing it in deeply, ridding my senses of the antiseptic smell that lingered. I glanced around, noting the full ambulance bay and hearing the chaos coming from the inside of the hospital every time a door opened. I had no doubt Gail would sort them out fast. She was an amazing charge nurse, and I was glad to work with her.

I stretched, my back and shoulders creaking and snapping in protest. It had been a busy night in the ER, and between nonstop patients and catching up on charting this morning, I was ready to head home.

I turned in the direction of the park, deciding I needed some coffee and a breakfast sandwich at the little café in the center. Being the weekend, it was busy, but I waited patiently for my sandwich and took it and a steaming cup of their cinnamon-laced brew over to my favorite bench. A little off the beaten track, it was quieter, fewer people around, so I rarely encountered anyone else when I went there. It was a great place to wind down after a long shift. I sat down, stretching out my long legs and placing my messenger bag on the empty space beside me.

I sipped and munched, enjoying the quiet. Leaning back my head, I let the breeze ruffle my hair and the solitude settle into my brain. My shoulders loosened, and I began to relax. I finished my sandwich, wadding up the paper and stuffing it into the empty coffee cup. I was about to stand when I heard the sound of running feet and two distinct voices. I turned in the direction they were coming from, the voices getting louder as they approached.

"Chloe! Come back!"

"No, Momma! I gots to find him!"

"Chloe! I said—" The voice cut off with a gasp, and suddenly, from the bushes burst forth a small child. She stopped short seeing me, her brown eyes large and startled in her round face. Corkscrew curls were a chaotic, riotous mass around her head, the color of wheat—bright, golden, and sunny. I judged her age as about four, maybe five. I smiled at her, wanting her to know she was okay with me.

I waggled my fingers. "Hi."

She startled me by racing over, stopping in front of me. She placed her tiny hands on my knees and tilted back her head, regarding me seriously.

"Hi. I'm Chloe. Have you seen my Stitch?"

"Pardon me?" I asked, immediately going into doctor mode at the word *stitch*. I cast my gaze over her, not seeing any open cuts or scrapes. "Stitch?" I repeated.

She nodded impatiently. "Stitch," she repeated. "My koala. I losted him. Mommy and me been looking everywhere!" Her voice rose to an almost wail, her chin trembling, and fat tears gathered in her big eyes.

"No, sorry. I haven't seen him. When did you last have him?"

Her brow furrowed, and she wiped away her tears, leaving a smudge of mud on her freckle-covered cheek. She was quite endearing with her serious expression.

"He was with me on the monkey bars. And when I had juice," she added triumphantly, looking at me as if that should answer the mystery of the missing koala.

"Sorry, ah, Pumpkin. I haven't seen him." I glanced around. "Didn't I hear your mommy?"

She sniffed and looked behind her, clearly surprised not to see anyone. She whipped her head around to face me, more tears racing down her face.

"Now I losted Mommy too!" she sobbed. Then in a move I hadn't expected, she launched herself at me. Without thinking, I gathered her up, letting her little arms wind around my neck as she cried.

"Hey, hey," I soothed. "It's gonna be fine. Mommy's probably in the bushes looking for Stitch. We'll go find her." I began to stand when a woman stepped out from the same place my little hugger had appeared. Although *stepped* might have been too strong a word. Hobbled was more like it. She gripped the small tree trunk as she stared, her mouth agape as she took in the sight of me holding who I assumed was her daughter. There was dirt on her cheek, and her face expressed pain. From the way she was awkwardly holding her foot, I understood the gasp I had heard earlier.

For a moment, I was speechless. She was the loveliest woman I had ever seen. Average height, with golden hair, the same wheat color as her daughter's, swept up off her face, and she had the most captivating eyes. Large, wide, dark pools set in a face I could only describe as *mesmerizing*. Rounded cheeks, full lips, and a stubborn chin that, at the moment, was raised in confusion. I cleared my throat and spoke.

"Look, Chloe. There's your mommy."

Before she could move, I hurried toward the strange woman, talking fast. "She was upset and jumped up for a hug. I wasn't—"

She cut me off with a wave of her hand. "I saw." She opened her arms. "Chloe, baby, come here."

I transferred my little hugger to her mother, frowning when she bit back a grimace of pain.

"Are you hurt?"

She shook her head. "I twisted my ankle. It's nothing."

Before she could protest, I dropped to my knees, peering at the appendage. It was slightly swollen over the top of her sneaker, and I frowned.

"You should let me look at this."

"And why should I do that?" she challenged, glaring down at me. Her brown eyes were filled with fire, pinning me with her gaze.

I stood, meeting her fire with determination of my own. "Because I'm a doctor."

"A doctor?"

"A pediatric doctor."

"I'm not a child," she stated dryly.

I didn't tell her I had noticed exactly how un-childlike she was. Instead, I smiled. "Bones are bones. That never changes."

"S-S-Stitch," Chloe hiccupped.

"We'll find him," her mother promised, turning to leave.

"After I look at your ankle," I insisted, halting her departure by gently grabbing her arm. "Please."

She hesitated but agreed. As she tried to step forward, she made a low sound of pain. I stopped her forward motion. "Wait. Give me Chloe."

I wasn't sure who was more surprised when Chloe didn't argue, but instead, she reached out her arms. I placed her on my hip, then wrapped my free arm around her mother's waist. "Lean on me," I instructed.

We limped to the bench, and I set Chloe on the wooden seat, then helped her mother lower herself down. I bent over her foot. "May I?" I indicated her ankle.

"Do I have a choice?" she asked humorously.

I had to chuckle. "Of course, but I'd prefer you said yes."

She regarded me for a moment. "Thank you," she said simply.

I tugged off her sneaker, then examined her foot, taking care to move it slowly and gently.

"Not broken," I assured her. "But sprained."

"Okay."

I reached into my messenger bag and pulled out a tensor bandage. I didn't expect the sudden bark of laughter. I glanced up in surprise, enthralled once again by the vision of prettiness in front of me. Her dark eyes were lit with amusement, and her smile was wide. Two deep dimples appeared in her cheeks. She was enthralling, and I found myself returning her smile.

"What's so funny?"

"You carry bandages with you?"

I winked. "Today, yes. Yesterday, I had some enemas in my bag."

"Guess it's my lucky day."

"Guess so."

Still chuckling, I bent over and swiftly bandaged her foot. After slipping back on her sneaker, I had her stand, and she took a few test steps.

"It feels better," she said with a sigh. "Supported."

I stood. "Good. Ice it. Try to stay off it. Keep it up. It should be fine in a few days."

"Okay. Thanks."

I turned to Chloe, who was watching us quietly, her knees tucked up to her chest. "Now, you, Pumpkin. This koala of yours. You had juice together? Then he disappeared?"

She screwed up her face, thinking. "Yes," she stated emphatically.

"Where was this juice fest?"

Chloe tapped the bench. "Here."

"Hmm." I scratched my neck. "I didn't see him, ah, her when I got here."

"Him. Stitch."

"Stitch. Right."

I glanced at Chloe's mom. "With your permission, I'll walk around a bit with Chloe, and we'll look for Stitch." I handed her my phone. "You take this and give me yours. I'll film where we go so you know I'm not trying to ah, *nab*, her or anything. You can track us. You stay off that ankle."

"On one condition."

"Sure."

"You tell me your name."

I held out my hand. "Ian. Ian Taylor."

"*Dr.* Ian Taylor?" she asked.

"Yes. Should I just call you Chloe's mom?"

That smile appeared again. The one that lit her face and brought out her dimples. "Samantha." As she spoke, she slipped her hand into mine. I closed my fingers around hers, feeling the warmth and softness of her skin. How well her hand fit with mine. I also noticed she didn't wear a wedding ring.

"Nice to meet you, Samantha."

There was a strange feeling of regret when her hand slipped from mine. I held out my hand for Chloe. She took it and tugged me away.

For some reason, I kept looking back at Samantha.

And every time I did, she was staring right back at me.

CHAPTER 2

IAN

I sat dejected, the sounds of Chloe's distressed sobs still echoing in my ears long after she and Samantha had walked away.

We had failed.

Despite our search, we never located Stitch.

I took Chloe everywhere she had told me they had been that morning. The monkey bars, the swings, the slide. Even the café. We asked everyone we came across, Chloe's description of Stitch getting more detailed as the minutes passed. When Chloe got tired, I set her on my shoulders, and we kept looking. She told me all about the adventures she'd had with her koala and how much she loved him. About his special place on her bed. His favorite food and color. His loose ear he got when she shut it in the door. How much he loved to wear the scarves her mom made him with scraps of wool. I even found out Stitch became her best friend after her dad left, so I had my answer to my unspoken question. With every word, I fell a little bit more under her sweet influence.

After an hour, we had to give up. We'd been everywhere they had been that morning. Chloe was quiet as we walked back to her mom, who was waiting with open arms for my little hugger. Chloe started to cry, telling her mom that Stitch didn't like the rain and it was cloudy and he'd be alone.

Samantha stood, holding Chloe. She handed me back my phone, took hers, her voice cordial but cooler than before. "Thank you, Dr. Taylor."

"I'm sorry I couldn't find him."

She shook her head. "You were very kind. I hope we didn't disrupt your day too much."

I didn't like the formal sound of her tone. I preferred her teasing, sweet one. I waved off her apology. "Not at all."

I stroked my hand over Chloe's wild curls. "Will she be okay?" The thought of her being sad bothered me.

"She will," Sam assured me.

"Ah…" I hesitated, wanting to ask for her number, but for some reason knowing she wouldn't give it to me. She had shut down, and I wasn't sure why or how to ask her. Before I could figure out what to say, she offered me a tight smile, then turned and walked away, her limp still there, but not as bad. Chloe lifted her sad face and waved before burying her head back into her mother's shoulder. I hated seeing the tears clouding her eyes. I also hated the sudden change in Samantha's demeanor.

I sat, feeling strangely bereft. What had caused the abrupt shift in Samantha's manner was a mystery. I picked up my messenger bag and headed toward home. My pocket vibrated with a reminder, and I realized I had missed a text. It was from Gail.

Gail: *I'm done with Marv. Meet me later, and we'll figure out our exit strategy. By midnight, we can be in the Bahamas.*

Normally, her text would have made me laugh. No doubt, Marv had called her with some inane question or, heaven forbid, made a decision without her.

Except, I knew Samantha had seen the message. She had no idea it was a joke, and she thought—well, I had no idea what she thought, but it was wrong. I wasn't running away with anyone. She had no clue it was all in fun.

I shook my head in frustration and shoved my phone back into my pocket.

"Thanks, Gail," I muttered. "You're always going on about me finding someone, then you yourself cockblock me."

I passed a garbage can and remembered my cup and wrapper were in my other pocket from earlier. I stopped to shove them into the can, only to miss the opening. I bent to grab them when I saw it. A furry paw sticking out of the corner of the overflowing waste bin. I yanked on it and pulled out a koala bear, wearing a knitted orange scarf with a loose ear.

I found him.

Too late.

Samantha and Chloe were gone, and I hadn't gotten her number.

I somehow doubted she took mine after seeing Gail's message either.

I was about to stuff Stitch back in the garbage, but I hesitated and for some reason shoved him in my messenger bag.

After all, it was going to rain, and Stitch shouldn't be alone.

I finished a chart and drained my coffee. I was having one of the unusual, rare days in the ER. We were steady but not slammed. I actually drank my coffee while it was still reasonably warm instead of ice-cold, and I was keeping up with charting. I glanced at the clock. Two hours to go, and I was off for three days. I was looking forward to the time away.

I headed to the nursing station and glanced at the board. Only three new cases since I'd slipped into the lounge. And only one with my color highlighted, indicating a child.

"Non-urgent," Gail said, sidling up beside me. "Little girl fell in the park, her wrist is sore, but the biggest problem is a huge splinter that got lodged in her hand. I can help if needed. Exam room three."

"Panicked?" I asked. I hated walking into rooms with panicked parents. They often caused the child more distress than needed.

"No. Mother and child both calm. Cute pair, actually."

"I'm sure the man in their lives thinks so. Not in the market for a ready-made family, Gail," I declared dryly.

A flash of riotous curls went through my head, and I shook it to clear my thoughts. That wasn't ever going to happen. I had been back to the park every day and hadn't found my little hugger or her mother. That ship had sailed, although I still held on to Stitch.

I headed to exam room three and walked in, stopping short when I saw the "cute pair" waiting for me.

Samantha sat on the exam bed, holding Chloe. Chloe's hand was wrapped in a towel, and she clutched it to her chest. There were traces of blood on the cloth. Her red-rimmed eyes met mine and widened. Samantha looked as shocked as I felt. It was Chloe's greeting that brought me back to the moment.

"Dr. Ian! Hi!"

I strode forward, pulling up the stool and sitting in front of them. I grinned at her. "Hello, Chloe." I glanced up. "Hello, Samantha."

She paused, then spoke. "Dr. Taylor, I didn't realize you worked here."

"Guilty as charged." I focused on Chloe. "Now, Pumpkin, I hear you've been removing wood from the park and hiding it under your skin while doing acrobatics." I tsked teasingly. "Dangerous stuff."

She shook her head, her curls bobbing. "I was running. I fell."

I held out my hand. "May I see?"

Without hesitation, she let me take her hand, and I examined it, then looked up at Samantha. "Well, like mother, like daughter. The wrist is sprained. I need to get that hunk of wood out of her hand, though, and I might have to add a stitch. It's deep."

Chloe's chin began to tremble. "Will it hurt?"

I shook my head. "Nope. Promise. I'm really good."

Gail walked in. "Dr. Taylor is the best. And he always has a treat for you after if you're good."

Chloe's eyes grew round. "A treat?"

I nodded. "The cafeteria here has the best milkshakes ever. If you're brave, I'll get you one."

I could feel Gail gape behind me. Normally, the treat consisted of a little toy we kept in a wooden chest. It was always fun to watch the child pick out something, forgetting for a moment what procedure had just occurred. But Chloe deserved a real treat.

"Okay," she agreed, although her voice was shaky. "Can Mommy stay?"

"Of course," I soothed. "She can hold you while I do my job. It won't take long, and you'll feel much better once that nasty piece of wood is gone."

Samantha was watching us closely, a small frown on her face.

"When was her last tetanus shot?" I asked.

"A year ago."

"Okay, good. I think I'll send her home with some pills. I'll clean it well, but I want to make sure there isn't any infection. Is she allergic to anything?"

"No." Her eyes grew misty. "It happened so fast."

Without thinking, I reached out and squeezed her shoulder in comfort. Her hair was down today, the same riotous curls as Chloe's tumbling past her shoulders. The coils felt soft under my fingers.

"Kids and scrapes happen all the time. It's part of growing up. I'm glad you brought her here instead of trying to dig that out yourself." I'd seen that happen too often, with disastrous consequences.

She nodded, not saying anything. I noticed her gaze drifted to my hand, and I wondered if she was looking for a ring, the way I had the other day. I knew I had to address the unspoken question between us. I just had to figure out how.

"Gail will get everything ready and she'll help me, so it goes fast. She's the best."

"I am," Gail agreed, moving around the room to get the supplies.

"I'll be right back. I have to get something," I informed them and hurried to my locker. I pulled out the koala bear that had taken up residence recently. Once I had gotten him home, I'd tossed him in the washer, cleaning him of the debris that had been dumped on him in the garbage can. I'd carried him with me for a few days in case I found the girls and could give him back, but finally, I'd tossed him inside the locker after giving up. He was fluffy and smelled clean, and I knew a little girl who needed him as much as he needed her. It would help distract her while I dug that nasty wood out of her little hand.

Back in the room, Gail had everything set up. Samantha was holding Chloe, and Chloe's arm was on the table, a small draping set up so she wouldn't have to see what I was doing. Chloe appeared anxious, and I could see she was shaking with fear. Samantha was trying to comfort her, smoothing her curls and talking quietly. I crouched beside them.

"Before I start, I have something I think you're going to like, Chloe."

"What?" She sniffled.

I pulled Stitch out from behind my back. "Look who I found after you left the park."

Instantly, her countenance changed. She reached for her beloved koala, one word escaping from her mouth. "Stitch!"

I stood and watched her love on her little bear. She petted and hugged him. Showed him to Samantha. Talked and cooed to him like a real live being.

"His ear is fixed!" she exclaimed.

"He was brave and let me stitch it," I explained, showing her the black thread.

"Did he get a milkshake?"

"Um, no. He got a bath instead."

"Where did you find him?" Samantha asked softly.

I leaned down close to her ear. "The garbage can. The bath was necessary."

She grimaced. "No doubt. Once again, Dr. Taylor, thank you."

"Ian. My name is Ian."

"Ian," she repeated. "Thank you, Ian."

I straightened and addressed Chloe. "You ready, Pumpkin?"

She clutched Stitch close. "Yes."

"Okay, then."

"All done."

It had gone well. The worst part was the freezing, and Chloe handled it like a champ. Gail kept her talking, and she was so happy to have Stitch back, she grimaced but didn't move. After that, I was able to swiftly remove the deep wood, irrigate and clean the wound, and add three small dissolving stitches.

While working, I made small talk, casually asked Gail about Marv, and she took care of my problem by telling Samantha about her husband of forty years and how he liked to irritate her. She tilted her head toward me.

"This one insists he's waiting in the wings for me, but every time I try to take him up on the offer, he finds an excuse for me to stay with Marv. I'm beginning to think he's nothing but a tease."

I met Samantha's wide gaze with a wink. "Marv's a good guy. The only person you should run off to the Bahamas with is him. I'm actually boring."

"I doubt that," Samantha murmured.

Before I could stop myself, the words were out. "Maybe you can find out for yourself."

If her hands weren't full, I was sure Gail would have clapped in glee.

I wrapped Chloe's hand in a bandage and used a small tensor on her wrist. I looked down at Samantha's foot as I was wrapping it.

"How's the ankle?"

"Much better."

"Good. The stitches will dissolve, but the hand needs to be kept bandaged and clean."

"I'll make sure."

Gail looked between us and cleared her throat. "Well, Dr. Ian, your shift is over, which works out well. You can take the girls for a milkshake with no worries. No time limit."

"Isn't that convenient." I smirked, knowing I had an hour left on my shift.

"Yep. We'll give Chloe a few minutes to relax while you finish the chart, then you're free." She winked. "All of you are free to enjoy a milkshake together."

I followed Gail to the door. "I know what you're doing," I whispered.

"I hope you know what *you're* doing," she replied smugly. "I got it all set up for you. Don't blow it. Your skills are lacking, you know."

I rolled my eyes, then glanced toward the girls. Samantha was snuggling Chloe, her head bent over, holding her tight to her chest. I couldn't tell where she ended and Chloe began, with their bright hair so similar.

"I'll be back," I told them.

Samantha peeked over Chloe's head. "We'll be waiting."

Those words made me smile.

I hoped I knew what I was doing too.

∽

SAMANTHA

Watching Chloe with Ian was fascinating. I had never seen her react to a man the way she had to him. The day we met him, when I had stumbled trying to catch up with her and had watched her run up to him, desperate to find her beloved Stitch, I was worried. He was a stranger, and she was alone with him. I had pushed through the bushes just as she flung herself into his arms. His facial expression and reaction calmed me. He was soft-spoken and kind, and I could hear every caring word he said. He wasn't a danger to her. His reaction to my injured ankle proved that even more. His innate gentleness surrounded him.

He stood after bandaging my ankle and insisted on trying to locate Stitch. I couldn't believe we had lost him—he had been Chloe's constant companion since before she was two. I had bought him for her just after Alan had left us. She barely remembered her father, but Stitch was her world. I was so used to him locked on to her little backpack. His Velcro-covered paws must have given away and he got left behind. I wasn't sure how Chloe would manage without him.

Ian questioned Chloe in a direct, calm manner. His hands were on his hips as he thought about her replies. He was tall—well over six feet—with sandy-colored hair and hazel eyes that twinkled when he laughed. An angular jaw covered in scruff set off full lips and a handsome face. His shoulders were wide, waist slim, and his smile was inviting and warm.

He seemed pretty perfect until I read that text and shut down. It hit too close to home, and once he returned with Chloe, empty-handed, I concentrated only on her. I'd already had my heart trampled on once; I wasn't letting it happen again—and I wouldn't allow my child to be hurt.

Except now, the teasing text explained and Ian sitting with Chloe on his lap, listening intently to her, and seeing how tender he had been with her earlier, my mind and heart were at war. When he had given her back her beloved friend, I almost wept. The rapturous joy on her face was a sight to behold. Since we'd sat down, Ian had peppered us both with questions, never rushing my answers, but obviously interested.

My mind told me not to get involved. My heart whispered this man was different.

Which one could I trust?

~

IAN

Over vanilla milkshakes, I had found out a lot about Samantha and Chloe.

Chloe was four. Her birthday was in the fall—only a week after her mommy's, she informed me. Samantha preferred Sam—at least to friends. They had moved here to Grimsby last month from Toronto. "I wanted a smaller town for Chloe to grow up in," she explained.

I was delighted to find out they lived in the same apartment complex as I did—four floors above me. Given my odd hours, it wasn't surprising we had never encountered each other in the building.

I planned to change that.

Sam was a book editor for a publishing house. She made her own hours, and as I realized, they rivaled my own at times.

She informed me she was divorced from Chloe's dad.

"Alan left us for a coworker," she clarified quietly. "He told me in a text —on his way to the Caribbean with her. The divorce happened quickly, and from what I understand, so did the end of his relationship."

I covered her hand on the table with mine. "No wonder Gail's text spooked you."

She lifted a shoulder. "I had no business being upset."

"Is it wrong to tell you I'm glad you were? I was upset I didn't get your number."

She glanced at Chloe, now sitting beside me, busy coloring a picture for Stitch to show him all he had missed in the past week, talking to him in her sweet little voice.

"Are you certain of that, Ian? It's not only me," she asked.

I thought of how I'd felt when they walked away from me in the park. How joyful I was, despite the circumstances, that I found them today in my ER.

"I am. But maybe I should ask you the same thing. My hours here are crazy. I volunteer at the local youth shelter. I get called in at odd times. I'm paying off student loans, and I live pretty simply." I held up my hand before she could respond. "Dating hasn't gone well for me, to be honest. But as bad as all that sounds, I felt something in the park. Something again today when I saw you. Something that told me maybe it was time to find a new priority in my life. That maybe that priority was you and Chloe."

She looked contemplative, then spoke low so only I could hear.

"My ex was wealthy and ignored us. Everything else came ahead of us. He walked away without a warning and blamed me for focusing on Chloe instead of him. She was then and is now my priority. She always will be. I don't need money and a fancy place. I need the person to be present, if that makes any sense."

"Understood." I took a chance and leaned forward, covering her hands on the table with mine again and squeezing her fingers. "But what if we agreed to carve out a little time for us and see where that takes us? If maybe we could be present for each other?"

She glanced at Chloe.

"We can take it slow," I insisted. "Friends."

"Friends?" she repeated.

"Well, friends who date." I grinned.

"Tell me, Ian," she murmured, bending low over the table. "Does this 'friends who date' thing include kissing?"

I dropped my gaze to her full mouth, unconsciously licking my lips. "Lord, I hope so. I mean, if you want it to."

"Yeah, I want," she breathed out, bending closer. "You're so sexy. Who wouldn't want to kiss you?"

I grinned. She thought I was sexy. She wanted to kiss me. Date me.

What a great day.

I moved closer over the table, caught in her spell, wanting to taste her lips.

Then Chloe piped up. Loudly.

"Mommy, are you *kissing* Dr. Ian? Is he your boyfriend now?"

We both pulled back. I was shocked how close we had been to each other. Chloe was watching us with wide eyes. I met the curious gaze of a few colleagues. Sam blushed as she picked up her coffee cup.

"We'll talk about it at home, Chloe," she said.

Chloe shrugged. "It's okay. I like him," she replied. "So does Stitch."

I met Sam's embarrassed gaze with a wink. "There you have it. Approved by the koala. Guess I'm your boyfriend."

"Oh, hush," she responded.

But she smiled. Dimples and all.

And it was a glorious thing to see.

CHAPTER 3

IAN

I was nervous as I tugged on my jacket, fiddling with my shirtsleeves. I hadn't been on a date in a long time—my schedule rarely permitted it, and I hadn't met anyone I was remotely interested in enough to try to change it. But there was something about Samantha that made me want to change things. She captivated me. Her gentle nature and intelligence. Her laugh and sense of humor. The loving way she was with Chloe.

That was another thing on my mind. I liked kids a lot—it was one of the reasons I chose to become a pediatrician. But somehow, I had never thought of having kids of my own or being involved with someone who did. But Chloe was special. She had wormed her way into my heart as quickly as her mother did.

I only hoped I wouldn't let them down.

I fidgeted all the way up in the elevator and had to pause before knocking on the door. I was surprised how much this evening meant to me. It felt like more than a simple date. It felt as if I was starting something important and significant in my life.

I gave my head a shake and lifted my hand to knock. I had barely lowered my arm when the door swung open and the sweetest little face peered up at me.

"Hi, Dr. Ian!"

I grinned down at her, unable to stop the surge of happiness seeing her brought me. Her wild curls bobbed around her face, and her dark eyes danced with mischievousness.

"Hello, Pumpkin. How's the hand?"

She fluttered her fingers. "Good." I captured her palm in mine and was pleased to see the fresh bandage over her wound. Her palm was cool and dry, and it looked as if it was healing well under the dressing.

"You're taking Mommy on a date," she stated as I stood.

"I am."

"Did you bring her flowers?"

Before I could respond, Sam appeared, looking gorgeous and upset. Her hair was swept away from her face, showing off her long neck. She wore a pretty blue dress that swirled around her knees and showed off her shapely calves.

"Chloe! How many times have I told you not to open the door without Mommy there? And you never ask someone questions like that!" she scolded.

Chloe sighed with all the attitude only a four-year-old could muster and looked at her mother. "I knew it was Dr. Ian. I heard you say you could hardly wait to see him, so I waited by the door, Mommy. I was *helping*."

Sam's cheeks flushed at her words, and I grinned, knowing she was as anxious to see me as I was to see her.

"And you love flowers," Chloe protested. "I was just asking."

I pulled out a bouquet from behind my back. "And I was just about to give these to you." I extended the flowers to Sam with a wink, then dropped to my knee in front of Chloe. "And these, little one, are for you."

Her eyes widened, and she took the small bouquet from my hands, staring at it. I had seen the bunch of sweetheart roses in the shop when I went in to get flowers for Sam and couldn't resist getting it for Chloe. She traced the edges of the little roses with her fingertip and lifted her gaze to mine.

"I never gots flowers of my own," she whispered, looking awed.

I glanced up at Sam, who was watching us, her eyes glossy. "What a lovely gesture." She held my gaze. "Let's go put them in water."

I followed them into the apartment, looking around the space. I lived in a bachelor apartment. One large room with a small bath and kitchen. It suited me since I was rarely home. Sam's place was one of the larger apartments in the building.

"Look around," she called. "I'll be there in a moment."

I took her up on the invitation, checking out the large living area. It was warm and homey, and they had a great view of the park across the street. The furniture was arranged nicely with comfortable sofas and a huge chair that looked as if it was well used. A table beside it held a pile of books, and a laptop sat on top of them. I assumed the hall to the right led to the bedrooms. I wandered into the kitchen, smiling as Chloe turned, holding out her vase.

"Look, Dr. Ian. Pretty!"

"They are," I agreed.

"Thank you," she said. "I love them."

"You are welcome." I bent and tapped her nose playfully. "You be good tonight, okay?"

She nodded her head so fast, her curls lifted. "I will." She turned to Sam. "Can I put these in my room, Mommy?"

Sam smiled indulgently. "It's 'May I,'" she corrected, gently. "And yes, sweetheart, you may."

Chloe went past me, carrying her flowers. Sam slid hers into a vase with a low sigh. She glided her finger over the petals of a lily, the same expression on her face as Chloe had had earlier.

"It's been a long time since I got flowers, too," she murmured. "Thank you, Ian."

I stepped closer, unable to stop myself from running a finger down her soft cheek. "You deserve pretty flowers all the time."

Our eyes locked and held. The same feeling I had sitting across from her the other day filled my chest. The want to get closer, to feel her mouth underneath mine, grew.

"I wonder if we should reverse the order of this date," I murmured.

She frowned. "Reverse it?"

"Maybe I could kiss you now instead of waiting until the end. Get that out of the way so we can enjoy the night, instead of sitting across from you feeling torn."

"Torn?" she repeated.

"Torn between the fact that I don't want the night to end, yet wishing it was over so I could know how your mouth feels with mine."

"Oh," she breathed, her gaze dropping to my mouth, then back up. "That would be…good."

"I thought so." I stepped closer, settling my hand on her hip. "Can I kiss you?"

Her lips quirked. "It's 'May I.'"

"Of course you may," I said and covered her mouth with mine, teasing and light, dragging my tongue along her bottom lip. "You gonna open up for me, sweet Sammy?" I whispered against her lips.

With a soft whimper, she did, and I slid my tongue along hers for the first time. Her warm breath filled my mouth, her taste overwhelming my senses. Sweet, minty, and Sam. Addictive. And somehow, right there, I knew—I would never get enough of her. Seconds later, she was pressed against the counter of her kitchen, one leg wrapped around my hips. It was only Chloe's voice calling for her mom that broke us apart. It let common sense seep back into my brain, pushing out the lust and desire that had swamped me.

I set her back on her feet and kissed her full mouth.

"Duty calls."

She stared at me, her eyes wide with desire, her hand still clutching my shirt collar. I smiled at her. "It's just the start, Sam. I promise."

She released my shirt, patting the wrinkled fabric. "I'm looking forward to it."

"As am I."

She paused before she went to see Chloe.

"Oh, I need the restaurant information to leave the babysitter. Just in case."

"I thought you might be a little anxious about leaving Chloe alone, so I made a reservation at DeGarmo's across the street. Great food and close in case."

She laid a hand on my arm. "That was incredibly thoughtful."

I ran a hand through my hair self-consciously. "I have to admit, my reasons were selfish."

She furrowed her brow. "Selfish?"

"The day I asked you out, you said that it would be the first time you've left her alone since your, ah, husband left. I didn't want you worried and distracted."

She chuckled at my confession. "It does make me feel better, to be honest."

I lifted her hand and kissed it. "Good. Now, go see what Chloe needs, and once your sitter arrives, we'll go."

There was a knock on the door, and I tilted my head toward the sound. "I'll get that if you want."

"Perfect."

~

Sam relaxed back in her chair, idly spinning her wineglass. "It's so nice here."

I sipped my wine, enjoying the heady flavor and the chance to spend time with the beautiful woman across from me. I had been pleased when I'd opened Sam's apartment door to find the superintendent's wife, Bonnie, on the other side. I got along well with her and her husband, Ray, and knew Chloe would be in good hands. She winked as she came in, her hands filled with a bag of games and a plate of cookies for her and the "wee one," as she called Chloe.

She had Chloe so busy with a puzzle when we left, she barely acknowledged us walking out the door. Chloe waved her hand, peering intently at the puzzle as she munched on a cookie. I knew it gave Sam some ease, knowing Chloe wasn't upset with her leaving.

"It's great," I agreed. "Comfortable and good food, without being pretentious."

I had held her hand on the short walk to the restaurant and stole a fast kiss or two in the elevator. She seemed to enjoy my touches, which made me happy. We had perused the menu then decided on an appetizer and two main courses, which we planned to share since neither of us could make up our mind. Our conversation had been continuous and relaxed as we drank our wine and ate our salads.

"You mentioned you work from home as a book editor?" I asked.

She swallowed a bite of her salad and nodded. "Yes."

"That must be interesting."

"It is. I love reading, and it puts my education to use. Today's methods are always changing, but the fundamentals of proper English are still the same. I take a lot of online courses to keep up-to-date with the ever-changing face of publishing, and I love doing it. I get to work, have a career, and still be home with Chloe."

"Have you been doing it a long time?"

"I started in a smaller position when I got out of school. I moved up, and when I found out I was pregnant with Chloe, they offered me a remote position. It was perfect—a job I could do from home."

I hated to ask but had to. "How did your husband feel about it?"

She made a face and took a sip of wine. "He would have preferred it if I edited nonfiction work, but that wasn't where my heart was. He was always embarrassed by my work. He thought the books I worked on were silly and inane."

He sounded like a pompous ass, but I refrained from saying so.

"What genre *do* you work on?" I asked, curious.

"Historical fiction."

"Like lords and dukes?"

"Yes."

I waggled my eyebrows. "With ravishing rakes and all that?"

A grin tugged on her lips. "Yes."

"Maybe you could send me a link to one of the books, and I can read it."

"Really? You would read a historical romance?"

"Why not? I like to read. I'd like to read something you worked on."

"Wow. Alan could barely stand the fact that I was somehow involved. He never read anything. Or talked about what I did. He called it my 'little hobby.'" She shook her head. "I hated that, and we argued over it a lot."

"I'm not Alan."

She shook her head. "No...no, you are most certainly not. What you *are*, Dr. Ian, is most certainly unexpected."

I liked being unexpected to Sam.

I sat back, regarding her. "You know, if you ever need to...*verify* a scene —make sure it's on the 'up-and-up,' so to speak, I'm your man. I can ravish with the best of them if needed."

The waiter appeared, placing a bubbling dish in front of us. "Your stuffed shrimp." He removed our salad plates, leaving us alone again.

Sam looked at me as she reached for the spoon and slid some shrimp onto my plate.

"I'll keep that in mind," she murmured.

"You do that."

~

"That was amazing."

I grinned at Sam, leaning over and wiping a small trace of chocolate off the corner of her lips. Partway through dinner, I had given in to the draw and moved from my side of the booth over next to Sam. We had shared from our plates, fed each other, held hands, kissed a few more times. I liked touching her. She, it seemed, liked it when I did so. It was a relaxing, enjoyable dinner—until dessert arrived. That was when I discovered another side to Sam.

She was addicted to chocolate. And she hated sharing, even though she had insisted she was full and couldn't eat dessert. When the double chocolate brownie with hot fudge sauce I ordered arrived at the table, she became possessive and growly. I had to fight for every bite.

It was adorable.

"It was *my* dessert," I reminded her as I licked the chocolate off my thumb. "You said you were too full."

"You're the one who moved close enough to tempt me."

I hunched closer to her, eyeing her full, sweet mouth. "Can I tempt you with anything else?"

She surprised me by cupping my face and pressing her mouth to mine. With a low groan, I slid my hand around the nape of her neck and kissed her back. She tasted of the chocolate we shared, the wine she sipped, and simply of Sam.

It was an intoxicating combination. *She* was intoxicating.

I knew the waiter had slipped the tab on the table. I ignored him. I kissed Sam until she was breathless. Until I was breathless.

I leaned my forehead to hers. "You are addictive."

She sighed, her breath washing over my skin. "You are dangerous."

I kissed the end of her nose before drawing back. I reached for the tab, sliding my credit card into the folder.

"But good, yeah?"

She tilted her head. "Yeah. Good."

"Then we're golden."

I laughed at her confused expression. "My mom says that all the time. It means we're good."

"I like it."

I signed the bill

"Next time is my treat," she insisted.

"I asked you out. I paid." My mother had raised a gentleman, even if my thoughts toward Sam were definitely not those of one at the moment.

"Then I'm taking you out next week. On me—since I asked."

I had to laugh. "Okay." Then I frowned. "So, I can't see you until next week?"

She smiled at my words. "What are you doing tomorrow?"

I grinned. "Day off."

"Then I'd like to make you dinner. If you'd be interested in having a meal with Chloe and me."

"I would love that." I pulled her from the booth. "Let me lay it on the line, Sam. Any time you want to give me with you, I'll take. Coffee. A visit in the hall. Dropping by the hospital for a milkshake. You name it, and if I can, I'll be there."

Our eyes locked, my words surprising even me. But I knew. Friends who date wasn't going to work for us. Somehow, I knew how important Sam and Chloe were going to be to me. And I wasn't playing games with her.

"Okay," she breathed out.

"Come on, I'll take you home."

She looked up at me, her beautiful eyes wide. "Will you come in for a while?"

"Absolutely."

When we arrived back at the apartment, Bonnie told us Chloe had been an angel. Then she left wishing us a "Good night," with a subtle wink.

I followed Sam down the hall and watched as she checked on Chloe. It was a girly room filled with pink and lace, with lots of stuffed animals around, although I was amused to see Stitch was still the one she held tight as she slept. Sam tucked her in and bent low to kiss her forehead. I peeked into the room across the hall, bookcases lining one wall and a desk with a pile of manuscripts stacked up on it facing the window. There was another chair with an ottoman, and I could picture Sam curled up in it, editing or reading.

Sam appeared by my side. "My office," she murmured.

"I figured. Looks well used."

She laughed. "It is."

She indicated the end of the hall. "That's my room."

I cleared my throat. "Maybe you should show me that another time, Sammy-girl."

"Sammy-girl?" She wrinkled her nose. "No one has ever called me that."

"Good. My special name. You are far too pretty to be a Sam."

A second later, her arms were wrapped around my neck and her mouth on mine. With a low groan, I hauled her up my chest and kissed her with everything I had. I loved how she felt in my arms. How she fit against me. How she tasted. The scent of her perfume. The heat of her skin. I wanted more of all of it.

"The sweet things you say drive me crazy," she whispered against my mouth. "You make me feel as if I matter. As if you see me."

"I do."

She eased back, still holding me. "Alan and I were over a long time before he left us. He changed after we got married. Money and power became his priorities." She sighed. "Everyone thought I was devastated when he left, but to be honest, I was relieved. We didn't work anymore, and I hated the way he ignored us."

"I'm sorry," I offered.

"I've been invisible for a long time," she confessed.

"Not to me. I see everything about you. And I like all of it."

"And Chloe?"

"I adore her. Both of you."

She blinked in the dim light of the hallway. "I think-I think we're going to adore you too."

"Good. Then we're on the same page."

Her expression was bright. "Yes, Dr. Taylor, I think we are."

Chloe's laughter rang out loud and clear as I pushed her on the swings. I had shown up early for dinner—five hours early—and taken the girls for a walk in the park while whatever Sam was making for supper cooked. Her apartment smelled amazing, the air heavy and rich with aromatic herbs and meat. My mouth watered. My apartment usually smelled of pizza or Chinese—cooking and I were not friends, although I could rustle up scrambled eggs pretty well.

"More, Dr. Ian! More!"

I smiled as I gave her another push, watching as her little legs pumped steadily to keep swinging. Sam stood on the other side of the swing, making funny faces at Chloe as she whizzed over her. Sam looked happy and relaxed, not at all upset about me arriving early and taking them to the park. She had looked delighted when she opened the door, greeting me with a fast kiss I had wanted to deepen and explore, but Chloe had appeared too quickly.

It had taken everything in me to leave Sam the night before, and I was pleased to see she seemed to feel the same way. It boded well for our relationship.

Twenty minutes later, we were in the park and eating ice cream. Then Chloe begged me to help her on the swings, and I was powerless to resist those big brown eyes and sweet voice. Stitch was clutched against the chains, squished, but I assumed, enjoying the ride.

Six weeks ago, if anyone had told me my day off would be spent this way, I would have scoffed at them. But there was nowhere else I wanted to be. The sun, the laughter, and the smiles of these two girls made my chest warm.

Chloe slowed, dragging her feet along the dirt to stop the swing, then ran for the slide. Sam and I followed, and I caught Chloe at the bottom a few times before she decided it was sandbox time. She raced toward another little girl she knew, and we headed to a bench close by. I made a detour to the little kiosk set up in the shade, buying some water for Chloe and an iced cappuccino for Sam and me to share. I sat beside her, lacing our fingers together as we watched Chloe and sipped the iced coffee treat.

"This is so good," Sam observed. "Different."

"Best kiosk in the park. He makes it with chocolate milk if you ask," I explained. "I always get it that way."

"My new favorite."

I leaned back, snagging my straw and taking a long sip from the cup. "Funny, I have a new favorite today too."

She looked at me, her brow furrowed. "Oh?"

I pressed my mouth to her cheek, nuzzling the sun-warmed skin. "You."

She blinked, smiled, then dropped her gaze for a moment. When she lifted her eyes back to mine, hers were bright and happy. "You say the nicest things."

"I'm simply stating the truth. It took all my restraint not to show up at your door when I woke up at six."

"You could have watched cartoons with Chloe."

I grinned. "I'll keep that in mind next time." I grazed her cheek again. "Not sure I'd be able to resist sliding into bed with you though for a little snuggle," I teased.

She surprised me by turning her head and pressing her lips to mine. "I might let you."

"Is that a fact?"

"You're hard to resist, Ian."

I bent my head and took another sip of our shared beverage. "I'll keep that in mind."

Hours later, I carried Chloe back to the apartment, her head resting on my chest, one arm flung over my shoulder. She'd worn herself out playing and sat beside me on the bench, sipping her water and falling asleep. In the apartment, Sam stripped off her shoes and socks, then covered her with a light blanket once I laid her on her bed. We sat on Sam's balcony, enjoying the late afternoon breeze.

"Dinner smells incredible. I don't get many home-cooked meals."

"You don't cook?"

"I can, but not particularly well or with much enthusiasm. I make great scrambled eggs and toast. I eat a lot of cereal or takeout, and a lot of cafeteria food."

She made a face, and I chuckled. "It's pretty good. They have a salad bar and decent sandwiches."

"You can't just eat that."

"My mom comes to visit sometimes and fills my freezer. I try to eke those out to last a while."

"Your mom doesn't live here?"

"No, after my dad passed, she moved in with my sister in Ottawa. She comes to visit every few months or so, and when I can, I go see her." I glanced at her. "You?"

"My parents live in North York. We see them regularly. I stayed with them when Alan first walked out, but once I found my feet, I moved here," she explained. "They live in a retirement village and are very active. They enjoy their life there."

I nodded in understanding.

I leaned back in my chair. "I was thinking maybe I could take you and Chloe to the zoo next weekend?"

"Oh, she'd like that."

I lifted her hand and kissed it. "And I think you were going to ask me out?"

She grinned. "I thought I might. What is your schedule?"

"It's a good rotation right now. I'm days all week. I'm working Saturday to cover a shift for a friend, then I have a couple days off. It's usually four on, three off, although I rarely seem to get the full three."

"You do nights?"

"Yeah. And some split shifts." I lifted a shoulder in apology. "Sometimes it's crazy."

She lifted one shoulder in understanding. "I understand. But I think, maybe, Ian Taylor, you might be worth the crazy."

I shifted closer and caught her mouth with mine. "I hope so, Sam. Because I'm crazy about you already."

She didn't say anything, but the way she returned my kiss spoke volumes.

I stepped into the elevator, rubbing at my temples. It had been a long and difficult week. I had been covering shifts, working extra, and barely home. I hadn't seen Sam at all and had to make do with a few calls and video chats with her. In the month we'd been seeing each other, this was the longest we'd gone without physical contact. She'd been more than understanding, but I missed her and Chloe terribly.

I'd gotten used to coffee with her in the evenings, having her drop by the hospital for lunch, sharing quiet moments in the early morning before I left for a shift. I missed Chloe's giggle and the way her face would light up when she saw me. Snuggling her on the sofa if she heard my voice and trotted down the hall in the evening.

I missed kissing Sam on the sofa. Feeling her in my arms. Talking to her about everything and nothing. Teasing her about one of her books.

We'd grown incredibly close, even though we had yet to move further into intimacy. I knew she was hesitant about that step, and I was being patient, even when sometimes I had trouble controlling myself. When she was ready, I was right there with her.

The elevator door opened, and as I walked down the hall, I saw a note on my door. I was already smiling as I reached for it, knowing it was from Sam. She often left me little notes and, at times, treats on my counter inside, or dinner in the fridge. I had given her a key, telling her to feel free to come and go as she wanted. I liked knowing she had been in my space. Opening the door and smelling the trace of her perfume lingering in the air. She had given me a key to her place as well, but I only used it when invited.

I opened the note and spun on my heel, heading back to the elevator.

Mom and Dad have Chloe until dinner. Come see me.

A few times, I had slipped upstairs in the early hours of dawn. I would sleep with Sam beside me, resting deeper than I thought possible. I always left before Chloe got up, but the short time I was there made the rest of my day bearable.

I slipped into Sam's place, the apartment dim and quiet. I dropped my messenger bag and walked down the hall, expecting her to be asleep, but she was in her office, curled in the chair, a manuscript on her lap.

"Hey," she called.

I sat on the ottoman and leaned forward to kiss her. "Hi."

She stroked my face, frowning. "Tough night?"

"Long." I turned my head and kissed her palm. "Why are you up?"

"I was waiting for you."

I couldn't help my smile. "Sorry I was late. Last patient was a little messy, and I had to shower before I came home."

She tugged on the collar of my shirt. "You look sexy in scrubs."

I chuckled. "I had nothing left in my locker."

"I did all your laundry. It's in my room."

I shook my head. "Sam, you didn't have to do that."

She shrugged. "I wanted to. I thought if that was done, you could relax and spend the day with me."

I frowned sadly. "I'm afraid the only place I will spend a great deal of it is in bed."

She met my eyes. "I was hoping you'd say that."

Instantly, I was awake. My body hummed with anticipation at her words. Our gazes remained locked on each other, and the heat around us built.

"Are you sure?" I asked quietly, knowing what a big step this was for her.

"We have all day," she replied. "Mom and Dad took Chloe last night so I could meet my deadline. I worked all night to finish this book. So if you want me—" she took in a deep breath "—I'm all yours."

I stood, pulling the manuscript from her hands and tugging her from the chair. I lifted her into my arms. "Yes, you are."

Our mouths didn't separate as I carried her to her room. They moved and caressed as I laid her on her bed. Broke apart only long enough for me to tear the scrubs over my head and send them flying into a corner before molding back together. We kissed endlessly, long, passionate moments of discovery. Of knowing, this time, the kisses wouldn't end until we were fully joined. I brushed my fingers against her smooth skin as our clothing disappeared. I learned her dips and hollows, tracing her body with my hands and mouth, marveling at the perfection she was under my tongue. Her breasts fit perfectly in my hands, her nipples a deep pink as I sucked them, the hard nubs like candy in my mouth. I kissed the tiny marks on her hips and stomach she tried to cover with her hands, the silvery feathers on her skin proof of her journey as a mother.

"These are part of you," I whispered. "There'll be more, Sam. Our children. And I'll kiss them every time, knowing how they got there. Because your beautiful body cradled them. You wear your love on your skin, my little warrior."

With a low cry, she brought my mouth back to hers, kissing me. I groaned as she wrapped her hand around me, stroking and learning. I ached with desire for her. I trembled as she explored me, her hands and mouth blazing a trail of fire across my skin. I called out her name as her mouth closed around me, the pleasure so intense I shook with barely controlled need. I grasped her, pulling her under me and hovering over her, our eyes locked as I slid inside her. One slow, glorious inch at a time— nothing between us masking the sensation, that conversation having happened weeks ago. There was only her. Only me. Only us.

I stilled at the intense emotional moment. Surrounded by Sam. Our bodies joined together so tightly, we were one. I stared down at her, over-whelmed and certain. She was it for me.

"I love you."

A tear slipped from her eye, rolling into the mass of curls spread around her head like a halo.

"I love you, Ian." She grasped my neck, bowing her back. "Love me now."

I covered her mouth with mine and began to move. I rocked with her, our bodies moving as if they had done this dance a thousand times. We surged and ebbed as my thrusts intensified. I was lost in a vortex of sensa-tion. Her soft skin, the clutch of her around me, her hot breaths drifting over my skin. My name being gasped in her throaty voice, the feel of her legs around me. Pulling me closer. She cried out as her body spasmed in bliss. I sped up, my orgasm barreling down on me. I clasped her tight, all reason leaving me as I gave in to the pleasure, moaning her name and coming endlessly.

Until I was spent. Until I collapsed on her chest, floating and mindless.

She nuzzled my head. I attempted to move, my body not cooperating.

"Stay," she pleaded. "I need to feel you for a few moments."

I managed to lift my head. "I never want to leave."

She ran her hand through my hair, a smile that took my breath away lighting her face.

"Then don't."

SIX MONTHS LATER

I slipped into the apartment, trying to be quiet. One of my fellow doctors had been called away on a family emergency, so I'd worked a double shift to cover him. It was almost five in the morning, and I knew my girls would be asleep, although Chloe would wake up in the next couple of hours.

I rounded the corner and stopped with a grin. Sam was asleep on the sofa, her laptop open, a cup of cold tea sitting beside her. I knew she was against a deadline and had no doubt taken advantage of the fact that I was occupied to finish the manuscript she was working on.

I looked around the room, still amazed this was my life now. Once I had made love with her, I knew I was never letting Sam go. Her gentle personality, her caring ways, her laugh, her smile, the way she mothered Chloe everything about her drew me in. And I adored Chloe. The two of us were buddies and, along with Stitch, had many adventures in the park, the pool downstairs, and the playground.

I had even nursed Chloe through a bad case of the flu, calling in favors to cover my shifts at the hospital. Worry I'd never comprehended before hounded me as I fought to bring down her fever and stop her nausea. She wasn't just a patient, and I wasn't just a doctor. When the fever broke and she fell into a restful sleep, I had almost broken down, finally under-standing what a parent experienced bringing their child into the hospital. It made me a better doctor. I had always been compassionate, but now it was tempered with empathy. It was a great lesson to learn.

While Chloe recovered, I stayed close. As I sat on the sofa with her one day, she looked up at me, her dark eyes pleading.

"You stay here with us, okay?"

I grappled to find the right words, looking to Sam to help me out. She surprised me when she smiled. "Mommy and Ian will talk about that, okay, Chloe?"

"Okay." Chloe patted my hand. "I like it when you're here. It makes me and Stitch happy."

So did I. After a brief discussion with Sam, I began spending more time with them and staying over, allowing Chloe to get used to having me around. When a three-bedroom place opened up in the same building, Sam had slipped the listing in front of me, looking nervous. I had kissed her long and hard, then called the manager. There was no discussion needed. My girls were it for me, and I was ready. We moved in together the following month, and my life became a dizzy calendar of all things Chloe, Sam, and me.

I kneeled in front of Sam and gazed at her. I had some news to share with her, and I wanted to tell her before Chloe woke up. I slipped her laptop onto the table and leaned forward, nuzzling her mouth. I felt her smile as she woke, her lips moving with mine effortlessly.

"You're home."

"I am."

She cupped my face. "You must be so tired."

"I grabbed a nap. I see you've been working too."

"Yeah, I finished the manuscript and sent it back."

I quirked my eyebrows. "A dashing rake in this one? Or is he a duke?"

She grinned. "Both."

I had discovered a guilty pleasure in reading the books she edited, often amused by the antics, and turned on a great deal of the time. I loved it when she printed out a steamy section and left it on my pillow. We had reenacted several scenes, and my favorite nickname for her was *wench*. She giggled when I would lower my voice and call to her.

"Come to me, my wench. Show your duke how much you love him."

"You'll have to tell me all about it."

She waggled her eyebrows, looking adorable. "I will. There is one scene I think you'll like. How do you feel about wearing a kilt?"

It was my turn to grin. "Bring it on, lassie." I kissed her, then moved away, knowing if I stayed close there'd be no more talking, and Chloe would be up soon.

I sat across from her, taking her hand. "Did the package come?"

"Yes."

"Great. I'll give it to her today."

"You spoil her."

I kissed her knuckles. "She deserves it. You both do." I drew in a deep breath. "I have some news."

"Okay?" She looked anxious, her brow furrowing.

"I accepted that job at Urgent Care."

"You did?"

"Yes. The salary is decent, my hours are set, which means I'll have more time for us, and the benefits are great. Once I'm settled, if I want, I can pick up a few shifts in the ER."

"You loved it at the ER."

I shrugged. "Yes. But a lot of that was so I stayed busy. I don't want to be so busy anymore. I want time with my girls. The Urgent Care facility is great. I met some of the staff, and I'm looking forward to the change." I sighed. "To be honest, with Gail leaving to retire and some of the new heads they have in the ER, it was time. They were talking more cutbacks and extra hours. I don't want to burn out."

"Then it's a good decision."

I met her gaze. "Yeah, it is."

"I, ah, did something yesterday."

"Oh?" I asked, curious.

Sam looked nervous. Then she lifted her chin. "I paid off your student loans."

I blinked. Then again. "What?"

"I paid them off."

"Why-why would you do that? How?" I sputtered.

"I used some of my settlement." She held up her hand before I could argue. "Alan paid a lot to get rid of us, and I put most of it away for Chloe's education. But I wanted to do this—for you, for us."

I sighed heavily. "I don't want you paying my debts."

"I'm not. You can repay me at a much slower rate and with no interest. I figured it all out." She eyed me speculatively. "I wanted to do that, Ian. Please let me. Knowing it's less stress for you makes it less stress for me. Besides—" she flashed me a grin "—it would piss Alan off if he knew his money went to help you, so it's a double bonus for me. Please accept it."

Alan hadn't been happy to find out his ex-wife had moved on. I had met him once, and our dislike of each other was mutual. I was worried he was going to try to use Chloe against Sam and me, but my fears were groundless. He had zero interest in being a father or a husband to them, but he hated not having the upper hand. He was a typical narcissist. He didn't want Sam or Chloe, but he didn't want anyone else to have them. Luckily, he grew tired of the game quickly and faded into the background, moving on with yet another new woman. I was glad he wasn't part of Chloe's life.

I sat back, amazed at this woman and how lucky I was to have her.

"I will pay you back."

How had I missed the signs?

She laughed, making me realize I had said that out loud.

"I did too, Ian. We've been so busy. I figured it out yesterday."

"Did you take a test?"

She slipped a slim white case into my hand. "Yes."

I stared at it. Sam was pregnant. With my child.

I pulled her back into my arms, laughing and crying at the same time. "This is the best news ever."

I stood, carrying her, pacing and planning. "I'll get Cindy Friesen. She's the best in the baby field. And a license. We'll get married next week. We'll need a house. With a yard. Maybe I should consider private practice. We have to tell Gail and Marv. Your parents. My mother." I stopped midstride. "How will Chloe take it?"

Sammy looked up at me, amused and alarmed. "Your head is going to explode. First, you can't do anything carrying me around, so you should put me down. Then we'll figure it all out, step by step. I'm six weeks along, Ian. Lots of time so we don't need to make any major decisions right now." Then she grinned. "Although I do want to marry you. But maybe in a couple of weeks? Give a girl time to find a dress."

I sat down, still holding her. "Anything you want. Sam," I breathed out. "I love you." I spread my hand across her stomach, knowing inside, our child was there, growing. "I love you so much."

Her eyes glowed. "I love you. And Chloe will be thrilled. Everything else is just noise, Ian. I don't care where we live or what people think. I just want to be with you and be a family."

I kissed her. "Me too, sweet Sammy. Me too."

EIGHTEEN MONTHS LATER

I pulled up to the house, stopping for a moment to enjoy the vista in front of me. The sun was bright, the flowers in the front garden blooming, their vivid colors setting off the green grass. The bungalow gleamed with a fresh coat of paint, and it looked cared for and homey.

And inside, was my family. I grabbed the flowers I had stopped to pick up and headed to the front door, grinning as it burst open and a little girl tore off the porch, her arms open wide.

"Daddy!"

I lifted her up, kissing her cheek. "Hey, Pumpkin. Have a good day?"

She bobbed her head enthusiastically. "Mommy made a picnic for the backyard!"

"Awesome. Did you help?"

"Yes. I mixed the brownies and looked after Theo!"

I kissed her again and handed her a bunch of daisies. They were her favorite these days. "These are for you for being such a good girl."

She squirmed from my arms, heading for the door. "Mommy! Look, I got flowers!"

Smiling, I followed her, enjoying the feeling of home when I walked in the door. Sam had created a warm, loving space for us. The bungalow had needed a lot of TLC when we found it, but we liked the area and the huge backyard. There was a newer pool, which I had fenced off, and we were still working at making it ours, but it had come a long way since the first time we saw it. The hardwood floors gleamed under my feet as I made my way to the kitchen we had gutted and redone. It was Sam's domain, and she chose every single detail that went into making it hers.

She turned as I entered the room, holding Theo close to her chest as she gave a small vase to Chloe. I set down my messenger bag, handed Sam some flowers, and took my son into my arms.

Then I kissed my wife. It was a long, lingering kiss of "Hello" and "I missed you."

"Hey," I murmured against her hair.

"Hi," she whispered back.

Theo squirmed, and I glanced down, grinning. "Hey, buddy. I see you. And I didn't forget about you." I slipped a new squishy bunny into his hand, laughing as he grabbed on to it, flinging his arm around and grunting in curiosity.

"I hear there's a picnic happening."

Sam chuckled. "We're celebrating we get you for six months."

I grinned. "We'll see if you're celebrating at the end of it."

Sam and I split the year-long parental leave that the Canadian government allowed. I kept working and she took six months off, and now our roles were reversing. I wanted the time to spend with my son. He changed so much every day, and I hated to miss it. I had barely taken a day off since I went to medical school, so the prospect of six months with just my family and no patients was both exhilarating and frightening. Sam was only returning part-time for the next six months, so we would have lots of downtime together. She planned to work around Theo's schedule, and I planned to accomplish some renovations and quality time with my wife and children.

After a lengthy conversation, Alan had relinquished his parental rights, and now, legally, I was Chloe's dad. I never wanted her to think she meant anything less to me than Theo or any other siblings. She was my daughter, and I loved her.

I settled Theo on my shoulder, and we carried the picnic out back. Sam had the table set, and we enjoyed the fun meal she had made, finishing it off with brownies.

I sat back, Theo asleep in his carrier and Chloe happily swinging on the set Marv and I had built for her. Her family of Stitches sat on the table watching her—the original Stitch looking his age and definitely worse for wear. Or as Sam would say, "Well-loved." I lifted him from the table, examining his many repairs.

"He needs to be retired," Sam commented.

I chuckled. "Little guy brought us together. I owe him."

"Our little matchmaker."

"That he is. Without his penchant for getting lost, I never would have found you."

Sam smiled. "Then I guess we better keep him around."

"Yep."

I took Sam's hand, kissing the palm. "I can't wait to see what the next six months bring."

She laughed, leaning over to tuck Theo's blanket a little higher. Then she pressed her hand to my face. "The time since I met you has been wild."

I pretended shock. "What are you talking about? Don't other people meet, fall in love, get married, have a baby, adopt a daughter, buy a house, move, and change jobs in a short time frame? That's not normal?"

She smirked. "Maybe for us it is."

"How about we chill, hang with our kids, demo a couple rooms, and just enjoy life, then? Try something a little different?"

"As long as it's with you, I'm game."

I leaned over, kissing her.

"Always, sweet Sammy. Always."

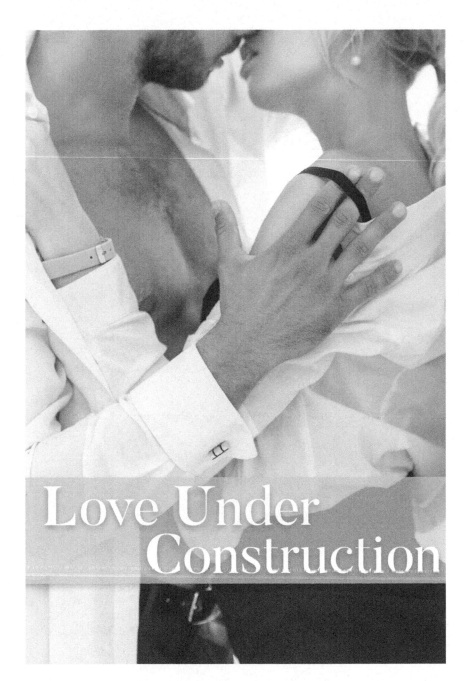

Love Under Construction

CHAPTER 1

JACKSON

There was a loud crunch of gravel as tires going too fast spun on the loose rock, shooting dust and debris into the air. Brakes squealed as a vehicle shuddered to a halt.

Someone was obviously in a hurry.

"Shit," Tom muttered. "Heads up, Jackson."

I glanced around and stifled a groan as the driver's side of the large black pickup was flung open and a pair of shapely legs slid out, the delicate feet encased in shoes that had no business being close to a construction site. Those small feet marched my way, carrying the petite, dark-haired woman—the boss's daughter—Laura Simmons.

"Jackson," she greeted me, her tone caustic. "I was worried you'd perhaps fallen into a cement mixer or off the scaffolding when you didn't return my calls. I'm *thrilled* to see you alive and well."

I resisted the urge to laugh. I was pretty sure "thrilled" wasn't the word she wanted to use.

I feigned surprise. "You called?" I made a show of pulling my phone out of my back pocket. "The damn thing's been acting up lately. I must have missed your voice mails."

She glared at me, crossing her arms, which pushed her pert breasts together, the hint of cleavage peeking through the vee of her dark-red shirt. I snapped my eyes away from the glimpse of the smooth skin and instead focused my attention on the tall man following Laura at a leisurely pace.

"Jackson," he said with a tilt of his head and a smirk playing on his lips partially hidden by his heavy moustache. His gray hair gleamed in the sunlight, and his blue eyes twinkled in amusement. "Phone trouble again?"

I smirked back. "Damnedest thing, Hank."

Laura snorted—a distinctly unladylike sound—and held out her hand. "Give me your phone, and I'll take it into the Apple Store and have them check it out."

"No, I'll take care of it."

"I insist." She smiled sweetly. "It is, after all, company property."

"No, really," I ground out between clenched teeth. "I'll take care of it."

She opened her mouth to protest, but Hank interrupted her. "Leave it. If Jackson says he'll take care of it, he will."

She snapped her mouth shut, those pouty, plump lips thinning out. Her blue eyes, the exact shade as her father's, spoke volumes, though. They were shooting lasers at me, which I ignored.

"What's up, Hank?"

"We need to go over the budget. I asked Laura to set up a meeting with you, but she was, ah, unable to get in contact. I decided to come see you, and she tagged along."

"I understood you were out of town, Laura."

"I got back early."

"Awesome." I nodded and turned back to Hank. "You want me to come to the office, or you want to do it here?"

"Come to the office after you're done."

"You want me to grab us dinner?"

"Angelo's?" he asked hopefully.

"No," Laura snapped. "No pizza for you, Hank! You know what the doctor said."

He rolled his eyes. "He said to watch it, not that I couldn't have pizza on occasion."

"When's the last time you had it?"

"Weeks ago—maybe longer."

She pivoted my way, her hands on her hips. "Jackson?"

I held up my hands. "I'm not your father's keeper. I have no idea what he eats."

She pursed her lips, her foot tapping on the gravel, glaring at both

Hank and me. It was a nice change not to be the only one with whom she was annoyed.

"No bacon or sausage," she snapped. "Light on the cheese."

"Sure."

Hank caught my gaze and rolled his eyes, letting me know what he thought of her command. I could work something out and keep them both happy. She'd probably only stick around for a few minutes. Maybe I'd grab two pizzas—one to make Laura happy, and one for Hank and me, and once she left, I'd bring in the latter.

My plan would have worked—except she didn't leave. That evening, back at the office, I spent a couple of hours being grilled by her over the budget and glared at by Hank for handing him a pizza covered in vegetables and a dusting of cheese. The fact that half had pepperoni on it didn't help since Laura watched which half he ate from, slapping his hand when he reached for the pepperoni. His mood darkened even more when she had the audacity to eat the pizza he felt should be his. He got even by sitting back and letting her pick apart every decision I had made.

When she got up to get a file, I growled, "Thanks for the backup."

"Thanks for the lousy dinner."

"I have a full works in the truck."

"Oh yeah?"

"Good luck getting it after you let 'The General' at me," I snarled, using the nickname the guys had for her.

He smirked as Laura swept back into the room, her skirt hem flipping up as she sat down, giving me a glimpse of her knees. Her soft, rounded knees.

"Now, about the overtime," she started.

Hank held up his hand. "The overtime was necessary. The client wanted the changes and knew it would cost them." He crossed his legs. "In fact, I'm pretty sure I remember okaying most of these expenditures. The ones I didn't I know about, Jackson wouldn't have spent if they weren't necessary."

We both gaped at him. He stood, stretching. "You head home, kiddo. You must be tired. I need to talk over a couple other things with Jackson. I'll call you on the weekend."

She gathered up her files and left the office, muttering. I waited until I heard her car leave the parking lot, and I glared at him. "Just like that? Suddenly, everything is fine because you want to get your hands on that other pizza? You're such a jerk."

"That was only part of it. I do enjoy watching the two of you spar. I can't believe you let her tell you what to put on the pizza."

I groaned. "You're my boss, Hank, but let's face it—she runs the show. I didn't dare bring in the other one."

He huffed. "Will you ever get along?"

I wasn't sure what to say, so I shrugged. "Maybe one day."

He shook his head. "The two of you drive me nuts. Go get the other pizza before she thinks of something else and comes back to keep arguing."

I laughed, because she would.

A while later, I pulled into the garage, smiling in anticipation. My girl's car was parked on the other side of mine, which meant she was here—waiting for me.

I stopped in the mudroom, shedding my clothes and stepping in the shower, ridding myself of the dust and dirt of the day. The hot water pounding against my aching back felt great, but I kept it short since I was anxious to see her. Wrapping a towel around my waist, I grabbed another one and ran it through my hair. I studied myself in the mirror. My hair was still a sandy brown, a few silver strands around my forehead starting to make an appearance. My face was still unlined, aside from the crinkles around my hazel eyes. I kept in shape, hard work and time at the gym making my muscles strong and my posture straight. My girl called me sexy and like to show me how much she appreciated my body. I enjoyed it immensely and returned the favor as often as I could.

Tossing the towel I used on my head in the hamper, I made my way down the hall to my bedroom, pushing open the door. She was curled up on my bed, her dark hair spread out on the pillow, smiling *that* smile—the one only I ever saw. Filled with warmth, light, and love. Love for me.

I dropped the towel and slid into bed, pulling her to me. "God, I missed you. I hate it when you go away."

"I hate it too," she whispered.

"Tell him no next time," I murmured against her lips.

"I can't."

"I know."

Fisting my hands in her thick hair, I brought her sweet mouth to mine. Our breath mingled, lips ghosting together. Her velvet tongue touched my bottom lip, and I was lost. With a deep groan, I crushed her to me and kissed her deep. Hard. Our tongues met, stroking and delving, wet and wanting. She clutched my shoulders as I clasped her tight, my need for her overwhelming and strident. My body hummed with arousal; the feeling of her lush curves molding to my hard planes was perfection. She was made to fit beside me. She belonged right here. I hovered over her, staring into her lovely blue eyes, caught in the emotions they reflected back at me.

"I need you," I rasped.

"Have me," she moaned, wrapping her legs around my hips, guiding me to her heat. I thrust forward, hissing at the sensation of being joined with her again. Every time was like the first time. Every time, I was overcome by the feeling of coming home. I moved within her, groaning her name against her skin as I ran wet, openmouthed kisses on her neck, burying my face in her hair and breathing her in.

The intense pleasure of her mouth against my skin, the press of her body on mine, and the heat of her surrounding my cock were too much. I came forcefully as she gasped and shuddered around me, her muscles clamping down, milking my orgasm as I shouted and slammed into her as deep as I could.

She wound her arms around me, pulling me to her chest. Gentle, long strokes of her fingers in my hair caused a slow, contented sigh to escape my mouth.

"You were a sight for sore eyes today."

"I missed you so much, I caught an earlier flight. When Dad said he was going to see you, I almost ripped the keys out of his hand," she admitted. "I couldn't wait another minute—even if I had to act pissy."

I grinned against her neck, nipping the silky skin sharply. "You do it well, sweet girl. I almost bought your act."

"It was hard. All I wanted to do was fling myself into your arms."

"You're here now."

"Why didn't you answer my calls?"

"I wanted to—but I was surrounded the whole day. I thought you were still away, and I missed you so fucking much I was sure anyone hearing me talk to you would know. I was going to call you back as soon as I was free."

"So, you weren't ignoring me?"

"I could never ignore you. Ever."

"Good."

I chuckled as I kissed her head. "Nice try getting my phone away from me, though. After what you did to it last time, I am not falling for that again."

"I thought you liked the ringtones."

"Barry White? I don't think so. Never mind the pictures you put on it. Christ, I had a raging hard-on every time I looked at my screen." I paused. "The 'reminders' popping up didn't help either."

7 p.m.—Lick my girl's pussy until she screams.

8 p.m.—Take my girl hard.

9 p.m.—Make my girl suck my cock.

She smirked. "It worked, though. You didn't forget."

"I could never forget needing to fuck you." I growled, knowing it would make her giggle.

She didn't disappoint, her breathy little sounds filling the room. Then a large exhale of air left her mouth.

"What was that sound for?"

"I hate acting angry at you all the time. I feel like I'm two different people."

"I know. It's the only way we can be together—at least for now." I nuzzled her head. "We'll figure this out."

"Promise?" she asked, her voice anxious.

"Yes." I tightened my grip. "How was your mother?"

"Worse than ever. This house needs to be done—and soon."

I chuckled. When Hank's ex-wife had decided to fully renovate her house, she insisted Hank make the arrangements for her, even though she lived halfway across the country. Still unable to deny her anything, he did as she requested, but she was a horrible client, constantly changing her mind, causing everyone grief. Mimi's phone calls were endless, and being the coward Hank was, he sent Laura to deal with the problems when they couldn't be fixed over the phone.

"You need to tell him to deal with this shit. He's the one who can't say no to the woman."

"I know. I'll talk to him and make him go next time." She snuggled closer. "I could hardly wait to get back to you."

"Welcome home, baby."

"I love you, Jackson."

I sighed into her hair, content now she was back where she belonged, even if it had to be in secret. "More than I can say, Laura. Love just isn't a big enough word."

She relaxed, slipping into sleep. I held her tight—the two women in my life once again melded into one.

Laura Simmons—the bane of my existence by day.

Laura Simmons—the love of my life and the one woman I was forbidden to have.

CHAPTER 2

JACKSON

Hank hung up the phone, passing a hand over his face. I glanced over from the desk I was using with a frown. "Problem?"

"My daughter's coming home. She's decided to take me up on my job offer."

"This isn't good news?"

"It should be. With Sheila leaving, Laura is the perfect person to take over her job. She's got experience, she's organized, and she won't take shit from anyone." He ran his finger over the picture of her he kept on his desk. I had seen the picture often—his daughter, Laura, was a pretty girl; long, dark hair with blue eyes that sparkled with mischief.

I had worked for Hank for two years but never met his daughter. He usually went to visit her, and the occasions she was in town, she never came to the office. A couple months ago, Hank had shared the news she was separating from her husband—news he wasn't exactly upset about. Craig, in Hank's opinion, was lazy, always willing to take the easy road for everything and didn't look after his little girl the way he should. Laura, it seemed, had been carrying the load for far too long. Hank had been after her to come home and work for him so he could keep an eye on her. He worried about her constantly and talked about her so much, I felt I almost knew her.

"You don't think she can handle the job?"

He sat back in his chair, staring out the window. "It's not the job I'm worried about. Running this place and running the big, fancy office she used to work at won't be the problem. It's…the crew. I don't want any of them around her. She's vulnerable and has a heart of gold. She's also beautiful—I don't want her overwhelmed or bothered."

I nodded in understanding. Hank had always been protective of his daughter. "I'm sure the guys will be respectful. I can have a word if you want, Hank. Tell them to stay away."

He turned in his chair, his expression serious. "She's off-limits to everyone here, Jackson. She isn't just another employee. She's my daughter." His fingers drummed on the desk. "Maybe I should implement a new policy—no dating within the company."

I had to laugh. "Since Laura will be the only woman here, Hank, that might be a bit obvious. It would make her uncomfortable, and frankly, it might make it more tempting for a few of them." Then I smirked. "Besides, you'll break Tom's heart. He's been after Simon since he got here. You can't do that to him when he's so close."

Hank laughed. We all knew how Tom felt about Simon. Except, it seemed, Simon.

"Maybe you're right. They're all the right age, but I want more for her." He sighed. "At least I don't have to worry about you."

I chuckled. "Oh? Not her type? Too rough around the edges?"

"She's twenty-six, Jackson. That's twelve years younger than you. I don't think you're into cradle snatching." His eyes narrowed. "Are you?"

I shook my head, amused at his fierce expression. I wasn't looking for a relationship —especially not with someone I worked with. The complications would be enormous. Never mind adding in the layer of her being related to Hank—not interested.

"Nope—too young for me. I like them walking and talking on their own." Then I winked at him. "Relax, Hank. Your daughter sounds as though she can hold her own. I'm sure if any of the yahoos step out of line, she'll put them in their place."

He nodded but didn't look convinced.

"I'll talk to them."

"Will you watch out for her? I'd feel better if I knew you were looking out for her."

"Consider it done."

"Maybe you could be friends."

Friends. I wasn't used to being friends with a girl—but I would try for Hank.

"I'm game if she is." Then I grinned wryly at him. "She isn't six, you know. You can't pick her friends for her—but I'll help her any way I can."

"Thanks, Jackson. I knew I could depend on you."

I waved him off. "Not a problem. Happy to help. I look forward to getting to know her."

Hank frowned, and I hastened to assure him.

"Relax—as a friend, Hank. It'll be like having another little sister around. It'll be great."

~

I was in trouble in about five seconds flat. Laura stepped into the office, and any and all thoughts of being her friend went out the window. And I certainly didn't feel this way about my little sister, Amy. The picture Hank had on his desk didn't do Laura justice—and she was no little girl. She was small, curvy, with hair that hung down her back in deep waves of chocolate, and large blue eyes that were bright and filled with intelligence. Then she smiled—full, pink lips curved into a warm, enticing smile that made my body tighten with want. She was dressed in a simple navy skirt and a cream-colored blouse and low heels—attire that was totally appropriate for the office, gave nothing away, yet on her, was completely sexy.

So sexy and alluring, I was hard instantly.

So hard, I couldn't even stand up to greet her. There was no hiding my reaction.

Instead, I was back to being fifteen again and hiding behind a large piece of furniture. When Hank introduced us, all I could do was remain seated, extend my hand, and offer her a gruff hello. His eyebrows shot up at my seeming rudeness, and Laura looked confused. Still, she placed her small hand in mine, greeting me politely. A subtle shock ran down my spine as my hand closed over hers, and it took everything in me not to pull her onto my lap and kiss her—even with Hank standing there. I wanted to feel those inviting lips moving underneath mine. Her eyes widened, and she pulled back her hand, her tongue peeking out as she bit her full bottom lip.

I wanted that tongue in my mouth. I wanted to bite that bottom lip, then run my own tongue over it and tease her until she begged me for more.

I grabbed a file and my laptop, muttered something about seeing a client, and ran.

Like a coward.

Inside my truck, I slammed my hands on the steering wheel. Desire was coursing through me, hot, pumping, and needy.

I wanted her.

Laura, the boss's daughter. The boss who expressly stated she was off-limits to everyone in the company. The boss who wanted me to look out for her, be her friend, and keep the other men away from her.

I felt a growl building in my chest.

That was the only thing Hank and I would agree on at this exact moment.

No one was fucking getting close to her. They wouldn't touch her.

She was mine.

It didn't matter that she was too young for me, just out of a bad marriage, or that she was Hank's daughter and was strictly forbidden.

I wasn't sure how I could stay away.

I ran a hand roughly over my face.

I had to.

～

My avoidance worked well for about six weeks. When we were forced to be together, I was polite but distant. At meetings, I sat as far away from her as possible—one inhale of her light, feminine scent was enough to start my dick twitching, which invariably led to inappropriate thoughts of burying my face in her neck, fisting her thick hair in my hands as I fucked her. On my desk. Her desk. In my truck. In Hank's truck. Anywhere I could.

I saw the flickers of hurt cross her face every time I was curt with her. Her shoulders curled in a little at my tone, and I hated knowing I was the one causing her pain. But it was the only way I could stay away from her. Other times, she squared her shoulders, and we went toe-to-toe over some minor infraction she felt I was perpetrating. Her eyes would flash, her voice rising, and she refused to back down. She was magnificent.

My cock agreed and wanted her even more. I'd have to hide again, often taking matters into my own hands—literally—when I couldn't stand it anymore. I hid a bottle of lotion in the bathroom for occasions like that. The fact that I was almost forty years old and having to rub one out in the bathroom to make it through the day without humping a woman I barely knew was more than humiliating.

I started spending more time on the jobsite we were currently running. I told Hank the guys were slacking off and needed me there, but it was the only way I could keep my sanity.

But she was everywhere. I heard her laughter in the office, and I wanted to be the one who made her smile. When she would bring in cookies she baked, I wanted to steal them all and keep them for myself since she made them. Instead, I would shake my head when she would offer the container, ignoring the way her smile fell away, and sneak some later when she was busy. I covertly stole looks at her during meetings, wishing I could smile at her and see that wondrous smile of hers in return. But if our eyes happened to meet, I would glance away, dismissing her. If she appeared on-site, I would snap at her about wearing steel-toe boots and a hard hat, without even greeting her. The truth was, I was terrified she would be hurt wandering around the site, but I couldn't tell her that.

I was shocked when a new emotion—one I had never experienced before—ran hot and free in my veins. Jealousy.

Coming out of the trailer one day, I saw one of the crew, Larry, standing next to her car, joking and laughing with her, causing a slow burn in the pit of my stomach. Stalking toward them, I growled at him. "Are we on a coffee break?"

He frowned. "I don't drink coffee, Jackson."

"Then I guess the break is over. Back to work."

Laura glared at me as he walked away, looking confused. "That was rude."

"I don't pay them to flirt with you."

"He wasn't flirting. He was talking about his mom. We were comparing the kinds of cookies she makes!"

"Whatever," I sputtered. "And for the last time—wear a fucking hard hat when you're on-site!"

She reached into her car and pulled out a pink hard hat, setting it firmly on her head. "I have one. I was leaving when Larry came over, so I had just removed it. Stop snapping at me, Jackson."

She glared at me as she spoke, which did something to my chest. She was adorable in her pink headgear, which only made her more appealing to me.

I returned her glare, pointing to her feet. "You forgot the boots."

I stomped away, knowing she was watching me, no doubt cursing at me under her breath. She rarely swore, but when she did, I found it rather sexy. I found everything about her sexy. It frustrated me to no end.

She was the opposite of everything in my life. In my world of dust, gravel, and hard steel, she was fresh, sweet, and delicate. Her voice was warm honey compared to the raspy tenors I dealt with all day, her mannerisms gentle and feminine compared to the roughness that surrounded me. There was a tenderness she hid from everyone that I could see when she thought she was being unobserved—usually when dealing with her father on a more personal level after hours. I wanted some of that tenderness in my own life.

I wanted her tenderness. I wanted her.

She took over the running of the office seamlessly, her actions always smart, direct, and honest. She was brilliant, and Hank beamed with pride.

Hank groused at me about not being friendly enough to her, and I scowled at him. "I told you, Hank, you can't pick her friends. It's a personality thing. Leave it alone."

After a couple of weeks, she started standing her ground more and arguing with me all the time. We'd trade barbs and thinly veiled insults, even during meetings. I began thinking maybe the best thing would be to find another job. With my qualifications, I could easily move along, except I liked and respected Hank, and until Laura showed up, I enjoyed my job. Now, I dreaded some days, knowing I'd have to deal with her at any given moment. Yet, the thought of not seeing her made me miserable. And on the occasion when we found common ground and worked as a team, it was magic. It was as if she knew exactly how I was thinking and would respond perfectly, our ideas meshing in complete sync. In those moments, being in her company was effortless and made me want more.

I was so fucked.

I eased back in my chair, running my hands through my hair in vexation and tugging on the ends. We'd had another sparring match this afternoon, and I stormed out of the office and spent the rest of the day on-site, snapping at everyone around me. I came back to the office to do some paperwork, knowing it would be deserted and I could get my work done in peace. I had heard Hank and Laura making plans for dinner earlier, so the area was clear.

Or at least, I thought it was. A throat clearing softly had me snapping my head up in surprise. Laura was standing in my doorway, holding a file and looking nervous. "Jackson? Can I talk to you for a moment?"

"I thought you were going to dinner."

"Change of plans." She hesitated. "May I come in?"

"Sure." I indicated the chair in front of my desk. "What have I done now? Is my cell phone bill being audited?"

"Oh." She squirmed a little in her chair. "No, nothing like that. Actually, I wanted to show you last month's figures."

"Is there a problem?"

"No." She handed me the file. "Your suggestion about the staggered shifts was a great cost- and time-saver. Hank was very pleased. It was-it was a really great idea."

I glanced at the numbers, nodding and hiding my face. My chest warmed at her quiet praise. "Good," I said gruffly. "Glad I did something right." I handed her back the file. "Anything else?"

She bit her lip and drew in a deep breath. "Jackson, I'm not sure how we got off on the wrong foot, but can we start again? My dad thinks the world of you, the crews respect you, and the other staff think you're the cat's meow. I'm not sure why you dislike me so much, but I promise, if you let me try again, you'll see I'm really a nice person." She offered me a shaky smile. "Maybe you could give me a chance?"

She looked vulnerable and sad. I wanted to take that sadness away and make her smile. "I don't dislike you, Laura."

Her eyes were confused. "But…"

I held up my hand, interrupting her. "It's my problem, not yours. I'm very sorry I've upset you." I huffed out a sigh as I studied her. She looked tired and weary, and suddenly I wondered if it was because of me. "I think maybe I need to move on. Look for another job."

She was on her feet in an instant. "No! You can't do that!"

I frowned at her. "Pardon?"

"Hank needs you, Jackson. He depends on you. I'll leave—you've been here for years. I've only just got here, so I can be replaced. You can't go work elsewhere. You can't!"

I gaped at her. She was so upset, her hands clenched at her sides, angry tears glistening in the corners of her wide eyes.

"You're Hank's family. He needs you more than me. He'll find another project manager."

"No. You're the best—he says so. He needs you," she insisted.

"I don't think I can stay here," I confessed.

"Because of me?"

I decided to be honest. "Yes."

"Why do you hate me so much?"

I regarded her for a moment, then spoke quietly. "I don't hate you, sweet girl." My voice dropped further. "Quite the opposite."

"Sweet girl?" she repeated.

"It's how I think of you. In my head," I admitted.

"But…you barely talk to me."

"It's-it's a survival thing." I beseeched her with my eyes to understand. "I'll talk to Hank on Monday."

She shook her head, her expression one of shock. "I wish you wouldn't."

"I have to."

She turned and left. I heard the outside office door close, and I knew I was alone. I looked out the window, knowing I had to do this. As much as I hated it, I had to go. My feelings for Laura were only growing stronger, not diminishing as I had hoped.

I sat lost in thought for a while, then gave up even pretending I was going to work. I had to go home and figure out my next step. I grabbed my coat and stepped outside, taking in a deep inhale of air. I glanced around the parking lot, seeing one of Hank's trucks there. I hadn't noticed it before—I must have missed it with my preoccupation and my thoughts. But as I walked toward my own vehicle, I saw the truck wasn't empty.

Laura.

She was bent over the steering wheel, hands wrapped around the leather, and her shoulders were shaking, the truck actually moving with the force of her sobs. My heart clenched at the sight of her.

There was no thought, only reaction. My feet crossed the pavement and I was in the truck before I even realized what I was doing. Reaching over, I dragged her onto my lap, wrapping her in my arms and holding her to my chest.

"Shh, Laura. Don't do this."

"You…can't…go… Please, Jackson." She lifted her head, her tear-ravaged face breaking my heart. "I don't want you to go…please!"

Her pleas, the pain in her voice, were too much. I cupped her face, wiping the tears with my thumbs. "Sweet girl," I murmured.

She covered my hands with hers, gripping my wrists. "Please," she whispered.

And then my mouth was on hers.

Her lips, so soft, molded to mine. I could taste the salt of her tears, the sweet of her lip gloss, and flavor of her—Laura. It was intoxicating, and I knew I wanted that taste for the rest of my life. As my tongue slid along hers, we both groaned.

I needed more.

I pulled her tight to my chest, one arm holding her close while I used my other hand to pull her hair free of the clip it was caught up with. Her hair tumbled down in a wave of silk that I wrapped my hand in, tugging on the tresses to tilt back her head. I sought out the skin of her neck, kissing, licking, and biting my way back to her mouth, needing her taste back on my tongue. She pulled on my hair, twisting the short strands roughly, holding my face tight to hers. Dropping a hand to her hip, I tugged her shirt out of her skirt, running my hand up the bare skin of her back, trailing over the bumps and ridges of her spine, jerking her closer. She whimpered into my mouth as I ghosted the swells of her breasts, tracing the hardened nipples with my thumbs.

She started to flex and move on my lap, her skirt riding up as she shifted. I groaned as my sheathed cock pressed into her warmth—the heat of her blazing, even through my pants.

"Please, Jackson," she panted.

Weeks of forbidden desire, raging want, and unending frustration burst. With a growl, I tore away her scrap of lace, slipping my fingers into her wetness, claiming her mouth even deeper. Her head fell back with a groan as I stroked her, building her desire, praising her. "That's it, Laura. Feel me. Feel what you do to me. Come on my fingers and show me you want me."

"Jackson!"

I brought her mouth roughly back to mine, my tongue stealing in and taking her breath. She rode my fingers, the muscles clamping down as she shattered, her cry muffled with my mouth.

I hissed with satisfaction as she fumbled and yanked at my belt and zipper. Lifting my hips, I felt the rush of cool air for only an instant before I was surrounded by her wet center. Cursing at the overwhelming feeling of being buried inside her, I grabbed her hips, stilling her motion. "Give me a minute, baby. I want to feel you."

Her head fell to my shoulder, and she shuddered, letting me set the pace. I slid my hands up her hips and slowly started to thrust, pushing her down to meet my movements. Pushing—pulling—in—out—faster and faster, the blistering heat building between us. The truck was filled with the sounds of our lovemaking—moans, whimpers, sighs, murmurs of endearments, the echoes of our skin meeting and separating. Nothing existed outside this cab—nothing mattered. All that mattered was the intense act happening between us. She pulled her head back with a gasp. I wrapped my hand around her neck, holding her gaze, still thrusting as she climaxed, her eyes huge and filled with ecstasy. My orgasm slithered up my spine, exploding with force, and I gripped her tight, her name falling from my lips as I groaned, emptying myself inside her.

She fell forward, her head resting on my chest. I wrapped my arms around her, a feeling of intense affection filling me. Nuzzling her hair, I inhaled her intoxicating scent. Her fingers traced lazy circles on my neck.

"That was…unexpected," I murmured. "Fucking amazing, though." I kissed her brow. "I've wanted you for so long."

"Was it what you imagined?"

I chuckled. "Except for the location, yes. I hadn't planned on our first time in the front seat of a company truck."

She giggled. "No?"

"Maybe our third or fourth."

That got me another giggle.

"I liked it." She shifted and grimaced, a small smile on her face. "We're a little messy, though."

"We are." Then I groaned. "Fuck, Laura. I didn't…I didn't even think… Fuck… baby, I'm clean, but I should have used protection. I wasn't expecting… I didn't plan…"

She pressed a finger to my mouth. "I'm clean and on birth control, Jackson. We're fine."

"Tell me you don't regret what just happened," I beseeched.

"Tell me you won't leave."

"I can't leave you now," I admitted. "I don't want to stay away from you anymore."

She lifted her head. "Then don't."

CHAPTER 3

JACKSON

I smiled as I looked over at Laura. We were in bed—our usual Saturday morning ritual well underway. I made coffee; she made her infamous breakfast sandwiches. We carried both back to bed with the paper. I spent a lazy hour enjoying the tranquility of perusing the headlines, while Laura worked on the crossword puzzle, often interrupting me with a query.

"Flightless bird—three letters?"

"Emu."

"Storage area—six letters?"

"Hmm…locker?"

"Oh, that works!"

I smirked and kept reading.

"Thrusting implement?"

I looked up with a frown. "What?"

"Four letters—starts with C…or it might be a D—definitely ends in K though."

"Are you shitting me with this?"

"Yes."

Then she fell backward, laughing at her silly joke. Chuckling, I lifted her feet on my lap and stroked her ankles, the way I knew she liked. She sighed in pleasure and smiled at me, tucking an arm under her head. She was relaxed, her dark hair spilling out around her, her eyes warm as they looked at me.

I loved seeing her like this.

In the office, she was Laura—cool, professional, and a force to be reckoned with. She hadn't earned the nickname "The General" for nothing. She dealt with the crews, suppliers, and problems efficiently and without apologies. She dressed the part, her outfits businesslike and feminine yet never crossing the line. She wore her hair up, often tucking an errant strand back into place. Some days, it took everything in me not to be the one who reached out and smoothed the curl behind her ear while I dropped a tender kiss to the skin for good measure. It was getting harder to resist.

When dealing with her father, she was still efficient and bossy, although her words were tempered with fondness—unless they were arguing over budgets or his terrible eating habits.

But alone with me, she became my Laura. Her body language changed, and she became fluid and supple. All soft curves and rounded edges—like liquid mercury. Her smiles were filled with light, her gaze warm and gentle, and her words uttered in the gentlest tone, the tenderness I had longed for on full display. Her laughter was low and sultry and happened often. I loved making her laugh.

"You're such a nut."

She grinned at me. "But you love me."

I tightened my hands on her feet. "I do."

Her face turned serious. "Tell me."

Lifting her feet off my lap, I moved and hovered over her, holding her gaze. "I love you, Laura. More than anyone or anything. You're my entire world."

She became peaceful, her smile shy. "I love you."

Lowering my head, I traced her collarbone with my tongue, swirling it on her delicate skin. I dragged my mouth up her throat, tugging gently on her earlobe, smiling at her shiver. "Now, about that crossword puzzle. Maybe I need to help you with a physical demonstration of that thrusting implement?"

"Yes...*Jackson*...God...*yes*...show me."

～

She was wrapped in my arms, snuggled close. The newspaper was scattered all around us on the floor, one overturned cup of coffee dripping a dark stain onto the paper. I traced the skin of her arm with one finger, up and down, over and over again.

"What are you thinking?" she whispered.

"How good it feels when you're in my arms."

She snuggled tighter. "I know."

"I want you here all the time."

She tilted up her head. "Jackson?"

"I hate it when you go away and I can't talk to anyone—say anything about how much I miss you or worry about you. I hate hiding how much I love you."

"Then we need to make changes."

I yanked on my hair in frustration. "I know. I just don't know how."

"We sit down with my father and tell him."

I snorted. "That's going to go over well. Pretty sure by the end of the conversation, I'll have a busted lip and no job."

"Do you really think he'll be that upset? He thinks so highly of you."

"In addition to being opposed to the age thing, and me not being good enough for you, I think he's going to be angry over the fact that we've kept it hidden all this time. He's gonna be mad on a lot of levels."

She shook her head. "You *are* good enough for me—and good for me. He'll see that. He may be mad at first, but my dad loves me, and he wants me to be happy. *You* make me happy."

Cupping her cheek, I smiled. "I like making you happy. I'm not sure about how fast he'll come around. He was pretty insistent on no one in the company getting close to you."

"Then we should face it now, and it's done." Her voice became even quieter. "Are you worried about his anger personally or professionally?"

"Some of both," I admitted. "I like my job a lot. I'm good at it, and I like working for your dad."

"More than you like me?"

"Of course not."

"Are you embarrassed by our relationship? Are you ashamed of me?"

"No! It's nothing like that."

"Yet we still hide."

"Laura…"

"You were going to leave when you thought we couldn't be together. What about now? Would you leave so we could be? Or didn't you mean it?"

"At the time, I guess I did, yes. I didn't want to leave, but I thought it might be for the best."

"But not now? Even if it meant we could be together—out in the open?"

"What about you? You said the same thing," I challenged. "You thought it was important I stay working with your dad. Or doesn't that matter anymore?"

She stood, suddenly very angry. "Is that what you want? For me to give up my job?"

I stood as well, tense. "Don't put words in my mouth."

And then, we were arguing. Angry words, accusations, and denials flew between us. All over a situation neither of us had a solution to, brought up at the wrong moment, when we were anxious, unsure of the future, and weary of hiding our feelings. What I *should* have done was take her in my arms and tell her we'd talk to her father. Face it together. If he was furious and completely against us, I *would* walk away from a job I liked—because I loved her, and she trumped everything.

Instead, we continued to argue until she was furious enough to storm into the washroom with her clothes and leave. And I was angry enough to let her go.

The slam of the door behind her echoed in the house, and in my heart, for hours.

Sunday, I was miserable. I woke up alone and exhausted, having tossed and turned all night, our argument on repeat in my head, my bed too big and empty without her. I kept picking up my phone to call her, but I didn't want this conversation to happen via airwaves. I wanted to see her face-to-face, but going to her place was risky. She always came here, since I lived across town from Hank. Her place was two blocks away from him, making the chance of him seeing my truck far too high. I paced the house, frustrated and angry, eventually saying fuck it and getting in my truck, determined to make this right.

But when I slowed down by her driveway, I saw not only her car parked there, but her father's company truck behind it. Cursing, I drove away, and I spent the afternoon doing errands and drive-bys, but Hank's truck remained a silent sentinel. Giving up, I went home and sent her a simple text.

Jackson: I'm an ass. Call me when the coast is clear so I can apologize properly. I love you.

I waited in vain—the phone never rang, and the message remained unanswered.

Monday morning, I was sullen, tired, and desperate to see her. Glancing at my schedule, I bit back a curse, realizing we had a staff meeting, directly followed by a meeting with a new client. I had met him once and disliked him immediately. I thought he was a pompous ass and hoped we wouldn't see him again, but as luck would have it, he'd scheduled another sit-down.

Laura would be attending both meetings—and unless I managed to get to her before they started, we'd still be on unfriendly terms when they began, and I didn't want that.

At the office, her door was closed and her car not in her spot. Hank was there, on the phone, and I waved as I went by. In my office, I sorted through some notes and listened attentively as the office became busier. When I finally heard Laura's voice calling out greetings, I relaxed and, after a few minutes, stood, a file in hand, preparing to go and talk to her. At my doorway, I paused as she came into view. My hand grasped the edge of the doorframe as I swallowed hard.

She didn't.

To everyone else, she looked normal. To me, she was fucking sin.

A silky wrap dress in a deep blue hugged her curves and ended just above her knees. The bow resting on her hip begged for my teeth to grasp it and pull it open. She was wearing high heels for a change, which made her legs seem long and endless—I wanted them wrapped around my hips, the heels digging into my ass as I pounded into her. There was nothing unusual about her outfit, except it was one of my favorites. I told her once how fucking sexy she was in it.

But it was her hair that caught my eye and made my breath catch in my throat. Her glorious fucking hair I couldn't resist, cascaded over her shoulders and down her back in waves of dark chocolate satin. She'd left it curly, which she hated, but knew I loved—the riotous mass swirling around her face as she moved. I wanted to lace my hands in the curls and pull her face to mine and kiss her. Bend her over the closest desk and bury my face in the sweet fragrance as I begged for her forgiveness. Fuck her until she moaned my name and showed me with her body that we were okay.

Instead, I was paralyzed as our eyes met. Her anger-filled gaze was challenging. My apologetic one ignored. She knew what seeing her hair down would do to me. How much I'd want—need—to touch her and not be able to. She was still angry at me, thinking I valued my job over her.

Taking in a deep breath and pushing off the door, I crossed the office, aware we were being watched. "Good morning, Laura."

"Jackson." Her voice was clipped, and this time, I knew it wasn't an act. Up close, I could see how tired she looked, and the hurt was evident in her gaze.

"I have a couple thoughts on that file we were discussing. I wondered if you could spare me a moment before the staff meeting." I paused and cleared my throat. "I thought about what you said, and I really wanted to talk it over with you."

Her eyes flickered, and she blinked—a glimmer of moisture appearing. I inched forward, needing to be closer. I inhaled deeply, the scent of her washing over me. "Please," I added, fighting the incredible urge to say *fuck it all* and drag her into my arms, not caring about the consequences.

Before she could answer, Hank strode out of his office, clapping his hands. "Great. I need to see both of you before Harris comes in. My office —now."

Our bubble was broken. Laura closed her eyes and stepped back, her guard once again returning. "Of course, Hank," she acknowledged and moved past me, her long tresses brushing my hands. Unable to resist, I pulled one curl with my finger, its texture silky against my callused skin. It took everything in me not to wrap the curls in my fist and yank her back to me like a caveman. Claim her in front of everyone. The curl unwound and escaped my finger as she walked away.

"We'll talk later, Jackson."

I followed her silently, realizing I would follow her anywhere.

I had to make sure she understood that.

CHAPTER 4

JACKSON

Laura smiled at me from the corner of the sofa as I handed her a cup of coffee. I'd helped her right her clothing and removed her from my lap. I slid over to the driver's side of the truck, and she looked at me questioningly. "I live five minutes from here—I often leave my truck in the lot. If Hank sees yours, he'll wonder where you are."

"Are we going somewhere?"

"Yes. You're coming home with me, and we're going to talk."

"Okay."

Once we reached the house, I gave her a set of sweatpants and a shirt to change into, while I made the coffee, quickly changed myself, and waited for her. When she emerged from the guest room, her hair brushed and back up, and dressed in my clothes, I couldn't suppress my smirk. She was beyond adorable—the sleeves of my shirt rolled up several times and the pants hanging off her hips. I drew her close, kissing her temple, finding the clip and letting her hair loose again.

"Leave it down. I love your hair."

She tilted up her face, biting her lip. I pulled on the plump flesh. "Keep doing that, and we won't be talking," I warned.

Color stained her cheeks, and I chuckled as I drew her to the sofa. How she could blush after what we'd just done was beyond me. She was a mystery to me still—one I wanted to solve.

She sipped her coffee, gazing at me over the rim of her mug. She was too far away, so I moved closer and laced our fingers together.

"I thought you hated me," she confessed.

"Anything but."

"Then why…?"

I kissed her hand and released it. "Your father was very specific when you were moving back, Laura. You're off-limits. To everyone." I shook my head as I chuckled without humor. "He asked me to be your friend. Look out for you—like I would my own sister. Except the way I feel about you isn't brotherly. The only way I could stop myself from acting on how I felt was to distance myself."

"But he really likes you—respects you. If we talked to him…"

"I'm twelve years older than you are, Laura. He'd fucking freak out."

Her chin lifted. "It's just a number."

"A big number."

She shrugged. "Your age doesn't bother me." She sighed, looking down into her mug, her voice low when she spoke. "The way you treated me bothered me."

I lifted her face and stroked her cheek. "I'm sorry," I murmured. "I hated doing it, but I didn't know what else to do. You…you affect me deeply, sweet girl."

"How?" she whispered, turning her face and pressing a kiss to my palm.

"You bring out feelings I've never experienced before," I confessed. "I've never felt this…need for another person. I want to protect you, keep you from harm. I want to touch you all the time." I trailed my fingers along her neck at the slight reddish skin from my scruff. "I want to mark you and let everyone know you're taken." I shut my eyes briefly, opening them to meet her intense gaze. "I want to know what makes you laugh and cry. All your hopes and fears. I want to make your dreams come true. I want to be part of your life." I drew in a deep breath. "I want to make love to you…to fuck you and hear you cry out my name again. I want…I want to be everything to you."

"But?"

"We're at different stages in our life, Laura. Your father wouldn't approve of our relationship. Even if he didn't fire me over it, he'd be unhappy."

"I don't care about his feelings."

"Yes, you do," I stated gently. "You adore your father."

"I adore you."

My breath caught.

"How do you know we're at different stages, Jackson? We're both healthy, happy with our jobs. I'm not a normal twenty-six-year-old. I don't enjoy clubbing or late nights. My dad has always said I had an old soul—I've never fit in with people my own age. I live a quiet life, and from all I've heard, so do you." She covered my hand with hers, pushing it into her skin. "I want to get to know you. Be your friend…and more. Is that such a bad thing?"

"You already are more."

"Then can't we…try?"

146

"I want to."

She placed her mug on the table and took mine from my hand, placing it beside hers. She slid onto my lap, wrapping her arms around her neck. "I want to as well. Please stop fighting this, Jackson."

Resting my hands on her hips, I studied her open expression. I slipped my fingers under the loose material of the shirt she was wearing, stroking the supple skin of her back. "I'm tired of fighting you, Laura. I want you, I want you with me. I just don't know how this will end. I don't want to hurt you even more than I have already."

"Then don't."

"You've already been hurt—your marriage…"

She shook her head. "Craig and I weren't right for each other. The divorce was a relief." She laughed ruefully. "He wanted a life of fun and glamour. He never wanted to grow up and be responsible. I thought he was what I needed to be less serious. I was serious enough for both of us."

"But?"

"I learned there was a difference between being serious and being responsible. His constant need to party and lack of ability to keep a job became very tiresome. I tried. I honestly did. I worked, he played. It just became too much, and when I told him to grow up, he told me to take a hike."

"He's an idiot. He should have taken better care of you."

"Hank would agree with you."

"I want to take care of you."

"I want to care for you as well." She hesitated. "What about you, Jackson? Dad mentioned you were divorced."

I nodded. "Much like you, I got married for the wrong reasons. We'd been dating a while, and all our friends were getting married. It seemed…the right thing to do."

"What happened?"

I shrugged. "We were too young. We changed, and what we wanted changed." I chuckled dryly. "Or what Wendy wanted changed. She hated everything I did. My job, my life—everything. She wanted a businessman—someone who carried a smart attaché case and drove a BMW. Not someone who wore a hard hat, dragged in dust at the end of the day, or drove a truck. We parted ways after a couple of years."

"I'm sorry."

"Don't be. She wasn't right for me."

"Since then?" she asked.

"I've dated—I'm certainly no monk. But I've never connected with anyone the way I connect with you. It's as if…" I trailed off.

"As if?" she prompted.

My mouth hovered over hers. "As if I've been waiting for you."

"Jackson," she breathed out.

As soon as my mouth touched hers, I was lost. Minutes passed as we shared the same breath, our lips melded together, tongues dancing and stroking, learning the taste and scope of each other. Slowly pulling away, I rested my forehead against hers.

"What do we do now?" I asked. "Tell me what you want, Laura. I'll give it to you—I'll give you anything."

She tossed her head defiantly. "We're both adults, what we do in private is our business—no one else's."

"Your father?"

"Just us for now—we'll deal with him when we're ready…when we know how it's going to end."

"How do you want it to end, sweet girl?"

Her eyes were fathomless. "With forever."

With a groan, I pulled her to my chest and covered her mouth with mine.

That was exactly what I wanted.

I shook my head, clearing my thoughts of memories, as I sat down. Hank bent over his desk, handing Laura something. "You left this in my truck."

Laura's hand closed around her cell phone. "Thanks, Dad—I wondered where I'd put it."

"I didn't see it until this morning. I hope you didn't miss anything important."

"I'll plug it in and see."

I wasn't sure if I imagined the glance Hank shot me, but I remembered my text, which Laura obviously hadn't seen. She had no idea I'd tried to contact her—but suddenly I wondered if he did.

"Couldn't break my password, Hank?" she teased, and I relaxed when he shook his head.

"I would have tried, but the damn thing was already dead. If you refuse a house phone, kiddo, you need to remember to keep it charged—and remember where it is."

She nodded, running her finger over the screen. "I usually do, I just forgot." Then she slipped her phone into her pocket. "What did you need Jackson and me for?"

"Harris has some more questions, but I think he's going with us. I want both of you to work closely with him. He's going to need a lot of hand-holding, I think. Put our best people on it, Jackson."

"All our people are the best, Hank," I countered.

He laughed. "The best of the best, then."

I gave a curt nod. "Will do."

He narrowed his eyes. "You have a problem with Harris?"

"Besides the fact that he's arrogant, a know-it-all, and I have a bad feeling about him? No, nothing."

I didn't add the fact that I didn't like the way he'd looked at Laura when he was here last time—as if she were the star in some twisted fantasy in his head. I didn't have the right to say that, I reminded myself.

"Work with him. He has a lot of projects on the go. We do a good job with this, it could be the start of some new business. Lots of it."

I nodded, hating the idea.

"Kiddo, I want you in on all the meetings. He liked your ideas last time. Develop a rapport with him."

"Sure, Hank."

I hated the idea even more now.

I stood. "Anything else?"

Her brow furrowed. "No. I expect both of you to be on top of this."

We both nodded and walked out of his office. "Jen," Laura called over to our new assistant. "Tell everyone ten minutes in the boardroom. I just have to get my notes and go over them." She turned away, and before I could stop myself, I grabbed her arm.

"Tell them fifteen minutes," I instructed Jen, leading a startled Laura to my office. "I need to go over this file with you before the meeting, Laura. It's *important*."

Ignoring Jen's surprised expression and Laura's glare, I pulled her into my office, shutting the door and flicking the lock. Seconds later, I had her pushed against the wall, trapping her between the hard surface and my chest.

"What are you doing?" she hissed.

"Talking to you."

She pushed on my chest. "It doesn't feel like talking. You're the one who said no touching in the office."

"Screw the rules. I'm tired of them," I growled, grasping her thighs and lifting her up, forcing her to wrap her legs around my hips—exactly the way I imagined them.

She gasped when she felt me hard and pressing into her softness. "*Jackson.*"

"You didn't get my message," I murmured into her ear, slowly thrusting my hips forward, making her quiver.

"You…you sent me a message?"

"Yes. I wanted to apologize. I came to your house—several times—but Hank was there. I asked you to call me."

"I didn't see it. We went for lunch, and I left my cell in the truck. I looked for it after he left. When I couldn't find it, I sent you an email saying I was sorry, but you didn't respond either."

I quirked my eyebrow at her. "I didn't check my computer."

"You need to embrace technology and add email to your phone, old man."

I grinned at her teasing, relieved to know she was no longer as angry with me. She knew I hated all that technology shit. She loved it.

"I like my private time, sweet girl." I pushed closer, stroking her upper thigh with my fingers. "I especially like my private time with you."

She whimpered, and I covered her mouth with mine. I kept the kisses light and indulgent, gentle sweeps of my lips against hers, tiny nips of my teeth to her bottom lip, and tender passes of my tongue over the plump flesh. Small, silent symbols of apology.

"I'm sorry, Laura. I hate arguing with you. I hate not being able to talk to you."

Her eyes glimmered.

"Don't cry. Please don't cry."

"I'm sorry too."

"We'll talk tonight? You'll come over?"

"I have a business dinner with Hank."

"Come after."

She smirked, arching back into me, making me groan at the contact. "It'll be late, Jackson, and we both know if I show up late, coming will be all that *will* happen—there'll be no talking. You'll be all sleepy and sexy. Your cock will be all smirky and winky… There won't be any talking— we'll end up making love instead."

"You think I'm sexy when I'm sleepy?"

"Definitely. You get all tousled, and your voice gets all growly. I love it."

I filed that piece of information away for later use. I grinned at her. "My cock…winks?"

"Smirks too—flirty little bugger does it constantly."

I lowered my mouth to her ear, tugging on her lobe. "Obviously, it's been too long since he winked at you. Otherwise you wouldn't be referring to him as 'little bugger,' Laura. I think you should *come*…over later tonight so I can remind you how *not* little he is."

She sighed, her hands caressing the back of my neck. "I love you," she whispered fervently, her hands pulling me close and my cock closer. "Maybe he'd like to wink at me now."

"Baby, we have to go. Jen will knock any minute."

"We have seven minutes."

I fingered the bow on her hip, desperate to feel her wrapped around me. "We shouldn't."

"I want you," she breathed.

"You'd have to be quiet," I warned, yanking on the bow and slipping my hands under the fabric, groaning. "No underwear, Laura?" I bit her earlobe. "Naughty, naughty girl."

She moaned low as my fingers found her slick center, stroking her hard.

"We have to be fast."

"Six minutes," she panted as my pants hit the floor with a quiet thud.

"I only need three," I moaned, burying myself deep inside her. "I'm going to make you come so fast."

"Two," she moaned. "I only need two."

She was right.

It was the best two fucking minutes of my life, my orgasm hot and fast, my groan lost in the sweetness of her mouth.

It left me four minutes to pull up my pants, help her retie her pretty bow, and then simply hold her. The tension had drained from her frame, her stiffness easing even more as I stroked her head—long passes of my fingers through her thick, wonderful hair as I whispered my adoration for her into her ear. She became fluid in my arms, and I felt myself calm and center holding her. She always did that for me.

"Forgiven?" I murmured into her hair.

"Yes." A yawn escaped her mouth, and she sighed.

"Good." I chuckled. "I can't believe we each tried to reach out and neither of us got the message. It would have saved some lost hours of sleep for both of us."

"What a pair," she agreed.

Regretfully, I tilted up her chin. "The best pair, Laura." I drew in a deep breath. "And it's time everyone knew exactly how great."

"Really?" she whispered.

"We'll figure it out. I'll talk to your dad later this week."

"We should talk to him together."

"United front?"

"Yes."

Affectionately, I ran my nose up her cheek. "Okay. He might not kill me if you're there to witness the act."

Jen knocked on the door. "Everyone's in the boardroom!" she chirped.

I moved back, cupping Laura's face, her gaze once again calm and tender.

"Tomorrow," I promised.

"Tomorrow."

CHAPTER 5

JACKSON

Two hours later, her eyes were anything but calm or tender. They shot daggers at me as Hank yelled, his face almost purple in rage.

"You better have a good fucking explanation, Jackson. You just cost me a huge amount of business!"

I stood, slapping my hand on the desk. "He was out of line, Hank! I couldn't sit there and listen to that shit. He was hitting on your daughter!"

Hank turned to Laura. "Is this true?"

"I could have handled it. I *was* handling it until you went all caveman, Jackson!"

I gaped at her, reminding myself she hadn't heard the disgusting remarks he'd muttered when she left the room to grab a report from her desk. He'd actually winked in my direction as he had the gall to ask me if anyone in the office was "tapping that hot ass." Then he went on to mutter some of the depraved things he'd do to her ass.

I'd had him pinned against the wall, my arm pressing on his throat, when Laura walked back in, Hank following her.

Chaos ensued; Vince Harris insisted I had attacked him unprovoked. He threatened not only to pull his business, but also screamed about legal action and insisted I be fired.

I shook my head at her. "You didn't hear what he said when you left. You *couldn't* handle that shit. Trust me."

Laura's eyes widened and her face blanched.

153

I met Hank's gaze. "I couldn't allow him to disrespect her, or you, like that." I straightened my shoulders. "Fire me if you want."

He ran a hand over his face and stood. "I'm not going to fire you. You said you had a bad feeling about him. I had just hoped he'd be a pain about budgets. Not hit on my daughter. I don't want his business."

"You want me to call him?"

"No, I'll take care of it." To my surprise, he reached out his hand. "Thanks for looking out for her."

I shook his hand. "You're welcome."

Hank left the room, and I sighed. "I suppose you're mad at me again?"

"What did he say?"

Quietly, I told her. "I couldn't sit here and listen to that, Laura. Even if you weren't...*mine*, I couldn't. But the fact that you *are*...I couldn't risk him ever trying anything. I couldn't bear it if anything happened to you because I held back and played it safe for the sake of some business."

Her hand slipped into mine. "I've never seen you like that."

"I'll do whatever I need to do to protect you."

She bit her lip and grinned a little. "That's rather hot, Jackson. No one has ever wanted to protect me, apart from my father. I hope you don't go to jail for it. Your face is too pretty for that to happen."

I chuckled, grateful she wasn't angry. "Let me get this straight, Laura." I lowered my voice. "You think I'm sexy, growly, *and* pretty? And my cock is smirky?"

"And winky."

"Right. Winky, too."

She nodded. "That about sums it up."

"Wow, a man finds out a lot of things on a Monday he never knew before."

She stood up, dropping a quick kiss on my mouth. "Wait until you see what I show you later."

"I can hardly wait."

A few days later, I sat at my desk in the trailer, trying to concentrate on the file in front of me. It wasn't working. All I could think about was Laura. About us. Telling Hank. Wondering if the past few days would make what I had to tell him easier or harder. He had calmed Vince Harris down—no charges would be laid, but there would be no business happening between them either. When I told him what Harris had said, Hank paid him a visit, and after that, the matter was closed. An angry Hank was a scary Hank—I knew this from experience. I also knew Hank was discreetly making some calls to other companies, warning them about Harris.

The door opened, the loud noise of the site flooding the trailer, and Hank stepped in. I accepted the cup of coffee he offered me.

"Hey," I muttered. "I wasn't expecting you."

"Laura needed one of the new guys to sign some papers."

"So, you brought them down?"

"Nah, she came with me. She'll be here in a moment. She said something about needing a conversation outside the office and wanting you involved." He sat down heavily, taking a deep swallow of his coffee. He looked out the window with a sigh. "I think she's fixing to leave, Jackson."

I shook my head. "No, she isn't."

"If she does, it's your damn fault!" He slammed his hand on the hard wood in front of him. "Why can't the two of you get on?"

"Hank—"

He interrupted me. "She's my daughter, Jackson! You're my right-hand and my goddamn friend! Why can't you get along? You came to her defense the other day, so you must like her a little."

I took in a deep breath. "*Are* we friends, Hank?"

"What kind of fucking question is that? Of course we are. I'm as close to you as anyone—you know that."

"Why?"

"Why what?"

Resting my arms on my thighs, I studied Hank's irate face, an idea forming. "Why are we friends?"

"Again, I ask… What kind of question is that? What are you on about this morning?"

"A fair one. Aside from the fact that you're my boss, you're fourteen years older than I am. What could we possibly have in common?"

He looked at me as if I were crazy. "What the fuck does age have to do with friendship? We have lots in common, we enjoy the same things, we get on well… I don't care if you're four years or fourteen years younger than I am."

"What about other relationships?" I asked quietly.

"What do you mean?"

"Does age have to play a role in any relationship as long as it's a good one for both parties? Despite what other people may think?"

He frowned and had just begun to speak when all hell broke loose outside. Shouting, yelling, and the sound of some catastrophe happening, had me leaping to my feet and racing to the door, flinging it open.

My eyes flew open in horror at what I saw, my blood freezing in my veins into icy shards of glass that pricked and stabbed at my flesh.

The large crane that was lifting equipment had clearly malfunctioned, the load now swinging freely, pieces of building supplies flying like debris in a windstorm. The crew was scrambling, yelling and trying to clear the area.

And knocked off her feet, frozen, in the middle of the chaos, her hard hat lying on the ground beside her, was Laura.

Behind me, Hank cursed and yelled for Laura to move. The only words in my head, though, echoing time and again: *not her—dear God, not her.*

There was no thought. In seconds, I was off the steps, moving faster than I thought I was capable of, screaming her name.

"Laura! Baby—get back! Move, Laura—move!"

I reached her before she had even turned her head, scooping her up in my arms and propelling her back into the safety of the overhang. The force of my lunge knocked us both back to the ground. I rolled so I landed on my back, Laura on top of me. My breath left my chest with a large oomph, my embrace like a steel cage around her. Gasping for air, I stared at her. "Baby—are you okay?"

Before she could answer, I saw it. A piece of broken scaffolding flying through the air, aiming directly toward us. With a loud curse, I rolled again, ignoring her grunt of discomfort as my body covered hers.

Heavy pain lanced across my foot, causing me to shout in distress. My eyes met Laura's fearful ones. Her gaze widened and her mouth opened in warning, my name a terrified gasp on her lips. *"Jackson!"*

There was more pain—searing agony that buried into the back of my head, exploding with a fiery, burning eruption.

Then the world went black.

There were voices, distant and muted. I tried to open my eyes, but the pain was too much. I attempted to turn my head to the sounds, but it was as if I were locked down, unable to move.

The voices droned on…

"Too early to tell… He needs time… Swelling…"

A different voice, angry and low. "You could have been killed… Why didn't you tell me…"

A tender voice, one I knew, whispered, "Come back to me, Jackson—please. I need you. I love you."

My own voice pleading, "*Laura.*"

The darkness claimed me again.

~

The world was clearer the next time I came to—the pain barely having changed. I forced my eyes open, blinking in the dim light. The room around me was stark, machines beeping a low, steady rhythm. My eyes moved and fell on the figure beside me, meeting the stoic gaze of Hank. His expression was serious, his stare inscrutable.

Panic fluttered as memories seeped into my addled brain. Despite the pain, I struggled to lift my head, rasping out the only word that mattered.

"Laura?"

He stood, looming over me, pushing me back into the pillow. "She's fine."

"Where?" I groaned, needing to know how close she was. I wanted to see her, make sure she was okay.

"She's sleeping."

"Please," I begged, fighting the darkness. "I need… I love…"

And I was gone again.

~

The next time I woke up, I wasn't alone in bed. Curled beside me was my girl, her hand clutching my gown, head on my chest. One arm was wrapped in tensor bandages, and I could see bruises forming on her pale skin. My arm was around her, holding her close. The pain in my head was less but still there. Grimacing, I nuzzled the top of her head.

"Laura," I whispered. "Sweet girl."

"She refused to leave again."

I looked up at Hank, who was watching us with narrowed eyes.

"She's stubborn."

A small smirk appeared on his lips. "Like her mother."

"Like her father as well."

157

I cleared my throat and gratefully accepted the water Hank offered me, taking several sips before handing him the glass.

He leaned back in his chair. "She may be thinking by staying there, she's protecting you."

"Do I need protection, Hank?"

"You have something you want to tell me, Jackson?"

"I'm in love with your daughter."

"And?"

"She loves me."

"How long?"

I hesitated, wondering how much to say.

"How long, Jackson?"

"I've been in love with her since the first day she arrived."

"You've lied to me all this time?"

"I tried to fight it, Hank. *We* tried. I stayed away from her as long as I was able to—I even tried to make her hate me. But…we love each other."

"Yet you hid it."

"We were worried about your reaction. You yourself told me no one was good enough for her—that she was off-limits to everyone. Remember? I tried to respect that, I tried to fight it." I brushed my hair off my forehead in an impatient gesture, ignoring the pain that simple action caused. "I didn't know what else to do. She's everything to me, Hank. She completes me. It's as if I've been waiting all my life to find her.

"We had decided to tell you—" I indicated my supine form "—then this happened."

He didn't say anything for a minute, and I used the time to look down at Laura. Her long eyelashes rested on her cheek as she slumbered, a slight frown on her full lips. I traced her mouth with my finger, smiling when her lips formed into a pout and she kissed the tip. I sighed heavily, trying to find more strength to keep talking. I was exhausted.

I looked up to see Hank watching us. "I know I'm not what you had in mind for her. I'm not rich. I can't provide her with all the luxuries she deserves. And I'm older than she is."

"I don't care if you're rich—it's how you treat her that's important. But you are older. A lot older," he grumbled.

"You said it yourself the other day. Age has nothing to do with how well a relationship works. Or does that only apply when you choose to allow it?" I challenged him.

He glared at me for a moment.

"You've said yourself she's an old soul. She's perfect for me. We mesh so well.

"I'll do anything I need to do in order to make her happy…in order to keep her." I sucked in a deep breath. "Including leaving the company, if that's what you want."

"You'd do that?"

"Yes."

"You saved her life. You risked your own life to save hers."

"I'd do it again—a hundred times over."

A glimmer of a smile appeared on his face. "I can't go through that a hundred times."

"Maybe we need to ban her from the work sites, then."

"I'll let you tell her," he chuckled.

"Do I still have a job?"

He scrubbed his face. "Jackson, when I tell you to give everyone the day off for doing a good job, do I include you in that statement?"

"Not usually."

"When I tell you to kick everyone's ass because we're behind schedule, are you part of that ass-kicking?"

"No."

"When I said off-limits to everyone…I wasn't necessarily including you either."

"You weren't?"

He shook his head. "I have a confession to make. I can't tell you how often I thought the two of you would make a great team. How many times I wished she'd find someone just like you to be part of her life. Someone strong and caring."

"That's not what you said," I pointed out.

"I know. I thought the age difference was too much and you working in the same company wasn't a good idea. I hated the thought that if things didn't work, I'd have to choose between you."

"No," I said quietly. "If that happened, I would leave. I wouldn't make you choose. But it's not going to happen, Hank. She's it for me. I've been waiting so long for her that I'd almost given up."

"Guess all the hiding has been hard on you, eh?"

"You have no idea. You could have said something. Given me a clue."

He grinned, lifting one shoulder. "I didn't want to make it too easy for you. Challenge is good for a man."

"You're an ass."

"At first, I thought you honestly didn't like each other, so I didn't bother trying to push it. But seeing how well you worked together gave me hope. Lately, though…"

"We weren't fooling you anymore?"

He chuckled. "No. The two of you were far too in tune with each other. If Laura was upset, I knew you would be too. On the days she was glowing, I knew you'd be flying high as well." He held up his hand. "And I don't want to know why."

I grinned. I had no plans on telling him either.

"The bottom line was, I saw how you were with each other, and I hoped it was because there was something there. And after the Harris incident, I was sure of it. I've never seen you rage the way you did that day. I knew then she was in good hands—you'd look after her."

"So…we're okay?"

He ran his fingers over his moustache, staring at me. I tightened my fingers on Laura's arm, pulling her closer to me. Hank leaned forward.

"No more lies. You show the world how proud you are to be with my daughter. You protect her and love her the way she deserves."

"I want to."

"Then do it."

"I will."

He stood up, placing his hand on top of mine that was holding his daughter. "I'm glad she has you."

I smiled at him. "Thanks, Hank."

"And I want grandkids—soon." He grinned. "Neither of us is getting any younger."

I blinked, then snickered. "I'll be sure to discuss that with your daughter."

"Okay. Enough of this emo shit. I'm going to go get coffee. I'll tell them you're awake." He paused at the doorway. "And, Jackson?"

"Yeah?"

"You hurt her, I have enough sites and concrete—they'll never find your body."

"I'm aware."

"Good. Keep that in mind." He chuckled darkly, pulling open the door and walking out.

Reaching for the glass, I took another sip, hoping when the doctor arrived, he'd give me something for the pain. I smirked down at Laura.

"I know you're awake, sweet girl. You're a pretty bad actress. No wonder he didn't buy it."

"He does, you know," Laura mumbled into my chest. "He has access to a lot of concrete."

"I'll remember that." I kissed the top of her head. "How much did you hear?"

She tilted up her head. "Enough."

I gazed down at her. "You scared the fuck out of me."

She blinked, her eyes filling with tears. "It happened so fast. I knew I had to move, but my feet wouldn't go, and then...you were there."

"I had to get to you."

"And you got hurt."

"My head can take it. Some Tylenol would be good, though. "

"Jackson," she admonished, half sitting up. "You have a concussion, stitches, your foot is broken, you have contusions all over your shoulders and back—it's way more serious than a headache!"

I glanced down, realizing for the first time my leg had an air cast on it. I already knew my head had stitches, and I could feel every ache in my back.

"How long was I out?"

"Most of the day. You're going to have to be off work for a while."

"Huh. Well, I guess it's a good thing I have you to look after me."

"I will."

"Then I'll be fine."

"I was terrified. The piece of equipment hit you, and you were knocked out. People were yelling, and Hank was there. The ambulance came." She shook her head. "I was crying, and I refused to leave you. I kept trying to tell my dad why, but he grabbed my face and stared at me, saying he knew, and he understood. He told me to calm down and go with you so I could be looked at. He followed the ambulance, and he's been here with me with us—until now."

"Sweet girl..." I breathed out.

"He's been so strong, Jackson," she continued. "I told him how much I love you, how you look after me, and he's been great once he stopped being annoyed. He was worried sick about you as well."

"I'm fine."

She sniffed. "We're both fine."

"When can I get out of here?"

"You just woke up, Jackson. I'd say not for a couple days."

"Ugh. I want to go home. I'd rest better there. Especially with you to look after me—at least, once your arm heals."

"It's just a sprain. It got pinned when you rolled us."

"I'm sorry."

"You saved me. You have nothing to be sorry for."

I frowned at her. "You shouldn't have been on-site. You should have come to the trailer, and I would have had the crew member come to you."

"I will next time."

I snorted. "There won't be a next time. You're banned from all work sites in the future. Permanently banned."

She got that stubborn look on her face I knew only too well.

"No arguing. Your father agrees."

"Great. Now, I have the two of you ordering me around."

"Get used to it."

Her eyes began to dance. "What if I wanted to drop by for…another reason, Jackson?"

"Another reason?"

"Like the other day?"

I shifted slightly under the covers and chuckled. "I might bend the rules for that."

"Yeah?"

"You'd have to come directly to the trailer. No wandering about."

She slipped her hand under the covers, slowly trailing her fingers down and cupping me. "No wandering at all?"

I groaned. "Laura, a nurse or doctor could walk in any minute—never mind. God forbid, your father sees what you're doing. I'm not sure he will ever be ready for that. If you keep doing that, there is going to be smirking and winking…"

"I like smirking and winking," she whispered.

"I promise to show you lots of it when we get home and my head isn't about to explode."

She withdrew her hand right away. "Sorry."

"Don't ever be sorry. I love it when you touch me, but I think we need to wait until we get home."

"Home?"

"My house, Laura. It becomes home when you're there. And I'd like it to be home all the time—for both of us."

"Jackson…"

"We've wasted enough time. I want you with me. I want to make a home and a life with you."

"I want that too."

"Marry me. Move in with me. Have babies with me."

"In that order?"

"In whatever order you want. Just do all of them with me. Please."

Her smile was as bright as the midday sun. "Yes."

I kissed her and eased back onto the pillows. "I want to celebrate, but I think the only thing I can manage is some painkillers and a nap."

She sighed. "Life with an old man. Guess I'd better get used to it."

I chuckled. "I'll make it up to you."

She slipped out of my embrace. "I'll go get the doctor."

She paused at the door. "Jackson?" she called in a low lilt.

"Hmm?"

"Whenever you're ready, I'm happy to work on those grandkids."

"Kids, as in more than one, Laura?"

"Definitely."

"I look forward to the smirking and winking. Lots of it."

Her voice was tender. "I love you."

That was all I needed. She was all I needed.

"I love you too."

CHAPTER 6

JACKSON

Laura plumped my pillows, then helped me settle back on them. She moved to the end of the bed, lifting my leg and sliding two more cushions under it, settling the removable cast in place.

"How's that? Do you need another pillow?"

I smiled at her fretting. She'd been fussing over me ever since I came home, barely leaving my side. Reaching for her hand, I grabbed it, bringing the smooth palm to my mouth. "I'm fine, sweet girl. Relax, please."

"Do you need any pain meds?"

"No. I think I need a nap." I rolled my eyes. "Having a shower has never been such an exhausting endeavor before now."

I finally felt clean. Laura had removed the air cast for a few moments, and thanks to the fact that I had a walk-in shower, I was able to sit on the bench and let the hot water pour over me, washing away the last of the hospital smell. I was dressed in clean clothes and tired, and the bed felt great.

Laura handed me a couple pills and a glass of water. "Take these and sleep for a while."

"All I do is sleep," I grumbled.

"Jackson," she began, resting her hand on her hip and looking at me with exasperation. "You were badly injured. Your body needs time and lots of rest. And that, mister, is exactly what you're going to get."

I smirked at her. "I love it when you're all bossy. Such a sexy little nurse you are." I held out my arms. "Come here."

She eyed me suspiciously, making me laugh.

"I was a good patient and took my meds. I'll rest, but I want to hold you."

Gingerly, she slipped in beside me, letting me pull her into my arms. I tugged her head to my chest and sighed in satisfaction at her closeness. "That's what I needed."

"I don't want to hurt you."

"Baby, lying on my chest and snuggling beside me is *not* hurting me. It's helping. I like you close. I feel better."

"Oh, okay," she murmured.

I kissed the top of her head, inhaling her warm scent. She had been running herself ragged the past few days, and I knew she had to be tired. "Sleep with me, sweet girl. Just for a little while."

I could already feel her body growing heavy. I lifted my hand, caressing her hair, letting the silky strands slip between my fingers.

"I need to figure out dinner, though."

"Chinese," I stated. "I feel like some spicy beef and noodles. All that takes is a phone call and some chopsticks."

"Hmm," she mumbled drowsily. "Sounds good."

"Sleep, baby."

She was out in seconds. I knew she was worn out, and although her arm seemed better, I hated causing her extra work. But she was determined to look after me. There were instances I felt her looking at me, and I knew she was reliving those terrifying moments, thinking of the "what-ifs." I did as well, but having her close helped. I hoped it did the same for her. I was fine and would recover. We both would, and we could move forward. Together.

With a long exhale of air, I fell asleep holding her.

"God, these are good."

I smirked at the vision in front of me. Laura, at the end of the bed, dressed in one of my old shirts and a pair of my socks, with her hair piled up, looking adorable. She was eating her noodles, or at least trying, doing a terrible job as usual with her chopsticks. Most of the time, she gave up and grabbed a fork, but she always tried.

"It works even better if you get them in your mouth," I observed as another noodle landed on my shirt. "You're gonna need a lot of bleach to get that shirt clean."

She looked down, giggling, then back at me, her gaze filled with amusement. I grinned back at her, pleased to see the nap we'd had earlier erased some of the weariness from her face.

"Of course," I drawled, bending my arm behind my head and leaning back as I looked at her, "You could lose the shirt."

"The noodles would land on my skin."

"I'd lick them off."

"*Jackson.*"

"*Laura.*"

"The doctor said—"

I interrupted her. "The doctor said when I felt I was ready. I've been home for two days. The accident was over a week ago. I *am* ready."

"Your head…"

"I'm not talking hanging from the chandelier." I dropped my voice, knowing how much she loved it when I did that, and let my gaze drift over her leisurely. "Just us—together. I miss you, baby."

She swallowed, and her cheeks darkened.

"Soon," she promised.

I growled low in my throat. "Damn soon." I waggled my eyebrows at her. "Maybe my sexy nurse needs to come give me a sponge bath. I'd be most appreciative. I know someone who would throw you a wink…or two."

"Jackson," she warned, trying to sound stern. It really didn't work considering how breathless she sounded.

She swung her legs off the bed, the action causing the shirt to ride up on her thighs. I almost began panting, remembering how they felt wrapped around me. How it felt when I was buried inside her.

"Where are you going?"

"I'm going to eat my moo goo gai pan in peace."

I patted my knee. "Why don't you come over here and I'll happily eat *your* moo goo gai pan?"

She blinked, then burst out laughing. She came forward and kissed my cheek. "Nice try, Jackson."

I heard her laughing all the way to the kitchen.

I crossed my arms and huffed in resignation. I guessed no sex today either.

"It wasn't that funny!" I yelled.

"Yes, it was," came drifting down the hall.

"Gin," Hank said smugly, laying his cards on the table.

I flung down my cards in disgust. "You are seriously pissing me off," I returned with a grunt.

He grinned, taking a long swallow of his beer. "You've been like a bear with a thorn in his paw since I got here. What the hell is eating you?"

I couldn't tell him the truth. His head would explode if I told him I desperately needed to fuck his daughter until she screamed my name and her tight pussy milked my cock.

Instead, I ignored him.

"Where's Laura again? When is she coming home?"

He sighed and sat back. "She's doing a couple things for me, and she had some errands. I came to sit with you and keep you company. "

I huffed. "You came because she told you that you had to. I don't need to be babysat."

"You need something to soothe that grumpy ass of yours. I brought pizza. I thought you'd enjoy it."

I laughed. "You brought pizza because *you* would enjoy it. The same with the beer." I knew I was pouting. "I can't even have one." Then just to tick him off, I added, "She is gonna be so pissed when she finds out you're eating pizza and drinking beer at lunch."

"I'm not gonna tell her—and neither are you."

I burst out laughing. "This is Laura we're talking about. 'The General' ring a bell? She'll know what you brought the second she walks in the door. And what's even worse is she'll know you hid it in your truck until she left so she wouldn't find out."

"Damn it." He stood, grabbing the box. "I'll get rid of the evidence. The key word here is deny, Jackson. Deny, deny, deny."

I smirked. "She has a nose like a bloodhound."

"Fuck!" Panicked, he glanced around the room. "Light some of those smelly candles! She'll never figure it out."

"Like she won't wonder why the two of us are sitting here, enjoying the candlelight, Hank?"

He sat down, dropping his head into his hands. "We are so fucked."

"*We?* I think you mean *you*. You are so fucked. I didn't do anything."

"You ate some!"

"Did I?"

"You know you did!"

I looked around. "There's no evidence." I looked down at my shirt. "No crumbs." I sniffed my hands. "No pizza smell." I smacked my lips. "My breath is minty fresh."

"You fucker. That's why you cleaned up *after* we ate."

I grinned at him. This was the most fun I'd had since I got home.

"I might be persuaded to help."

"Name your price."

"Get your daughter to move in right away."

"She's already here."

"Only because I'm laid up. I can't pin her down to stay."

"What's in it for me?"

"Besides the lack of a lecture that will last longer than it took you to scarf down that pizza?"

"Yeah, besides that."

"I plan on marrying her and then working on those grandbabies for you. She'll be so busy with them, you'll be free to eat pizza anytime you want."

I lied like a rug, but it worked.

"Deal."

"Okay. Grab the Febreze and crack a window. I'll light a candle. Put all that shit in your truck."

"Done."

~

Laura got home an hour later, walking in carrying groceries. She glared at me as she came toward the couch. "You should be resting."

"I am."

"I mean lying down. Have you had your meds?"

"I did. But I wasn't tired. Hank and I have been playing cards."

"Did you have lunch? I left some sandwiches."

Luckily, Hank had noticed those. They were in his truck, along with the evidence of the lunch he had brought with him.

I nodded. "They were great, thanks."

She sniffed the air delicately. "Why do I smell Febreze?" She narrowed her eyes slightly. "And why do you have a candle burning?"

Hank stiffened, and I frowned at her. "I'll explain later."

Her toes began to tap. "Explain now."

I crooked my finger, and she hunched down. "Hank's a little, ah, gassy. He made his famous chili last night. I sprayed the couch and lit the candle. It was really bad, baby. Don't say anything—he was pretty embarrassed."

I knew Hank could hear me, but the bastard couldn't say a word.

Laura looked at me, and I nodded, keeping my face impassive.

She straightened. "I'm going to make coffee."

Hank glared at me. "You're fired."

"Okay. I'll call her back and tell her the truth." Then I laid down my cards. "Gin."

"You are going to pay for all this, Jackson. Somehow, someday, I will get you."

I smiled at him. "Game on, my favorite father-in-law-to-be."

CHAPTER 7

JACKSON

I woke up from my nap, yawning and stretching. After Hank left, Laura insisted I lie down. It really didn't take much to convince me—I was rather tired, so I agreed easily. She had helped me to bed, then puttered around, chatting as I fell asleep. I was hoping when I woke up, she'd be beside me, but I woke up alone.

I glanced around the room, confused. All the lights were out, except one burning in the corner, the dim bulb throwing more shadows around the room. In the middle of my night table sat a bell. Frowning, I reached for it, wondering where the hell it had come from. I certainly didn't own any bells. Did Laura buy it? Had I been calling her so much that she bought it so I would stop shouting for her? I felt bad if I had. Did she actually want me to ring it?

I hesitated, then gave it a shake. After a couple of seconds, I heard Laura coming down the hall. I opened my mouth to tease her, but the words died in my throat as she walked in. She was dressed in the shortest, tightest nurse uniform known to man. White garters and silk stockings encased her legs. Her hair was pinned up, and nestled on top was a starched replica of a nurse's cap. Ruby red stained her plump lips, and her eyes glinted with mischief.

She was the very epitome of the world's sexiest nurse.

She wet her lips with her pink tongue. "You rang, Mr. Cooper," she breathed, her voice raspy. "You need something?"

In an instant, I was hard, the sheet covering me tenting as I stared at her, speechless. My blood ran faster, my breathing picked up as desire grabbed me, snaking down my spine with lust.

"I...I..."

She came forward, bending over me, her cleavage spilling from her tight top. "Can I help you with something?"

"I feel a little warm."

She inched nearer, but still too far away for me to touch. "You do look...*hot*."

"Laura," I moaned. "Baby, don't tease."

She smiled, her finger drifting up my chest. "I need to examine you, Mr. Cooper. Find the source of your, ah, fever."

"Yes," I panted. "Examine me thoroughly."

"I need to remove your shirt."

I had it tugged over my head in a flash.

"Hmmm," she murmured, tapping her chin. "Patient is short of breath and feeling warm."

"Hot. I'm feeling *hot*. And needy."

She laid her hand on my stomach, her finger running over my skin, my muscles contracting under her touch. "I need to check your vitals."

I swallowed. "Yes."

Her lips hovered over mine. "I have to make sure you're okay. It is my job."

"You do it well," I whispered and grabbed the back of her neck, pulling her down to me. Her lips pressed on mine, and she slipped her tongue into my mouth, teasing me. She slid her hand down, fondling my chest, playing with my nipples as we kissed. Our tongues brushed together, touched and savored. I groaned at her taste, having missed it so much. I fumbled with the hair clip, pushed the hat out of the way, and wrapped her hair around my fist, keeping her close. I tugged her down to my chest, smoothing my hand up the back of her small skirt, caressing the skin on her back.

"You need to lose your skirt, Nurse."

"You need to let me do my job." She pulled back, frowning at me. "I'm not finished my examination."

I couldn't conceal my smirk. Her lips were swollen, her hair falling down around her shoulders, and the cute hat askew on her head. Her nipples pressed against the white of her shirt, hard and pebbled. I waved my hand. "Continue."

171

She tugged off my sweatpants, looking up with a mischievous grin when she saw I was commando. It took her a minute to pull the pant leg over the cast, but then I was free, and my sweats were tossed over her shoulder somewhere.

"Spread your legs, Jackson. I need you comfortable."

With a low moan, I followed her command. Knowing her eyes were on me, I stretched, feeling her gaze travel over my body, lingering on my erection. I arched my back a little, watching her gaze widen. Slowly, I reached down, cupping my balls and stroking my hand over my leaking cock. She scrutinized every movement.

"I think someone is winking at you."

"Smirking too," she breathed.

"He's smirking, all right—he's ready for you, Nurse."

"I'll be the judge of that, Mr. Cooper."

Reaching behind her head, she pulled off her skimpy uniform, leaving her in the tiniest scrap of lace and her sexy garter and stockings.

"I think my fever is getting worse." I shifted, needing to be closer to her.

She crawled up the bed, like a lioness coming for her prey. I was a willing victim.

The next ten minutes were pure torture of the best kind. She used her mouth and hands, trailing them over my torso and legs. She teased and nipped, her tongue swirling on my skin, her teeth pulling my nipples, her lips sucking at the base of my throat, leaving her mark.

"You do seem hot, Jackson," she whispered as she licked up my neck, placing wet kisses as she went.

"I'm fucking hot for you," I hissed, grabbing her face and kissing her hard.

We were both panting when she pulled back.

"I need to check your temperature."

"Stop teasing," I begged. "God, baby, I *need* you."

She quirked her eyebrow, then shifted back, sitting beside my good leg. She stroked her hand up my thigh, her fingers gentle and seeking. Over and over again, she stroked, each time going higher, making my hands fist the bedding.

Her hot breath drifted over me. "He just winked at me."

"I bet he did," I groaned. "I bet his smirk got bigger too."

"It's about to."

Keeping our eyes locked, she lowered her head, taking my cock in her mouth. I flung my head back, shouting out a curse as her lips wrapped around my rock-solid erection. I was lost to the sensation of her talented, wicked mouth. Pleasure exploded, surging through my entire body. Laura worked me, using her tongue, her hands, and even her teeth. Warmth and wetness, intense pressure, then light teasing—the way she varied her caresses brought me to the brink of my orgasm, only for her to pull back and start again.

Finally, I couldn't take it anymore.

"Laura, baby, please."

She smirked, then tugged on the tiny bows at her hips, leave her bare. She flung her leg over my hips, bending low, being careful not to jostle my leg. She planted a wet kiss in the middle of my abdomen, then sat back, sinking down on my cock. Her wet heat engulfed me inch by inch until we were pressed flush together.

"Jesus."

She arched back, her beautiful breasts jutting out. She gripped one thigh, while her other hand tugged on her hair as she began to ride me. I began thrusting up as much as I could, and she pressed down, meeting my lunges, her hips rolling smoothly. I held her hips, guiding her. "Laura... *baby...so good...so fucking good."*

She sped up, leaning forward, and her hair brushed my skin. New waves of pleasure rippled through me at the different angle, and my balls began to tighten. Laura grasped my arms with her fingers, her body trembling. "Jackson...oh God..."

"Let go, baby. Let me see you come."

She threw back her head, a low cry escaping her lips. I followed right behind her, my orgasm powerful as her pussy muscles contracted around me, milking my cock as I filled her.

She stilled, shuddering, and I tugged her down to my chest, pushing the damp hair away from her head and brushing my lips across her skin.

"You are one thorough nurse."

She giggled. "I care about my patients."

I growled low in my throat. "I had better be your only patient."

She looked up at me, smiling. "My one and only."

I turned serious. "Stay, sweet girl. Come live with me now. I need you. Every day."

She cupped my cheek, stroking my skin. "I arranged the movers today, Jackson."

"You did?"

"I almost lost you. Do you honestly think I'm going to leave you alone?"

"You've avoided discussing it. I thought maybe you changed your mind."

"No. I wanted to make sure you hadn't."

"Never. I want you here. And I want to marry you. It's a big house. I want to fill it with our babies and lots of laughter."

"I want that too."

"When are the movers coming?"

"I'm going to pack up over the next few days. They'll move me in next week."

"Perfect."

She moved off me, propping herself up on her elbow. She studied me briefly. "So…today. Did Hank bring a large or an extra-large pizza?"

"Damn it, Laura. How do you know this shit?"

She grinned. "He is pretty lousy at hiding the evidence. Now, spill."

I sighed. "Large."

"I suppose it was the meat extravaganza."

"It had olives too."

She snorted. "Well then, I suppose it's fine."

I chuckled. "He said he did it for me."

"I'm sure he did."

I pulled her tight to my side. "Is this how it's going to be, sweet girl? No secrets, no sneaking pizza and beer with your dad—you'll know all and see all? I can't hide anything from you once you move in?"

"Yep."

I pressed a kiss to her head, smiling.

"I'm good with that. I love you, baby."

She snuggled closer. "I love you, Jackson."

CHAPTER 8

JACKSON

I stormed into the trailer, throwing my hard hat against the wall as hard as I could. I hoped it left a fucking mark.

Flinging myself into my chair, I leaned back, gripping my hair.

"I need a fucking Advil and a bottle of Jack Daniel's," I muttered.

"How about a nice dinner with me instead?"

My head snapped up. Laura was at the desk in the corner, a large basket perched on top. Just seeing her made me smile.

"Well, this is a nice surprise." Then I frowned. "I didn't see your truck."

"It's out back."

"Did you—" My voice trailed off when she held up her hard hat.

"I learned my lesson." Her face darkened. "Because of me, you got hurt."

I held out my hand, my frustration forgotten. "Come here, sweet girl."

She stood and walked toward me, her footsteps loud. I bent over the arm of my chair and whistled. "When did you get those?"

"Right after your accident. I haven't been to a site since, so you haven't seen them."

I grabbed her hand, pulling her down. "Sexy," I breathed against her mouth, kissing her. "I like you in steel-toe boots."

"I look like an idiot."

I ran my hand up her thigh, cupping her rounded ass. "You look totally sexy in a skirt and boots, baby."

She giggled, the sound making the corner of my lips twitch. I loved hearing her laugh.

"An added benefit." She smiled, but it didn't reach her eyes.

"Hey."

Her eyebrows rose in question, but she didn't say anything. I stroked along her soft cheek, down her jawline, and cupped her chin.

"It was an accident. Thanks to your care and patience, I've recovered. I'm fine."

"An accident I caused."

I hated that it still bothered her. "No. You didn't break the machine. It was an equipment malfunction." I sighed. "No matter what, I would have reacted the same way, Laura. I will protect you at all costs—that's my job. Always. So, no more blame, okay?"

Biting her lip, she nodded.

"Now, what is in that basket?"

"I got your text earlier saying you had to stay late, so I brought you dinner."

I groaned as I remembered why I was working late. "Do you have any alcohol in there?"

"Is Sven at it again?"

"He's decided he wants two walls moved." I snorted and added a thick Swedish accent. *"It's only two valls, Yackson. Two valls. Vy so hard to do?"*

I leaned my head back, feeling weary. "Two load-bearing walls. Walls which are already up. Then he wants the kitchen moved. God help me. It never ends. The design changes weekly now. This is why I hate taking on private homes. Give me massive office buildings anytime."

Laura hummed. "I have a meeting with him tomorrow to tell him how much it will cost with another redesign and structure issues."

"A lot." I sat up straight. "I'll go through the numbers and have it for you in the morning."

She walked around the back of my chair, her hands resting on my shoulders. "First, you need to eat and relax."

"I'm not sure I can do either."

"Yes, you can. I'll make sure of that—that's my job now."

"Is that so?"

She gently pushed my shoulders forward, her hands working on the tense muscles. I moaned in pleasure. Laura's hands were as talented as her mouth. How she worked those tiny fingers into my sore flesh, releasing the painful tension, was beyond me. I loved it when she gave me a massage. I loved it when she touched me. Anywhere.

I hissed as she dug her fingers into my neck.

"Jackson, your neck is like cement." She tsked.

"It's been a shit day."

Bending, she wrapped her arms around my neck, pressing her lips to my ear, placing a slow, lingering kiss there. "Can I help you relax?"

"Don't tempt me, baby."

She flicked open my shirt buttons and slipped her hands inside, her blunt nails pressing into my skin. "I had you pretty loose last week," she crooned.

I rested my head on her full chest, meeting her mischievous gaze.

"We should have stayed in Jamaica," I grouched.

"It was a lovely honeymoon."

I grinned up at her, pulling her face down to mine. Upside-down kissing had never been as good as it was with my wife.

We got married quietly at city hall with Hank and a few close friends around us. Laura insisted she didn't want a big wedding. *"I had the big wedding with the wrong guy the first time. I want it small with the perfect man this time," she stated firmly.*

She was beautiful, and the day *was* perfect because it was just *us*. Quiet, simple, and real. Then came a week away in a secluded bungalow with nothing but a warm, sandy beach, my sexy wife, and as few clothes as possible. We rarely left the cabin, having meals brought to us. We walked along the surf, swam in the ocean, danced under the stars, stayed up way too late, and slept in every morning. We made love in a huge net-covered bed, fucked hard on the wet, packed sand with the sunlight streaming down on us. We were together every moment, and the week went by too fast.

Laura's wandering hands brought me back to the present moment. She kissed me again, her tongue tracing my lips. "I bet I can make you stress-free again."

With a growl, I spun my chair and pulled her down to my lap. I grabbed her face, kissing her hard. I lost myself in the feel and the taste of my wife. Her lips were full and pliant underneath mine. She wound her hands into my hair, pulling me close. I held her hips, pressing her down onto my growing erection, then tugged up the back of her shirt, digging my fingers into her skin, stroking her spine, and groaning at how right she felt touching my chest.

"Did you lock the door?" She moaned against my mouth.

"I will."

"Shut the lights off, too."

For a second, I hesitated.

"The crew was packing up to leave, Jackson. I saw Larry and told him you and I were going to have dinner and go over numbers, and not to disturb us. He'll lock everything up." She grinned—a wide, wicked smile that made me grin back. "We'll have dessert first."

That was good enough for me. I would never let an opportunity go by to fuck my wife.

I lifted her off my lap, setting her on her feet. I captured her mouth, kissing her the way she liked it best. Hard. Wet. Possessive.

"I'll get the door and the lights. You lose the shirt." Then I winked. "Keep the skirt and boots on."

I sighed with contentment. Laura was curled against my chest, with the blanket she had brought to use with our dinner wrapped around us. I nuzzled her hair, feeling far more relaxed than I had when I'd slammed into the trailer earlier. Nothing calmed me more than being with my wife.

"Still need that Advil?"

Slipping my fingers under her chin, I lifted her face to mine, kissing her. "No." I grinned against her lips. "You're the best medicine."

She smiled up at me. "I wanted to make your day better."

"You did."

She bit her lip. "I have something else to make you smile."

"Oh yeah? You got some of your cookies in that basket?"

"I do have cookies, but I think you might like this better."

"Better than your cookies? This I gotta see." I held out my hand. "Gimme."

She handed me a strange-shaped parcel, wrapped in brown paper.

I arched my eyebrow at her. "Shopping at the adult toy store again, sweet girl? Should I be afraid of what's in here?"

She giggled, slapping my arm. "Open it," she insisted, her voice sounding strangely nervous.

I opened the paper and held up a toy tool belt and a tiny hard hat.

I frowned, looking into her watery gaze. "Very cute, but I'm not sure it's gonna fit. It's rather small…" As my voice trailed off, my eyes grew wide.

"Laura?" I asked, choking up. "Really?"

She reached over, pulled a white stick out of one of the pouches of the small tool belt and held it up. A bright-blue plus sign was in the small window. "Congratulations! You're going to be a daddy."

Sven, the bad day, and the entire world disappeared as I yanked her to my chest, dropping kisses all over her face. Joy I had never experienced before flowed through my body as I held my wife and our child within her.

"A baby. We're going to have a baby," I breathed. "Is it a boy? Is that why you bought me a tool belt?" I asked excitedly, laying my hand across her stomach and spreading my fingers wide. Soon, there would be a bump there. A baby bump. *My* baby bump. I grinned at her. "Is it?"

"I have no idea, Jackson. Right now, your baby is the size of a peanut. We won't find out the sex for weeks yet." She crossed her arms. "Are you saying only a boy should have a tool belt?"

I shook my head, grinning. "No. My daughter can wear whatever the hell she wants, tool belts included."

She cupped my cheek, stroking my skin. "Good answer."

I pressed my forehead to hers. "Are you okay? Everything…good?"

"I'm great. A little tired and I've been a bit nauseous in the morning. But I'm good. I saw the doctor today, and she said everything was fine." She slipped her hand into her pocket. "I brought you a picture."

I squinted at the image. "It *is* a peanut!" I exclaimed.

"It'll grow." She sighed. "So will I."

"You'll be even more beautiful. I can hardly wait to see you all rounded, carrying my child." I placed my hand on her stomach again. "Thank you, Laura. You just made my day, my week…my entire month."

Then I had a thought. "Does your dad know?"

"No. I thought we'd tell him together."

"I am so in for favorite son-in-law."

"Um, Jackson, you're the only son-in-law."

I waved my hand. "Doesn't matter. He wanted grandbabies, and now he's gonna have one! I'm *so* in."

She threw back her head, laughing. "Okay, whatever you say."

"I'll crunch numbers later. Let's go home. I want to hang up my peanut picture and spoil my baby momma."

She rested her head on my shoulder. "I'd like that."

I kissed her forehead. "Thank you, sweet girl. You made today amazing."

She snuggled closer. "You're welcome."

CHAPTER 9

JACKSON

Hank was on the phone when I walked into his office. I threw myself down on the chair in front of his desk, leaning my head against the cool leather and closing my eyes. Maybe his call would take a while and I could grab a nap. All too soon, I heard him hang up the phone, but he didn't say anything for a minute. Finally, he spoke.

"Jackson, you look exhausted."

"I am."

"Is Laura okay?"

"She's fine. More than fine." I grimaced. "She's...*full* of energy."

"Well, that's great news."

"Yep."

"You could be a little more enthusiastic."

I opened my eyes, leaning forward, resting my arms on my thighs. "I'm thrilled my wife is healthy. I am beyond relieved the first trimester is over and her morning sickness is done. The, ah, difference in her is—" I sighed "—*extreme.*"

A ghost of a smile made his lips twitch. He sat back in his chair, flipping his pen between his fingers. "I know we never talk personal shit, Jackson, your wife being my daughter and all, but Laura has always been very much like her mother. And I lived with her mother while she was pregnant with Laura. I know about the, ah, *extremes.*"

I dropped my head back on my chair. "Oh God. I could barely touch

181

her for weeks, and I thought I was going to explode… And now… *Jesus*… Now, it's like she can't get enough of me."

Hank held up his hand. "If you start to tell me any details, Jackson, I'm bound to unleash another wild crane full of scaffolding on you. No matter how sympathetic I am."

I shook my head wearily. "I have no desire to share any details with you, Hank—even if she weren't your daughter, that shit is private. But, man, I'm not sure I'm gonna survive this pregnancy."

Hank's shoulders shook with silent laughter.

I glared at him. "Glad I amuse you."

He shook his head. "Every man feels the same way. Your wife is suddenly amorous all the time, and you think you've hit the jackpot."

"I did. Until I realized she is never satisfied. I'm lying there exhausted and happy, and she wants to start all over again. I swear I'm too old for this shit."

He didn't hide his laughter this time, and I had to grin with him. He was right. When Laura's morning sickness had stopped and she suddenly was interested in sex again, it was like a dream come true. She was primed and ready for me when I got home and, again, later in the evening. It started all over again in the morning. Then the visits during the day to the trailer started, and I realized I couldn't escape her wandering hands and pleading eyes anywhere. And my damn cock had no problem rising to the occasion. It was the rest of my body that was objecting. I was exhausted.

The scariest part was, the further along in her pregnancy she was, the hornier she seemed to become. Last night, I had invented a late meeting so I could catch a nap in the trailer before I got home. But I knew I couldn't do that often. She was far too clever; even if she hadn't cut back at work, she would find out. Not only would her feelings be hurt, but she would also be furious. The thought of the passion she was experiencing turning to anger directed at me was a scary thought.

"All I can tell you is that it does level off." Then he smirked. "Once the baby comes, you'll be back in dry dock, so try to enjoy it."

I chuckled. "At least I'm safe here. Maybe I'll sneak in a nap later at my desk."

Hank's mouth opened to say something when we both heard it. Laura's voice out in the lobby.

"Did I see Jackson's truck, Jen?"

I stared at Hank in panic. I shook my head wildly. I'd already made love to her twice today. Surely, she wouldn't…

"I want to see him. Is he in his office?"

"No, he's with your dad," Jen replied.

"Oh God," I whimpered. I knew what was going to happen. She was going to come in here, all glowing and sweet, and tell Hank she needed to see me. Then she'd take me to her office and have her wicked way with me. She'd be energized and sated, and I would be a walking, shaking shell of a man.

Hank stood. "Hide."

"Where?"

He glanced around. "Get under my desk. Fast."

I was out of the chair and under his desk in a flash. He went around the front, and I heard the creak of a leather chair as he sat down.

Seconds later, I heard Laura's footsteps. "Hey, Dad."

"Hey, Laura. How's my girl?"

"Good."

"My grandson?"

"Doing great. I, ah, I thought Jackson was in here?"

"Oh, he was. He left a couple minutes ago. You just missed him."

The sound of the other leather chair creaking reached my ears.

"That's odd. His truck is still here."

"Oh. Um, did you check his office? The bathroom?"

"Both doors are open."

"No idea, then. Maybe he had an errand and is coming back later for his truck."

I stifled my groan. He was a horrible liar, almost as bad as Laura. We were both toast.

"Maybe."

"He said he was hungry. He probably went to get something to eat. If he comes back, I'll tell him you're looking for him."

"Trying to get rid of me, Dad?"

"Of course not! I…I just have a lot of work to do."

I heard the scratching of a pen, footsteps, then the door opening.

"I'll see you later."

"Yep."

The door shut, and I sighed. I felt bad, but I'd make it up to her tonight.

I waited a few minutes. "Is she gone?" I whispered. "Is the coast clear?"

"Oh, Jackson."

I froze. That wasn't Hank's voice. I swallowed heavily. Grabbing the edge of the desk, I hauled out my ass and met Laura's gaze over the wooden surface.

She shook her head. "Really, Jackson? Hiding under my father's desk?"

"I was looking for something?"

"Your pride, maybe?"

I sighed and stood, crossing to the front of the desk. I sat on the edge in front of Laura and held out my hand. "Sorry, sweet girl. I panicked."

"Why?"

"I heard your voice, and I thought…"

"You thought what?"

The words exploded out of my mouth before I could stop them.

"That you were coming looking for me to have sex. And I can't. Well, I can, but I swear I'll die, Laura. I'm exhausted. I can't keep up." I yanked on my hair. "Don't get me wrong, I love having sex with you. My cock wants it as much as you do, but I'm worn out! I need a day off."

I waited for her anger or her tears. I braced myself for either. She stared at me for a minute, then her head fell back and she laughed out loud. She laughed so hard, tears ran down her face. I crossed my arms, perplexed. Laughter wasn't the emotion I was expecting. Finally, she stopped laughing and wiped her eyes. She stood, wrapping her arms around me. Tentatively, I embraced her, wondering if this was a trick. She pressed a kiss to my neck then drew back.

"I have been on you a lot, haven't I?"

"I know I need my head examined…"

She shook her head. "It's fine, Jackson. I'll try to control myself around you a little." Her gaze danced with mischief, and she lowered her voice. "I just want you all the time—it's like I'm hooked on your cock. I'm addicted to him."

I gaped at her.

She was addicted to my cock?

"It's not my fault you're so damn sexy, and I know how amazing it feels when your cock is buried inside me," she continued. "Or the way he winks and smirks when he sees me, the little tease."

"Ah…" I swallowed, feeling the little tease twitch. He rather liked how it felt to be inside her, too.

"Hmm." I studied her for a moment. "How did you know I was under the desk?"

She reached in her pocket and handed me a piece of paper.

Under the desk.

He made me do it. Coward. Make him suffer.

It's payback time.

Bugger. He'd been trying to get me back for months after the Febreze incident. I thought he'd given up when he found out he was going to be a grandfather, but apparently not.

Well, two could play at that game.

Suddenly, I wasn't as tired as I had been earlier. She smelled good and felt right in my arms. I dropped my head to her shoulder, turning my face and peppering kisses along her neck. She shivered, and I smiled against her skin.

"You like that, baby?"

"I always like everything you do."

"Oh yeah?" I pulled her a little closer so she was standing between my legs. I tugged her lobe between my teeth, growling low in my chest as she ran her hands up my thighs. "Laura," I warned. "You're getting awfully close to Mr. Smirky."

"Is that what he's doing? Smirking?"

"I think if you got a closer look, you'd see some winking, too."

"What did you have in mind?"

I grinned down at her. "Two things. One, a heavy make-out session in here. Two, I'll come home with you and take you so hard, you'll be the one needing the nap."

"You up for that?"

"I'm getting there."

She giggled. "I was sure you were going to take me here."

"Part of me wants to, but I think your dad would actually explode. And now that I've gotten you pregnant, I've fulfilled my purpose. It would be cement time for me. But…"

"But?"

"We could let him think—"

She chuckled, her fist clutching my shirt. "How?"

Just then, I heard Hank's voice.

"Are they still in my office?"

I heard Jen answer, "Yes."

I grinned, lifting Laura into my arms. "Work with me, baby."

She wrapped her arms around my neck and her legs around my hips. "Do it."

I strode out of the office, holding Laura close. Her face was buried in

185

my neck, and I could feel her giggles. I nodded at Hank, who was looking completely shocked. He had been certain I was in deep shit.

"Thanks, Hank. Hold my calls, okay, Jen? We may be a while."

Then I walked into my office, shutting the door firmly behind me. I pressed Laura against the wall, making sure to be gentle.

"Was his face red?"

"Almost purple."

"We're awful."

I brushed my mouth over hers. "Awful good."

"I still get my hot make-out session, right?"

"Yep."

"And when we get home?"

"My cock and I are yours." I paused in thought. "Afterward, a nap?"

She laughed. "I can work with that."

"Good."

EPILOGUE

JACKSON

The hospital was quiet, and I was grateful Laura was alone in her semi-private room. I smiled at my wife as she held our son, cooing to him quietly. The click of the camera was the only other sound in the room.

She glanced up, meeting my eyes. "You've taken way too many pictures already, Daddy."

I shook my head. "Impossible to take enough pictures of something so beautiful." I bent forward, brushing my fingers over the soft down of my son's head. "He's so perfect, Laura."

With a gentle smile, she slipped him into my arms and leaned back against her pillows. "He looks so much like you."

I looked down, chuckling at the way he had his fist jammed into his mouth, sucking away. He was a big baby—long and lean, and weighed in at over ten pounds. Watching Laura give birth to him had been an amazing experience. Being there with them as he came into the world, holding her as she dropped, exhausted, onto my chest as he was born, yelling and protesting, had been the greatest moment of my life. Holding him for the first time, and every time since, had been life-affirming.

"Your dad is a bit pissed about not being here."

She yawned and nodded. "He insists you convinced the baby to come early just to mess with him."

I slipped my finger into my son's hand, in awe of how he clutched on tight. "He'll calm down when he meets him and hears his name."

"Mason Hank Cooper," she whispered. "It suits him."

"It does."

Mason blinked up at me, his eyes fluttering with fatigue. The same fatigue his mother was experiencing. I stood, gently setting him into the bassinette beside Laura. Then I turned to her, checking to make sure she was comfortable.

"You need to sleep, sweet girl. You and my boy have had a very busy day."

I knew how exhausted she was when she didn't argue. She moved gingerly, curling her fist under her chin, her eyes drifting shut.

"Love you," she mumbled.

I bent down, brushing kisses to her cheek. "I love you, Laura. Thank you for our son."

I settled in my chair and watched my family. They were both out, heads turned slightly, resting on their hands. In profile, he looked even more like me, which made me smile, but I hoped his eyes would stay blue like his mother's. He definitely had her dark hair.

She was the best thing that had ever happened to me, and he was the best of us combined.

The door opened, and her nurse, Sabrina, came in. "Everyone's settled for a while?" she asked, checking them out but not disturbing either of them.

"Yep."

"A Hank Simmons called. He said he's Laura's dad?"

"He is."

"He said to tell you he'd be here shortly."

I glanced at my watch. "It's past nine. Is he allowed in?"

"He's family. He can't stay long, but he can come in briefly."

"Okay."

She paused at the large arrangement of flowers by Laura's bed I had bought her. The roses and lilies filled the room with their scent. "Beautiful."

"Like her." I indicated Laura with a tilt of my chin. "She thought they were too much, but after today, I don't think they're close to being enough."

She smiled. "It's a life-altering experience." She patted my shoulder. "Your love is enough for both of them. The flowers, though, they add to it. Keep that up, and you'll be fine."

She left, and suddenly I was excited. I'd get to introduce Mason to

Hank. Show off my son. Place my child in the arms of my best friend and father-in-law. I had a feeling the two of them were going to be buddies.

Mason grunted, letting out a small cry, and I was out of my chair instantly, peering down at him. His tiny fists beat the air, and I lifted him, holding him close and sitting back down, tucking a pillow under my arm, grinning as he settled right away. I gazed at him, unable to stop. I started talking to him, much the way I had while Laura was pregnant. Silly thoughts and plans for the future. All the things I'd show him. All the wonders we'd discover together.

I blinked at the moisture in my eyes. My emotions were very close to the surface today. Mason's birth had opened up another protective streak I thought only existed for Laura. I knew I would do anything to keep my son safe. To keep my family safe. I would be their rock. They would be my focus for the rest of my life.

"You'll spoil him," Laura murmured drowsily. "You've hardly put him down."

I cleared my throat. "I intend to. I'm going to spoil both of you. Now, back to sleep. Mason and I are getting to know each other."

"I miss you both."

I laughed low and stood, pulling my chair close. I entwined our fingers, lifting her hand to my mouth, kissing the knuckles. "Better?"

"Hmm." She frowned. "Are you all right, Jackson?"

Carefully cradling Mason, I leaned over and kissed her. "Never been better." I kissed her again. "Thank you, sweet girl. For you. For my son. For making me happier than I ever thought possible."

"You do the same for me."

"Good." I ran my hand through her hair, humming quietly, knowing that would relax her.

Soon, her deep breathing told me she was out again. Mason wriggled, burrowing into the warmth of my skin. I shifted, getting comfortable, not planning to move until I had to. I had my son and my wife—both close, safe, and content. Tomorrow, we would go home. Hank would be here soon, and our family would be complete.

I nuzzled the tender skin on Mason's head.

Life couldn't get any better.

The door opened, and Hank peeked in, his eyes twinkling. I held my finger to my lips, and he came in, grinning and holding a huge teddy bear.

"She okay?" he whispered.

"Exhausted. She worked hard today."

He set down the bear and held out his arms. "Lemme see my grandson."

With a frown, I placed him in Hank's arms. "Careful with his head."

"I've held babies before, you know. Laura turned out all right."

"She told me about the time you almost dropped her. And she has that scar behind her ear from the day you showed her how to climb a tree and she fell on the branch."

He shook his head. "A man makes a couple of mistakes," he muttered. Then he looked down, a huge smile on his face.

"Look at him. Isn't he something else?"

I had to smile. "Yeah, he is."

"He looks like you."

"I know. He's a handsome devil," I chuckled.

"I was hoping he'd look more like Laura," he deadpanned. "Maybe he'll grow out of it."

"Gimme back my son."

"No."

"Will you two shut up?" Laura mumbled. "Neither of you are going to get to hold him if I kick you out."

"Now look what you did," I snarled.

"You were arguing too," Hank shot back.

Laura groaned. "I'm calling the nurse."

I leaned over her. "Are you in pain? What do you need?"

She met my eyes, her blue gaze amused. "Stop it. You are not setting a good example for Mason."

I bent closer, whispering, "It's okay. He doesn't know words yet. I can give your dad a hard time for a few more months."

Her lips curved into a smile. So did mine when Hank handed me back my son and showed Laura the teddy bear. He hunched over her, talking quietly, and I walked the small room, rocking my boy and giving them some privacy.

Hank was smiling as he joined me. "She's out again."

"Hardly surprising."

"So, she told me. Mason Hank Cooper." He smiled. "That's a good, strong name for my grandson." He held out his hand. "Thank you."

I rolled my eyes and gave him a one-armed hug. "You're my friend, Hank. My wife's dad. A huge part of our life. We wanted to honor that. I hope he grows up to be the kind of man you are. Loyal, compassionate, and strong."

Hank blinked. Blinked again. His dark eyes looked glossy, and he turned and looked at Laura. He cleared his throat. "Okay then," he muttered. Then he clapped me on the shoulder. "I'll be at the house tomorrow."

He leaned down and pressed a kiss to Mason's head. He paused at the door. "Jackson."

I turned. "Hmm?"

"My daughter and grandson are lucky to have you." He paused. "So am I."

Then he was gone.

I looked down at Mason. "If I knew the way to get him to leave was to get sentimental, I would have hugged him a long time ago."

Mason grizzled into his blanket in agreement.

"Good plan," I whispered. "We'll remember that for next time."

I sat back beside my wife, still holding my son. I held her hand in my free one and smiled.

Life was good.

Very good.

And as far as I was concerned, this was just the beginning.

House Arrest

CHAPTER 1

JENNY

I squinted in concentration as I leaned forward, trying to keep my balance and open my door. Why wouldn't the damn key go in? Frustrated, I heaved a sigh, causing my hair to lift away from my forehead as I tried once more. I desperately needed to lie down.

Damn Jackey. This was all her fault. When I called her earlier, *she* was the one who insisted we go out drinking to give me a chance to vent. *She* was the one who kept ordering the drinks. *She* was the one who picked up the bartender and left me alone in the bar.

Now, I couldn't get into my apartment. I studied the key, frowning. I was scratching up the door with the key instead of opening it. Why wouldn't the damn thing turn? Groaning, I kicked the wood in frustration, only to hiss in pain after my foot made contact. I placed my hand on the door and tried one last time to put the key into the lock. If it didn't work, I would have to find the super and ask him to let me in.

I gasped in shock as the door I leaned against swung open, and I lurched forward. The only thing that prevented me from hitting the floor was a strong pair of arms wrapping around me. Blinking in surprise, I looked up into the confused eyes of my very favorite neighbor.

Officer Connor Michaels. He was tall and broad, his shoulders filling the doorway, his barrel chest pressed to mine. His dark hair was damp, his T-shirt clinging to his well-defined muscles.

"Connor?" I slurred.

"Jenny." His amused voice purred my name.

"Why—why are you in my apartment?"

He pulled me upright, setting me on my feet as he smirked. "I'm not. You're in *mine*."

I gaped at him, then looked at the door.

Damn it.

His deep chuckle let me know I'd said that out loud.

I gazed at him, my already warm cheeks becoming even hotter. Good God, the man was gorgeous. I kinda wanted to lick him. I couldn't, but I wanted to.

"Sorry, Connor. I obviously went down one door too many. Sort of like the drinks this afternoon." I snorted in embarrassment. "Guess that explains why my key didn't work. I'm—I'm kinda drunk."

"I can see that."

"I keyed up your door." I waved my hand and hiccupped. "I'll fix it— but not today. I need a nap."

I turned to go and tripped over my own feet. Connor's arms shot out, keeping me upright. He lifted me, carrying me effortlessly into his apart- ment, and set me down on his couch. He sat beside me; his long fingers tilted up my head, and I looked at him with bleary eyes. God, he was so handsome. He had such beautiful eyes. They were blue and as deep and fathomless as the ocean. He was rugged and strong, his neck thickly corded, his face intense. For me, however, there was always a smile and a softening of his expression, a kind word and a gentle hug. I liked that. I liked *him*.

The way his eyebrows shot up made me wonder if I uttered that out loud, but I wasn't sure and he didn't comment.

Instead, his voice was quiet and concerned. "Why are you drunk at three in the afternoon, Jenny?"

Traitorous tears filled my eyes. "I broke up with my boyfriend."

"Ah. I'm sorry."

I lifted my arm. "I bought him a watch."

Connor grinned, that sexy dimple on the right side of his face deepen- ing. "I don't think you understand this whole breaking up thing. The last girl I broke up with slapped me so hard I had a bruise on my face for a week. She didn't buy me a watch."

I shook my head. He was so funny. Funny, handsome, and lovely. I frowned. Why would anyone ever break up with him? He was so wonder- ful. I thought he was pretty fucking perfect.

He was grinning at me again. I wasn't sure why. Did I say something? What were we discussing again?

Oh right, the watch.

"No." I tried to explain. "We hadn't been getting along well lately. He always seemed to be mad at me, and I thought it was my fault. So, I bought him a watch to say I was sorry."

"Okay?"

I sniffed. "He works from home a lot, so I took it over to surprise him. Only he surprised me. When I walked in…he was fucking his assistant against the wall."

"Oh."

"I don't think it was my fault now. He wasn't very happy to see me."

He cupped my face tenderly, wiping away the tears from my cheeks that rolled down despite my efforts to stop them. "I'm sorry that happened to you, Jenny. You didn't deserve that."

"I kept the watch. I think I can return it."

"Good decision." He rose and went into the kitchen, coming back with a glass of water. "Here, drink this."

I accepted the glass and sipped the cold liquid.

"What did you do? I hope you gave him a piece of your mind."

"I might have yelled a lot. And I might have bitch-slapped *her* when she got in my face about what a lousy girlfriend I was to John."

"And him?"

"I, um, I threw his cell phone off the balcony into the pool, then I kicked him in the crotch." I groaned, remembering my impulsive reaction. "I kicked him hard." I held out my foot. "These pointy shoes are lethal."

His lips quirked, and he had to look away as he tried to hide his smile. I didn't want him to hide his smile. I loved his smile. It was especially attractive with his sexy dimple. I wondered if it tasted as sexy as it looked.

This time when he grinned at me, *I knew* I'd said that out loud. *Damn it.*

"Well." He smirked. "I think that concluded his wall-banging fun for the day—maybe even two."

I giggled, clapping my hand over my mouth to cover the snort I knew would follow. I always snort-laughed when I was drunk. Jackey told me it was highly unattractive.

Connor leaned over and uncovered my mouth. "Laugh, Jenny. I much prefer you laugh than cry. And the bastard deserved it." He chuckled. "Just remind me not to let you too close when you're pissed at me."

I giggled again.

Connor frowned at me. "I get the crotch attack, but why his cell phone?"

"He loved that thing. That and his precious car. More than anything." I sighed. "Certainly more than me."

"He didn't deserve you. Anyone who would love their cell phone or their car more than you clearly isn't right in the head."

I giggle-sobbed, followed by a hiccup, while I rubbed the top of my arm, and winced a little. "Well, I guess he's not my problem anymore."

Connor's eyes narrowed as he watched my hand, and he pulled my sweater from my shoulder. "Did he leave a mark on you?" he hissed.

I looked down at the bruise that was forming where John's hand had gripped me. "Um, I guess so. He was really mad over the whore-cheating-girlfriend-slapping thing, and, I imagine, the crotch attack, but probably the angriest over the cell phone in the pool. He grabbed me hard when he threw me out of the apartment."

"What's his address?"

I looked at him, confused. "Why would you want that?"

"Your boyfriend needs a lesson in manners."

I blinked at him. "He's not my boyfriend anymore." I proceeded to burst into noisy, wailing sobs.

Connor wrapped his arms around me, and I found myself in his lap. His hands stroked my back in gentle, comforting circles as he crooned with a quiet voice in my ear, telling me everything would be okay.

When I calmed down, he handed me some Kleenex and smiled at me. "I know it hurts, Jenny. But he wasn't the right man for you. As clichéd as it sounds, you'll get over the pain."

Before I could stop myself, I shook my head. "That's the problem, Connor. I–I'm not upset we broke up."

"I don't understand."

I exhaled a deep, shuddering breath and kept my eyes averted. I needed to tell someone how I was feeling. I couldn't even tell Jackey since I was so ashamed of myself, but somehow, telling Connor seemed right. I wanted him to know. "I'm actually relieved. Things hadn't been good for a long time, and nothing I did seemed to be right or to help. A relationship shouldn't be that much work. Or make someone that unhappy most of the time."

He lifted my chin. "So, you're crying because...?"

My lips started quivering again. "Because I feel guilty. I know I wasn't a good girlfriend." I huffed. "Something changed for me a few months ago, and my feelings toward John were different. I was different." I shrugged. "They had been fading for a while and I tried to fight it, but it didn't work."

He frowned at me. "At least you tried. It sounds as though he just moved on and kept stringing you along."

We were quiet as I continued sitting on his lap. He made no move to push me off, and I made no move to leave. I liked how it felt sitting there. His arm was still around me, holding me loosely, and I was close enough to be able to breathe in his clean scent. His other hand still cupped my face, his long fingers dancing soothingly on my skin along the edge of my hairline. It was comforting and felt strangely right.

He spoke up, breaking the silence. "What happened to change your feelings, Jenny?"

I closed my eyes briefly. When I opened them, I looked into the deep blue of his warm gaze, and I swallowed. I realized I was still drunk enough to be brave and say what I had been hiding for so many months.

"*You* moved in."

His eyes widened. "*Jenny.*"

I shook my head. "It's okay, Connor. You don't have to say anything. You didn't do anything wrong. It's all me. John wasn't right for me. He never was…and I knew it before I met you. I just—" Embarrassment crashed over me, and I tried to push myself away. Connor tightened his arm around me and I glanced up, expecting to see rejection and pity on his face.

First, he'd found me drunk in the hall, and now, I'd confessed to having a secret crush on him that might have led to the breakup of my relationship. All that drama from the girl he had coffee with occasionally and borrowed the odd condiment from at times. Every interaction had been friendly and easy, and I found his presence soothing and enjoyable. Our encounters always left me wanting more time with him—and now I had just ruined it.

Except, it wasn't rejection or pity I saw. He was smiling at me, the most endearing look on his face. I stopped pushing on his chest, my breath catching as I looked at his expression. He pulled me nearer until our faces were so close, I could feel his breath washing over me. "It's *not* all you, Jenny," he said.

Then he was kissing me.

God, his mouth. It was everything I had fantasized about since the first time he'd smiled at me. His lips were warm and soft against mine, moving and guiding me. He dragged his tongue across my bottom lip, and my mouth parted. My senses exploded as he deepened the kiss, its nature becoming possessive and greedy immediately. I moaned deep in my throat as his arms tightened and his tongue demanded, claimed, swirled, and explored, leaving me breathless and clinging to him for dear life. My head began to spin, and I pulled away, gasping for air.

Glowing blue met dazed brown as we stared at each other. His hand came up, softly tracing my lips, which puckered against his touch. I blinked as the room began to pulsate around me.

"Connor..."

"Jenny?" His voice was husky and filled with want.

"I need..."

"What do you need, baby? Tell me."

CHAPTER 2

JENNY

I woke up, blinking and confused. I buried my head back into the pillow and burrowed under the soft blanket covering me. My bed had never felt so comfortable. I inhaled and frowned. My pillow didn't smell like Downy. It smelled like fresh-cut grass on a nice, sunny day. It smelled like Connor did when he gave me a hug.

Connor.

Oh no.

I sat up, my eyes wide as I looked around the room. I was not in my bed. This was not my room. I swallowed heavily. I was in Connor's room. My hands flew up to my mouth, stifling my gasp as I remembered exactly how I ended up in Connor's room. Images bombarded me—finding John, kicking him, slapping Tami, drinking and stumbling home, and ending up in Connor's apartment, crying in his arms. I shuddered as I remembered my whispered confession and kissing him. Oh God, how we had kissed. I never wanted to stop.

Except, the room had begun to spin, and I had pushed away from Connor, then ran to the bathroom and threw up. My embarrassment grew as I remembered him behind me, holding my hair, stroking my back, and making little hushing noises at my distress. I looked down, my humiliation complete as I realized I was no longer wearing my blouse and pants but rather a large T-shirt that had to belong to Connor. I pulled the T-shirt aside and saw my tank top was still in place, as were my boy shorts. I must have vomited on myself before passing out. Looking at the fading light, I judged it was early evening, which meant I had been out for a few hours.

I swung my legs over the edge of the bed and stood. I had to get out of there, as quickly as possible and with as little contact with Connor as I could manage. Then, I needed to pack up my apartment and move in the middle of the night while he was asleep.

Yeah. That was a good plan. I wasn't sure how I would do it with a pounding headache and no truck or help, but I would figure it out.

I listened, but the apartment was quiet. Cautiously, I stuck my head out the door and looked around. It was empty. I must have disgusted him so much he left. No doubt, he'd hoped I would wake up and leave before he got home. I was sure he'd be grateful when he realized I had moved in the night. It would save us the awkward embarrassment of reliving my drunken episode every time we passed in the hall. I was sure our coffee dates were over.

I scurried across the living area, grabbing my purse from the floor. I had no idea where my clothes were, and I couldn't see my shoes, but I didn't care. I had twenty pairs of flats in the closet, and I simply had to go down the hall. I reached the door and stopped dead at the large piece of paper hanging on it.

Jenny
If you are reading this, you are awake—or at least coherent and no doubt panicking.
Stop.
I'll be back soon.
Don't run. Go sit on the couch and relax.
I'm sure you need this.

Taped below was a new toothbrush. I reached out, touching the white handle. He was always so thoughtful. My gaze returned to the note.

Towels in the bathroom. Tylenol on the counter. Water in the fridge.
Did I mention, stop panicking?
Connor x
PS: You look cute in my shirt.

PPS: I know you're still panicking and want to leave. Your clothes are in the laundry. I took your keys and your shoes—you can't go anywhere.

PPPS: If you feel like you are being held against your will on house arrest, then I suggest you move on to the next phase of being kidnapped. Stockholm syndrome. In case you don't know, that is where you develop an intense bond and deep feelings for your captor—me. I already have them for you.

PPPPS: Please sit down. STAY. Back soon. Don't make me come find you. I will. I'm a cop. I can do that.

I blinked at the note and reread it. I looked down at the shirt and smiled, then laughed when I reread the PPPPS part. I reached out and tore the toothbrush away from the paper, returned to the bathroom, and used it vigorously. I also had a quick but refreshing shower and brushed my hair, emerging a few minutes later feeling human again. I padded to the kitchen, still wearing his T-shirt and my underclothes. I located the water and Tylenol and swallowed some pills, hoping they would ease the throbbing pain in my head. I desperately hoped they would ease the nerves in my stomach that had nothing to do with the alcohol I drank and everything to do with the confession I had spilled *because* of the alcohol I drank.

The sound of the key in the door made me turn my head, and I watched, wide-eyed, as Connor walked in, his hands full of bags. He stopped when he saw me regarding him warily from the couch. Setting down the bags, he crossed over and, before I could react, leaned over the back of the couch, dragged me up into his arms, kissed me soundly, and pulled back with a smile. "Stopped panicking yet?"

"Um, no?"

He leaned down and nuzzled my lips. "Stop now, please."

"Connor—"

"I kissed you, Jenny. I started it."

I grimaced. I was certain falling into his apartment drunk had started it. I looked up when he chuckled.

"You talk out loud a lot, don't you? I never noticed it before today." He grinned down at me. "Not much of an inner voice?"

I shut my eyes. It would seem that was all I did around him. Spill my innermost thoughts.

He stroked my head with his large hand, his touch light. "I brought dinner. We are going to eat and talk." He paused. "If your head is up to it?"

I nodded. "It's fine."

"Good."

"Do I get my keys and shoes back?"

"Nope."

"Oh." I hadn't expected that answer.

"Unless you really want them."

I shook my head.

He leaned down again, his face level with mine. "I like you in my shirt. And you smell like me."

"I had a shower, and I used your soap. I hope that's okay?"

He nodded. "Perfect. I *like* you smelling like me. Have you moved on in your kidnapped-adoring-your-captor-syndrome? You there yet?"

My breath caught. "Aren't you moving a little fast?" I squeaked. I had only broken up with John a couple of hours ago. Where was all that coming from?

He shook his head, his face getting closer. He wrapped his hand around the back of my neck, pulling me close. "I've been waiting for you since the day I moved in, Jenny. As far as I'm concerned, it's been too long."

Once again, I found myself drowning in his kiss.

When he finally released me and moved away, I stared after him in shock.

Since he moved in? He'd been waiting since he moved in?

That was six months ago.

I wanted him to come back and talk to me. My fingers brushed my swollen lips. They wanted him back as well.

I sighed.

The Stockholm syndrome had definitely started.

~

"Eat, Jenny. You need something in your stomach."

"I ate earlier," I protested. I remembered that part.

"You spewed up your poutine about three hours ago, Wren." He shook his head, chuckling. "Not much of a drunk, are you? You eat greasy foods the morning after. Not *while* you're drunk. They always come back."

I gaped at him. I had eaten poutine? I *hated* poutine. I shuddered. He had *seen* that? Oh God, that was so gross.

He shrugged. "Well, you ate it. So, throwing it up was a good thing, I guess, if you hate it so much."

Oh. My. God. My mouth had no filter today. None.

I stared at him in horror. I could feel my entire body flushing with embarrassment. "I'm so, so sorry," I muttered. "You shouldn't have seen that."

He waved his hand dismissively. "Nope. It's fine. I've seen lots worse in my line of work. No doubt I'll see it again."

"What?"

He nodded enthusiastically around his mouthful of noodles. "No doubt I'll piss you off, and you'll have to go drinking with Jackey sometime. Best we got the first one over with now."

I shook my head. I couldn't imagine ever being pissed at this man. He was perfection walking. I also knew I was never drinking again.

He laughed, slapping his knee as he guffawed. "Inner monologue, Jenny. You really need to work on that. Between no filter and that expressively beautiful face...I can read you no problem."

Huh. John always said I was closed off and removed to him. My inner monologue only seemed to fail around Connor.

Connor leaned forward, his chopsticks loaded with noodles. "Open up, Wren."

That was the second time he'd called me by that name. "Wren?"

He grinned. "Jenny Reynolds. *Jenny Wren.* It's how I always thought of you. You remind me of one of those little birds with your soft brown hair and those dark eyes. Do you hate it?"

"No," I admitted, feeling shy. "I kinda like it."

"Good. Now open up and let me feed you, little bird."

I opened my mouth, and he gently fed me the noodles, smiling in approval as I chewed. "You *will* drink again. I *will* piss you off. I promise you that." He traced my cheek with his fingers. "But I'm going to try really hard to be a good man for you. The kind you deserve." He handed me a container and a spoon. "I got you soup. Eat it, please."

I stared at him as he went back to his food.

The kind I deserve?

I wasn't sure what kind that was, but the thought of it being Connor made me smile.

~

Connor's phone rang, and he picked it up with a smile of apology. After listening, talking, and laughing for a couple minutes with whoever was on the other end, he hung up, his expression amused. I heard something about "smell" and "car" and "it'll never be the same," but I didn't pay it much attention. He grinned at me. "That was my partner."

"Everything okay?"

He chuckled. "For me, yep. Not so sure for someone else."

"Okay?"

"I'll tell you later." He moved closer to me on the couch, his hand clasping mine. "Feeling better?"

"I am. Thank you."

"Good. Your arm okay?"

"It's fine, Connor."

"He isn't going to touch you again. Ever."

"I don't plan on seeing him again."

"I hope not. He doesn't deserve to be in the same room as you."

I shook my head. No one had ever sounded so protective or caring. I wasn't used to the feeling. I stifled a yawn as I looked at Connor. If he was home this afternoon, I wondered if he had to work in the morning. He shook his head when I asked.

"No. I'm off until Sunday—three full days. I've been looking forward to the time off."

"I guess I should, um, go. I'm sure you have plans tonight."

"I do, and she is sitting next to me."

"Oh."

"Did I frighten you earlier, Jenny? All the talk about us?"

I sighed, lifting his hand and studying it in the light. His fingers were long and callused, his palm large and yet always so gentle when he touched me. I glanced up at him. "Frighten me? No. Surprise me, yes. It feels rather surreal, Connor. This morning, I bought a watch for John. This afternoon, that relationship ended badly. Tonight, I'm here with you, and you're telling me you have feelings for me."

"You said you had feelings for me too, Jenny." He hesitated, his voice wary. "Or was that the liquor talking?"

I kissed his hand. "No. The liquor made me brave, but I meant it."

"Did I break up the two of you?"

"No. We'd been drifting apart for a long time, even before you moved in. I think I stayed with him out of convenience and habit." I shrugged sheepishly. "Guess that doesn't make me a very good person, does it?"

"It makes you human." He sighed, his head falling back on the couch. "The first day I moved in here, I saw you. You were laughing at something Jackey said, and I thought you were the prettiest thing I'd ever seen. You came over, introduced yourself, and welcomed me to the building." He turned his head, his eyes serious. "You were so full of light and kindness. I fell for you right there."

"Oh."

"Oh, indeed. I found out you had a boyfriend, so I told myself I could just be your friend, at least for the time being. But I loved bumping into you or running out of ketchup."

"You eat a lot of it. You were always asking for it."

He grinned. "I never use the stuff. It was something I noticed you had a lot of in your fridge one day when I was over for coffee and grabbed the cream."

I rolled my eyes. "I kept it on hand for John. I never used it either. He put it on everything."

Connor's eyes crinkled as he smiled. "Well, at least he was good for one thing." He softened his voice. "I loved how you always offered me coffee in the mornings if you saw me. It was my favorite time of day—getting to sit with you for a few minutes and talk to you, see you smile." His cheeks flushed slightly. "I, ah, may have memorized your schedule so I knew when I'd bump into you. Coffee with Jenny days were the best."

My own cheeks tinted, and Connor frowned at me. "Jenny?"

"I may have noted all of those days, as well. I always made sure to brew extra coffee."

"Quite the pair."

I looked at him. "Quite."

The air around us grew warm, and Connor's gaze darkened as his hand squeezed mine. "I want to kiss you again. Will you let me?"

"Please," I breathed.

He pulled me toward him slowly, his eyes never leaving my face. He wrapped his hands around the back of my neck, burying them in my hair as his lips descended on mine. I had thought kissing Connor while drunk was good; nothing prepared me for the burst of heat that hit me while kissing him sober. Every sense in my body ignited. I whimpered as he pushed his tongue in, licking and exploring, his flavor filling my senses and my head. I couldn't get enough of him—his taste, his scent, his strength— as he held me against his hard body. I gripped his shoulders with my hands, as he tilted my head, controlling the kiss completely. I lost myself to him and the passion he brought out in me. It was only when he pulled back, I realized I was straddling his lap and we were both panting and flushed.

"God, you're amazing," Connor whispered. He traced his thumb over my bottom lip, his gaze hooded with desire.

Teasingly, I drew his thumb into my mouth, swirling my tongue around the tough skin, with my teeth nipping at the thick end. A strangled groan escaped Connor's lips as he stared at me, his eyes burning. I lowered my gaze, my eyes widening when I took in his growing bulge, his pants straining at the zipper. He pulled his thumb out of my mouth, crashing his lips to mine as he grabbed my hips, pulling me down on top of his erection, thrusting upward. We both groaned at the intense sensation as we rocked together, our lips fused, and our bodies locked in a rhythmic dance. My body was on overload, and I shuddered as long rolls of pleasure ran through me. I had never felt anything like it. My head fell back as I gasped for air, and Connor's lips nipped and licked at my neck.

"Tell me to stop, Wren," he murmured in my ear. "Tell me to stop, or I won't be able to… *God…Jenny.*"

I didn't want him to stop. I wanted him to come apart, and I wanted to see it happen. I sped up my movements, undulating over him and moaning his name. He pressed me down, pushing right where I needed him the most.

He spoke in a gruff voice. "*Baby*…I can't… You need to…" He then stilled, throwing his head back as he shuddered and cursed. I fell with him, my orgasm tearing through me. I watched him, my body locking down as I gasped his name. I was unable to tear my eyes away from his face as he climaxed.

Fuck, he was pretty when he came. I smiled. I did that to him. I made him pretty.

I fell forward, nestled against his torso, spent and exhausted. He pulled me to cuddle against his body, his chin resting on my shoulder as we slowly recovered.

"You're staying the night."

I smiled against his chest. It wasn't a request. I wanted to stay, but I still couldn't resist teasing him.

"I am? You're still holding my keys?"

"And your clothes and shoes." He growled into my neck.

"I guess I have no choice, then."

He groaned and stood, taking me with him. He strode down the hall, laying me on his bed. He hovered over me, his face close to mine. "I'm going to have a shower. You're staying here. Unless, of course, you want to join me."

I shook my head. I wasn't quite ready for that yet.

"Then you'll be here when I get back."

I nodded, my eyes drifting down to the front of his pants. I bit my lip as I looked back up. Connor smirked at me.

"Proud of yourself, Jenny? You made me come in my pants. I haven't done that since I was a teenager."

I tried to suppress my smile but failed.

Grinning, he leaned down and kissed me hard. "Smile away. You did it." He stood and walked to the dresser, grabbing a pair of sleep shorts before he paused and turned around. "But, Jenny?"

"Yes?"

"I am not pretty. Guys are never pretty when they come. We're sexy, hot, devastatingly handsome, but not pretty." Winking, he strode into the bathroom.

I grumbled as I rolled over. Inner monologue. I needed to find my inner monologue. I had to stop my mouth spilling out all my thoughts when I was around him.

But I strongly disagreed. He was hot and sexy, yet still very pretty.

CHAPTER 3

JENNY

"W hatever you're thinking about that is making you look like that needs to stop right now."

I looked up in surprise at the sight of Connor, leaning against the doorway, running a towel through his damp hair. His chest was bare, gleaming in the soft light cast by the bedside lamp. He strode forward, his long, muscled legs visible since he only wore low-slung shorts. His abs, arms, and pecs were well defined and taut. There was a tattoo on his shoulder of the police insignia, the ink strikingly black against his skin. He tossed the towel into the hamper before he lifted the covers, lying beside me. He cupped my cheek and frowned. "What is going on in that beautiful head of yours?"

I started shaking my head, and his hand tightened. "Don't say nothing. You look positively shattered right now." He leaned forward, pressing his lips against mine. "Tell me."

"What must you think of me right now, Connor?"

"I don't understand."

"I broke up with my boyfriend this afternoon, and I'm in your bed tonight. In between, I got drunk, confessed my hidden feelings for you, and then..." I couldn't even finish, and I looked at him in horror. "I don't act like this. I've never done anything like this before," I whispered, my voice pleading. I wanted him to believe me. I wanted him to know the kind of person I was. From the second he had left to go shower, my thoughts had been raging. I had been struggling with everything that had happened, the enormity of the day crashing over me.

"I *know* that, Jenny. I know *you*."

"How? How can you be so sure?"

"Because I see *you*. I've heard you on the phone with your friends and family when I was at your place. I've seen the pictures in your apartment. You've shared stories about yourself and your life with me. I could hear you talking in the hall with neighbors and friends. I know how caring you are with everyone. You help all the people in this building. I know about the meals you make for Mrs. Franklin and Mr. Smithers. I know you got them playing cards together so they aren't alone all the time. You look after everyone around you. Your friends adore you. I even heard how great you were with that jerk."

"You did?"

"I didn't mean to listen, but the walls are quite thin, and when I'd hear your voice, I just sort of became more alert." He shrugged. "It's the cop in me, I think. I always had to make sure you were okay. He was leaving one day, and you were telling him to calm down, that you felt he worked too hard and you never saw him anymore." He frowned. "I didn't like his tone when he talked to you, but I stayed out of it. Although, if he had done anything, I would have been out of the door and on him in a flash. But he brushed you off fairly quickly and left."

"I remember that day. You came over a little while after he left and told me your coffeemaker broke. You asked me if I could make you a thermos to take to work."

He smiled sheepishly. "I had to check on you."

"We've had a lot of coffee together."

"It was a great way to spend time with you. I could see you, and you were comfortable with it. It gave me a chance to get to know you better." He cocked his head to the side. "I don't think you realize how generous you were with me. You always sent me off with a snack or lunch. Are you even aware of how often you knocked on my door with dinner or some of your treats?"

I shook my head.

"I figured that. It is so natural with you. I loved hearing those knocks. I always felt so cared for."

"I liked how you reacted when I gave you something. You were so enthusiastic and grateful. And you made me feel less alone." I shrugged. "John was around less and less."

Connor smirked. "Working so hard."

I smiled ruefully. "I guess he wasn't working as hard as I thought he was—at least, not at his job."

Connor sighed and moved closer. He pulled me to him and held me silently for a minute. When he spoke, his voice was low but firm. "Listen to me, Jenny. I think, today, you ended something that wasn't right for you. You haven't been happy for a long time. You told me that. What happened today was simply you moving on from a relationship that has been dead longer than you realized." He paused, his hand ghosting up and down my arm. "I know this is fast and completely out of character for you. What happened earlier, on the couch? We didn't plan it, but it wasn't wrong. I'm sorry you're regretting it."

"I'm not regretting it, Connor."

"No?"

"I just need you to know it's not my usual style."

He chuckled. "I already knew that, but duly noted."

"John and I… We haven't been, um…"

He held up his hand. "That is none of my business, Jenny."

I grabbed his hand and held it tight. "Please, let me."

"Okay, Wren. Whatever you need."

"Things have never been very passionate between us. I always questioned that because it didn't seem right. My friends all talked about this connection they had with their partner, and I never felt it with John." I looked at Connor intently. "I've never felt anything like I felt with you on the couch. Ever."

A slow smile spread across his face, but he didn't say anything.

"The past few months, it got worse. I didn't like his touch anymore. It just felt wrong. He only stayed over twice since you moved in, and both times he was drunk and nothing happened. He thought it did, and I let him, so I didn't feel so guilty. But there was no spark." I sighed. "I should have broken it off months ago."

"So, you *liked* the couch?"

"Yeah. I did." I chewed the inside of my cheek. "I'm not sure I'm ready for more just yet, though."

"I can handle that. Just being here with you, like this, is more than I hoped for." He tapped my cheek, shaking his head. "Stop beating yourself up about not breaking it off with him sooner. Hindsight is a powerful thing. Okay?"

"Okay."

"And for the record? I liked the couch, too. That spark your friends talked about? We have a fucking inferno. When you're ready, I'm more than happy to show you just how hot we are together."

We both grinned at each other, his arms still wrapped around me.

He turned serious. "Jenny, have you ever had a feeling? Just a sense that told you something, someone was the *exact* right thing for you?"

"I don't think so."

He smiled down at me. "I have. Three times. My parents died when I was young, and a great couple named Kelly and Jason adopted me. They had come to the group home to see a little girl, but I took one look at them and informed Kelly she was supposed to be my new mommy. I remember looking at her and just feeling like she was what I had been waiting for. That once she loved me, I would be okay again."

"Connor—" My voice caught at the emotion in his voice.

His arms tightened, his hands splayed across my back, his fingers moving. "They took both of us—since I also refused to leave without Carly. As soon as I met her at the orphanage, I became her big brother, and I told Kelly and Jason we were a package deal. They came to see *her* and adopted us both."

I felt the tears gathering in my eyes as he shared his past with me. I wanted to know everything about this man. He was quiet for a moment, seemingly lost in his thoughts.

"You said three times?" I prompted quietly.

He stared at me thoughtfully, his fingers still moving on my skin. When he spoke, his voice was full of warmth. "First Carly, then Kelly and Jason. I knew I was supposed to have them in my life, and I was right. They're my family." His hand stopped its caresses and moved to cup my face. "I can't wait for them to meet you. They are gonna love you." He drew in a deep breath. "The third time was when I met you, Jenny. You offered me your hand, and when I took it, it was as if I had come home. I knew, one day, you'd be mine."

I could no longer contain my tears. They poured down my face as I looked at him. No one had ever said something as beautiful as that to me in my life.

He wiped away the tears and leaned in, his lips nuzzling my cheek, his voice tender as he spoke. "So, however it happened, how quickly we got *here*, doesn't matter. How I feel about you hasn't changed except to think this is exactly how it was supposed to be, Jenny. I'm yours, if you want me. I have been for months. I *will* be for as long as you let me. Please let me."

I could only get one word out as I gazed at him, awed by the passion in his warm eyes.

"Yes."

~

We were snuggled on the bed, our bodies entwined. We had been talking for hours, asking questions, sharing soft, loving kisses and caresses, and basking in the closeness of being together. I told him about growing up with divorced parents, being passed back and forth, never feeling secure. He told me about being adopted. I shared more with him in a few hours than I ever had in the months I'd been with John.

I hesitated before I leaned up on my elbow and looked at Connor.

"What?" he asked tenderly. "Just ask me, Jenny."

"Your job…"

He sat up, leaning against the headboard. "Yeah, we should discuss that subject."

"Is it very dangerous?"

"Well, it certainly is more dangerous than working at the local bingo hall." He grinned. "Although, I hear those old biddies get awfully handsy with their canes if you don't call the numbers loud enough."

I frowned at his attempt to make me smile. "I'm serious."

He picked up my hand, his long fingers tracing the veins on the back of it as he thought it over.

"It can be dangerous, Jenny. But I'm careful. I have a good partner." He smiled encouragingly. "Honestly, there are more days I don't draw my gun than I do. We don't live in a high crime city—Grimsby isn't like Toronto. It's not like anything you see on TV. I'm not knocking down doors every day and breaking up major drug rings. A lot of my job is helping people. I like that part."

"But there is crime."

"There is."

"Do you wear a bulletproof vest?"

"Yes. We all do." He paused and cleared his throat. "Is that something you can live with, Jenny?"

I sighed. "I'll worry about you."

"I'm careful. I promise. And you might not have to worry for too long."

"Why?"

He looked almost bashful as he grinned at me. "I spent some time in the forensic lab. I really enjoy that aspect. Putting the pieces together. Working with the police investigators. Solving cases with the collected evidence. It's usually long and tedious—again, nothing like you would see on TV, but I love it. I've applied to take the courses to become a CSI. If I'm accepted, I'll take a leave of absence from the force and see where it goes. I have some good contacts at the lab, which would help once I pass the courses."

"Connor, that is amazing!"

He nodded. "As much as I'd miss some of what I do now, I can see myself in the lab ten, twenty years down the road. I'll miss the force, but…"

"You love being a cop, don't you?"

His lips quirked. "Some days more than others."

"What was that smile for?"

"Um, nothing."

"Something, I think. Your partner called earlier, and you smiled like the cat that swallowed the canary when you were talking to him. You said you'd tell me later."

Pouting, he leaned forward, pulling my face to his and kissing me deeply until I was breathless. "Okay."

"Okay?"

"I'll tell you. I just had to kiss you in case you decided not to find this funny."

Crossing my arms, I glared. "Connor. Tell me."

"After you passed out, I was picking up your purse, and your cell phone fell out. Your contact list was open."

"And?"

"I looked up the jerk's information."

"Why?" I asked, confused.

"He hurt you, Jenny. He put his hands on you. That is *unacceptable*." He shrugged. "I wanted to check him out."

"Oh my God, did you have him arrested?"

"No. But I did find out he had three unpaid parking tickets."

I shook my head. "He always has some. He parks that stupid car in all sorts of places he shouldn't." I pursed my lips. There was more—I knew it. "Connor, what did you do?"

"I, um, arranged to have his car impounded. It was towed away this afternoon while you were passed out."

"He must have freaked out!" I gasped.

Connor nodded and grinned. "Oh yeah, he did. The idiot made it easy, though. He had it parked illegally when the tow truck arrived as well. I was told he acted like a complete ass at the impound. The only way he could get it back was to pay his tickets and the fines before they released it back to him. It cost him huge."

I narrowed my eyes at Connor. "There is more to this story." I thought about the call I had only half listened to. "You did something..." My eyes widened. "You did something to his car!"

"Not me. I did nothing."

"*Connor.*"

He held up his hands. "I may have had some help. That person may or may not have hidden a small dead fish or two somewhere deep inside the car."

I gaped at him. "But they'll go bad, and it's summer..."

His grin was evil. "They'll stink, really badly. The car will become undrivable and unsellable."

I stared at him, wordless.

He stared back, not at all apologetic. "You never place more value on a car than the woman in your life, Jenny." He narrowed his eyes. "You never touch someone I care about."

I continued to stare, my thoughts rampant.

He shifted uncomfortably. "Um, Jenny? You're not gonna like, kick *me* in the nuts now, are you?"

I gave in. I started to laugh and didn't bother stopping the snorts that were liberally scattered among the guffaws. I fell back on the bed, holding my stomach, as my mirth spilled over.

Connor leaned over me, his face wreathed in smiles. "Johnny is not having a good day. He gets kicked in the balls, his cell phone takes a swim" —he waggled his eyebrows— "his car is towed, and in the matter of a few days, will start smelling like ass. Really, *really* bad ass."

I kept laughing. I knew I shouldn't. I knew I should tell him off, not only for looking in my cell phone, but also for pulling such a childish prank. Part of me knew I needed to tell him to get the fish out of the car the same way he got them in. But I couldn't. He was gazing down at me with the most yearning expression on his face. It begged me not to be angry. So, I kept laughing until I was exhausted. The whole time, Connor hovered over me, his face expressing his enjoyment at my reaction.

I fixed a serious expression on my face as I cupped his cheek. "Don't do that again. Or I'll get mad."

"If he stays away from you, I won't. You took care of his precious phone. I helped with the stupid car. I have no reason to bother him if he stays away. I don't want you mad either." He grinned. "If you got mad, would you *punish* me, Jenny?"

"I might."

His grin grew wider, and he lowered his lips to my ear, his voice husky. "I, um, have handcuffs, if you really need to punish me. I'd take it like a man."

I couldn't help the shiver that went through me. "I think you'd enjoy that too much for it to be considered punishment, Connor."

He chuckled, his lips ghosting over my skin. "You may be right."

I sighed. "No more. Leave him alone, okay? He is out of my life. Gone."

"I will." He pulled back and kissed my palm. "I actually feel bad for him right now."

"Because of his smelly car?"

His face softened, and he lowered his voice. "No. Because today, he lost the most amazing woman in the world, and he has no idea how empty his life will be without her." His voice grew nervous. "And he is never getting her back."

"No?"

"You're mine now, Jenny. You're going to be my whole world. I know it."

We stared at each other, and before I could stop them, the words were out. They were right, and I meant them. I had felt it for months; I had fought it for months, but it was there.

"And you, mine." I hesitated. "I think I'm falling in love with you, Connor."

His eyes widened and he smiled. "The Stockholm syndrome has happened, has it?"

"No. You happened. You walked into my life and changed it."

This time when he smiled, it was different. It was a smile that promised a whole lifetime of laughter and caring. Of being cared for and protected. Of being together.

"You go ahead and fall. I'll be right there to catch you. I'm falling too, Jenny." His lips covered mine, his passion evident, his touch overwhelming.

For the first time in my life, I knew.

I'd found my home, too.

CHAPTER 4

JENNY

"Here." Connor tossed a box into the cart. "Next?"

I looked in the cart, already knowing what I would see. "I said Shreddies, Connor. Not Frosted Flakes."

"I like Frosted Flakes."

"They aren't for you. They're for me. For my apartment." I avoided lifting my eyes. If I lifted my eyes and saw his sweet, pleading gaze, I was toast. I was always toast when it came to him.

"But, Jenny, I like it when you have breakfast in *my* apartment, with me. In my bed. I like Frosted Flakes. I really like how they taste when I eat them off you."

Internally, I groaned, shutting my eyes. He shouldn't be saying things like that in the grocery store. When he said things like that, I wanted to say fuck the groceries and leave.

His arm went around me, his lips nuzzling my ear. "Instead of fucking the groceries, why don't we go home, and you can fuck *me*, Wren? I'm good with that."

Shit, that wasn't internal.

His chuckle was low and deep. "Neither was the toast remark."

I sighed and leaned back into his caress. I should never have wine with dinner and try to accomplish something afterward. Ever. Especially not with Connor around.

"We *can* accomplish something, Jenny. We just need to get out of the store before I bend you over the cart and accomplish it here." He flexed his hips into me, showing me exactly what he wanted to accomplish. "It's probably not a good idea for me to get arrested for public lewdness. I don't think my *pretty* face would survive jail."

I straightened up and pushed him away. "You and your accomplishing things is what has me in the grocery store aisle at nine o'clock at night on a Wednesday, Connor. I have no food in the house."

He grinned at me. "I keep telling you, you don't need it—I have food. I'm happy to share. You can just stay at my place."

I snorted. "You have about as much food as I do, Connor. We ordered out the last two nights. Now, give me the Shreddies."

Pouting, he tossed the box into the cart. "They taste like ass. You need like six teaspoons of sugar on them just to make them palatable."

"You bite my ass all the time and moan about how it tastes. Are you saying my ass tastes like Shreddies now? Do you need to sprinkle me with sugar, too?"

He stared at me, his eyes going dark as he licked his lips. That was not a good thing to say. I should never have said that. Connor did *not* need added incentive to be excited.

"You *and* your ass have no need for added sweetness. But I'm happy to try it—once."

"Connor—"

He grinned, a dark, mischievous grin, before he chuckled. "Okay, Jenny. Let's finish your list and go home. But the Frosted Flakes are staying."

I pushed the cart while rolling my eyes. "You're not eating them off me again," I muttered.

"Oh yes, I am."

"Not with milk."

He let out a bark of laughter as we rounded the corner. "I admit it was messy." He wrapped his arms around me, pulling me close. "But tasty." He kissed my forehead. "You make everything taste better." His breath sighed against my skin. "You make *everything* better, Wren."

Oh. My. God.

How did he do that? One second, he was all hot and sexy, dirty talk, and the next second, he made me feel as if I were the center of his universe.

His voice was low. "You are."

I shivered. If he kept that up, he was seriously getting laid as soon as we got home. Forget the perishables.

"That's the plan, Jenny."

I was never drinking and shopping with Connor again.

~

CONNOR

I bit back my smile at her indignation. She tried so hard to be stern and failed miserably. Nestled under my arm, she fit well next to me. She was about average height at 5'5", but given the fact that I was 6'4", she barely reached my chest. Her creamy complexion and full lips were set off with wide, dark-brown eyes and golden-brown hair that fell to her shoulders. She wasn't conventionally pretty, but to me, she was the most beautiful girl in the world. Spunky, with a smart mouth, she was fucking adorable. I loved her. She was sweet, funny, intelligent, and so responsive. She was also a fast drunk. One glass of wine got her giggly, and two destroyed any verbal filter she had without her knowing it. By glass three, she was sleepy, and four was a total TKO. Tonight, at dinner, she'd had two glasses and out came my favorite Jenny—chatty with no filter. I loved hearing her inane and funny thoughts. I especially loved hearing her thoughts about me. About us. Her perceived inner dialogue was music to my ears.

I looked down at her, tucked into my side, her hands wrapped around the handle of the cart. I had to smile as I watched her. Her cheeks were flushed, and I knew it wasn't just from the wine. She wanted me as much as I wanted her. When I had told her on our first night together we'd be an inferno in the bedroom, I'd had no idea how accurate that statement would be for us. She was everything I could have asked for in a lover— passionate and fierce at times, teasing and sweet at others. As well, she was achingly beautiful in her desire. Together, we fit perfectly, and I adored everything about her—even when she was bossy about cereal.

My mind strayed, thinking about our first time.

We didn't plan it; it simply happened. We spent all weekend together. I took her to return the watch, laughing when she picked out something pretty for herself instead. "Money well spent," I informed her with a kiss. "Much better."

We talked about everything. From our childhoods, schooling, parents, friends, what we wanted from our relationship, even birth control and being safe. We left nothing to chance. I was serious about this girl.

She stayed the night again Saturday. She slept in my arms, and for the moment, I was good with that. Sunday after dinner, she smiled as we finished the dishes and waved her hand toward the door.

"I should go. I have laundry to do and a little work I meant to do this weekend. Until I got, ah, got…"

I moved closer, slipping my fingers through the belt loops on her jeans, tugging her close.

"Sidetracked?" I offered.

"My boyfriend put me on house arrest."

I lowered my head to her neck, pressing kisses to the column of her throat. "I let you go back to your apartment yesterday, Jenny. You came back of your own free will."

She made a sound, a cross between a moan and a whimper. It was low and sexy. She tightened her hands on my shoulders.

"Do you really have to go?" I murmured.

With a sigh, she stepped back. "Yes. We both have things to do. Your shift starts at seven tomorrow morning. I have a meeting I need to be ready for."

She was right, and I knew it. The fact that she knew my schedule made me grin, even as I tamped down my disappointment. I leaned over her shoulder, snagged a spare key off the hook, and pressed it into her hand. "Use this whenever you want, Wren."

"Really?"

"Yes."

I pulled her in, hugged her close, and walked her to her door. "Sleep well, little bird. I'll call you tomorrow, okay?"

She rose up on her toes, and I met her partway, kissing her hard. It took everything in me not to follow her inside her place.

Hours later, I was lying in bed, an arm tucked beneath my head, staring at the ceiling, I couldn't sleep. My once-comfortable bed felt wrong without Jenny in it. Rolling over, I punched my pillow and tried to get comfortable. It was stupid. She had only slept there for two nights, yet my room seemed empty without her. I could smell her on my sheets, which only made me miss her more. Glancing at the clock, I groaned. It was 1:00 a.m., and I knew I wouldn't be falling asleep anytime soon. I was keyed up, and my mind wouldn't shut off.

I heard a noise and rose up on my elbows, listening. Not hearing anything, I began to lie back down when the noise started again. Certain I had heard my apartment door open, I swung my legs over the mattress and flicked on the light. The footfalls were soft and could only belong to one person. My heart raced, and I spoke loudly.

"I have a gun, and the license to use it."

The footfalls came closer. "So I've heard." Jenny's voice sassed. "You bragged earlier how big your gun was, if I remember right."

She appeared at my door, wearing a nightshirt, her hair up in a ponytail. She looked sexy and nervous.

"You should give a guy a warning before breaking in." I smirked. "My gun might have been loaded."

"It's not breaking in if I have a key." She peered around. "Where's this big gun of yours?"

"Come closer, and I'll show you."

She moved forward, and I pulled her between my legs. "What are you doing here, Wren?"

"I couldn't sleep. I couldn't stop thinking about you."

"Funny, I was having the same problem." I ran my hands up the backs of her thighs and cupped her firm ass, my cock growing as I realized she was bare under her shirt. "Thinking of anything in particular?"

"Your big gun."

She was under me in an instant. Our mouths fused together, kissing each other as if we'd been apart for days, not hours. Her hands roamed my back, running over my sides, clutching at my ass after she pushed the sheet down with her legs.

"Oh God, you're naked."

Seconds later, so was she. Skin-to-skin, we discovered each other. She pushed me onto my back as her hot mouth traveled the length of my torso, flicking her tongue on my taut nipples, over my abs, and down my thighs. She explored my muscles, swirling her tongue, tracing them and torturing me with her caresses. She wrapped her hand around my dick, whimpering with pleasure when she realized she needed both of them to go around it fully. She touched and teased, whispering dirty words that cranked me higher, telling me how many times she had fantasized about us, just like this, naked and yearning.

"Reality is so much better." Her breath washed over my skin as she bent and trailed her tongue across the head of my cock. "I want you so fucking bad, Connor. I can't take it anymore."

Then she engulfed me in her mouth.

I shouted, my back arching off the bed as she teased and sucked, nibbled and licked, her hands never in one place for long, her hair brushing my thighs, first on one side, then the other, as her head moved and her ponytail flopped. She did things with her tongue I was certain were illegal in this country—probably every country—but they felt so fucking good, I never wanted her to stop. Wave after wave of pleasure crashed over me, and I pleaded for her to stop.

"I want inside you, Jenny. Now, Wren."

I felt the hum of her laughter around my cock and the movement of her head as she refused. She cupped my balls, her hands stroking and teasing. She slipped her finger lower, rubbing and sending me over the edge.

I fisted my hands in the sheets, shouting, "Jesus, fuck! I'm gonna…"

Her response was to grab my thighs and suck deeper. Our eyes locked as I came. Hot, hard, and wet down her throat. Long spurts as I groaned and bucked; the ecstasy so great, it was almost painful.

Slow and sated, I sank back into the mattress. She crawled up beside me, lying with her head on my chest. For a minute, there was nothing but the sound of my labored breathing and the feel of her gentle touch as she ran her fingers over my skin.

"Proud of yourself?"

"Pretty much."

"You should be." I pulled her up, kissing her hard. I tasted myself, sharp and salty on her tongue. I explored her mouth fully, not stopping until we were breathless.

I grinned, moving fast and flipping her, hovering over her with a wolfish smile. "My turn."

She was so sweet under my tongue. So receptive. I discovered the soft spot behind her ear that made her whimper. Her nipples peaked and hardened as I flattened my tongue, then nipped and licked at them. She was ticklish on the left side, arching up as I ghosted my fingers along her rib cage. I kissed the inside of her elbows, her wrists, teased her neck and shoulders. I discovered all her dips and curves, first with my fingers, then with my mouth. Sliding down the bed, I started at her feet, kissing the soft skin of her delicate arches, up her ankle, twirling my tongue on the sensitive indent behind her knee. Her head thrashed, her hands fisting the sheets as I slid my tongue up her thighs, taking my time, drawing out the moment until I covered her with my mouth, tasting her for the first time.

She bowed off the bed, calling my name and a litany of religious figures. Her legs encased my head, her hand buried in my hair as she cried out. I lapped and flicked my tongue, stroked and pressed. I slid one finger into her, then another, adding my thumb to the mix as I drove her to release.

Her muscles fluttered, tightening around my fingers as she came, beautiful and free in her orgasm. I shifted, pulling her up my thighs and driving into her before she had come down. I lifted her, wrapping her in my arms as I thrust, groaning at her wetness and heat, how tight, how right, she felt around me. She draped her arms over my shoulders and lifted her face, her eyes wide and dark.

"Connor, please," she pleaded.

I covered her mouth, kissing her hard, and kept moving. I grabbed her ass, slamming her down on me, grunting my approval as she clung tight.

We moved as if we'd been lovers for years. I knew her body, and I knew what she needed. She took me inside, bringing me home, making me hers as much as I made her mine.

The beginnings of another orgasm started. My balls tightened; my spine snapped with nerves.

"Come for me, Wren. Let me feel you," I begged, needing and wanting that desperately.

Her head fell back, a soundless "O" forming on her lips. Her pussy clenched around me like a fist, sending me into my own release. I moved faster, groaning her name.

Until she was spent.

Until I was done.

Carefully, I laid her on the pillow, withdrawing from her. I relaxed beside her, smiling as she curled into my chest.

The room smelled like us. Sex, her, and me. We were sticky, sweating, and perfect.

I pressed a kiss to her head. "Told you. Fucking inferno."

She stretched, her toes dragging along my calf. "I've never felt anything like that until tonight."

"It's only going to get better."

"I may combust."

"I'll put out the flames, baby."

She giggled, running her finger between us where we were damp and hot. "Your fire extinguisher does double duty. Starts and puts out flames."

I laughed at her silly remark.

We were quiet for a while, and she looked up at me, her gaze filled with tenderness. "I don't want to go home."

I tucked her closer. "This is home, Wren. Stay."

"Okay," she breathed out. "We should get some sleep."

I glanced at the clock. "It's past three. Neither of us will get much tonight." I tilted up her chin. "You're gonna be tired tomorrow."

She slid her arms around my neck.

"I'm good with that because it's so worth it."

Strangely enough, I agreed wholeheartedly.

I shook my head to clear it, the mere memory of that night making my cock swell. I was already having trouble focusing. We needed to get home—I needed Jenny alone.

We turned the corner into the produce section, and I had to stifle a groan. She ate way too many vegetables—never mind the fruit. She was constantly filling my plate with them, and damn it, I ate them because she asked me to with those soft eyes and sweet voice. I was so whipped.

I sighed and grabbed a bag. I didn't even ask before I went over to the apples and started filling it up. They were always on the list—along with bananas, grapes, and, whenever she could get it, watermelon. Jenny loved watermelon. She said I picked good ones, so I was in charge of choosing one. I liked impressing her with my melon-tapping skills to find the perfect one. Normally, I made a great show of picking them for her; I loved making her laugh. But tonight, I just wanted to finish the damn shopping and go home. I wanted her. Alone. It wasn't melons I wanted to tap.

Well, maybe *her* melons.

Plus, I had some sugar sprinkling to do.

My hands were full as I turned and stopped dead. Jenny was across the aisle, her stance rigid, her expression appalled, and in front of her—John. I could tell from her body language she wasn't scared, but she wasn't happy to see him. I hurried over, stopping when I reached her side. He was talking, gesturing, telling her his sob story. He barely glanced my way as I dropped the bags in the cart and wrapped my arm around her waist in silent support. John was so busy blabbering, he didn't even notice the gesture.

"It's been awful, babe. It's as though my luck has changed. Nothing has been right since you walked out on me."

Babe? Walked out on him? He was fucking someone else when she walked in. *What the hell?*

Beside me, Jenny stiffened, and I tightened my arm, wondering if I was going to have to shut him up soon. I wasn't going to let him upset her.

Jenny stepped forward, my arm slipping off her waist. She reached out her hand, and I grabbed it with mine, holding it firmly.

"I didn't *walk out,* John. You threw me out. Forcefully."

He looked at our entwined hands and blinked, not even acknowledging her remark. Then he carried on as though nothing had happened.

"It started with some weird shit with my car. It got towed that day —*towed,* J, if you can believe it. I mean, who would tow a fine piece of machinery like that?"

I had to swallow my snort. He glanced at me, frowning, before he turned his attention back to Jenny.

"It hasn't been right since. I've spent thousands on it, J. It's as if there is a curse on it. It smells. I can't even describe it, like something died in it. It's been cleaned, detailed, and steamed… Nothing has worked. I think I need to replace the engine." He looked at her in all seriousness. "You know how much I love that car."

I choked back a laugh. It wasn't the engine that needed replacing. He needed to look behind a speaker or under the glove box—for starters.

Was he seriously talking to Jenny about his stupid car? The one he prized more highly than her? And why the fuck was he calling her "J"? Did he not know her name? Was *Jenny* too hard to say? I eyed the watermelon in the cart. I had an idea where I wanted to put it right now. He was certainly a big enough asshole to handle it. A small chuckle broke through my lips before I could stop it.

He looked at me, his expression curious. "Do I know you?"

I shook my head. "Nope."

He frowned and looked back at Jenny, who was gazing at him impassively. "Tami quit *and* dumped me."

Jenny's voice was dry. "What a shame."

"Did she buy you a watch?" I mumbled.

Jenny giggled, her hand tightening on mine. I squeezed back.

John looked at me, confused. "No."

I shrugged. "Too bad. A good source tells me that's the latest craze."

"Are you sure I don't know you?"

"Nope. Never formally met you."

He glared at me and returned his gaze to Jenny. "I think I've been cursed."

"Oh?"

"It never ends, J. I've gotten tickets for parking, speeding, littering, talking on my cell phone in the car—it's as if the cops are watching me all the time. Every time I do something remotely illegal, they're there. Just the other day, three of us stepped off the curb too soon, and I was the only one nabbed and given a ticket for jaywalking!"

It was all I could do not to laugh out loud at his morose expression. He made it all too easy. I could feel myself shake with repressed laughter, and I bit down on my lip so I didn't start guffawing.

Jenny's head snapped in my direction.

Oh shit. I was so busted.

I moved and wrapped my arm around her tightly. I needed to make sure she couldn't use her legs.

I knew how dangerous she was with her legs.

JENNY

As soon as John started listing off his problems, I knew. Beside me, Connor was almost vibrating in silent laughter. He was in so much shit.

"J!"

I looked back at John. "What?"

"Did you hear me?"

"I'm sorry you're having a rough time, John. But it has nothing to do with me."

Inside, I was fuming. It had everything to do with my current boyfriend, who had moved in closer, holding me tight against his side.

"I think you need to give me another chance."

I gaped at John as Connor stood taller and pulled me even closer.

"Excuse me?" he hissed.

John frowned at Connor. "Wait. I do know you. You're the neighbor guy. I saw you in the hall a couple times." He glanced down at the cart. "Shopping together?"

"I'm not the *neighbor* guy, John. I'm the boyfriend guy. Jenny's boyfriend. We're shopping together because we *are* together," Connor snapped in response.

John looked between us. "You have another boyfriend already? It didn't take long for you to move on."

I laughed. "That's rich coming from someone I found fucking his assistant. I'd say you moved on first."

"Well, it's not as if you'd been offering it up much, babe. I had needs, Jenny. You no longer met them."

"So, it was my fault?"

"Well, yeah. I'm willing to take you back, though. Give you a chance to make it up to me." He lifted his hand as if he expected me to grab on to it like a lifeline. Did he seriously not see Connor right there beside me? Or hear what he had just said? Could he not see how securely I was nestled into his body? I pulled back, not wanting John to touch me.

Before I could say or do anything else, I found myself tucked behind Connor. The cart was pushed out of the way as he stepped in John's direction. Connor's voice was almost eerily calm, and I realized I was hearing Officer Michaels speaking. "You don't touch her. *Ever.*" He breathed through clenched teeth. "Now listen, you scumbag. First off, her name is Jenny, not *J*, and not fucking *babe*. Not to you. Show the lady some much due respect. She is *not* interested in your problems, and she certainly has no interest in taking you back. I think you need to be clear on something in that tiny pea brain of yours. She is not at fault for what happened. You made the choice to cheat, not her. This was all on you." His hand settled on his hip, pulling his jacket away from his waist. I saw John's eyes look down before they snapped back to Connor's face. John's cheeks reddened, and he stepped back.

"*We* are a couple now, John, and I have no intention of letting her go. Unlike you, I'm not stupid. I look after the people I love—you understand me?"

John nodded, but he didn't say a word.

"I suggest you apologize to my lady and leave. Don't contact her, and don't come near her. I'd *hate* to see your bad luck get worse."

John took another step back, glancing between us. I had no idea what he had seen that made him so uncomfortable, but he looked downright ill. "Yeah, so I'm gonna go. Sorry to have bothered you. Um, have a good night and, ah, yeah. The whole Tami thing? My bad. Bye."

He turned and hurried away.

Connor stood watching him before he turned around. "You okay, Wren?"

"What just happened?"

Connor shrugged. "I said my piece. I wasn't going to listen to him degrade you in front of me."

I shook my head. "I get that, Connor. Why did he look so frightened?"

He shrugged and grabbed the cart. "He doesn't like dealing with someone his own size."

I narrowed my eyes and pulled his jacket away. My mouth dropped open. "Connor!"

"What?"

"Don't you *what* me. You know perfectly well. John saw your badge and your gun clip."

"It's empty, Jenny. My gun is at work, in my locker. I had left the clip on so I remembered to clean it tonight. It got some sticky donut stuff on it." He grinned, no doubt hoping I would laugh with him.

"He didn't know that. You only let him see you were wearing one. He thought you were threatening him."

"I can't help what he thought—or thought he saw. He was being an asshole and disrespecting you!"

"What if he makes trouble?"

"I have lots of witnesses that saw me lock my gun away. I always carry my badge. I forgot I was wearing my clip. There was no threat. I did nothing wrong."

"You forgot? You did *nothing* wrong? At all? Nothing in that conversation sounded familiar to you?"

He had the grace to look slightly ashamed, but he shook his head. "No."

228

"You always flash your badge at ex-boyfriends? As a warning?"

"No, I only do that for you."

I huffed out a sigh and shook my head.

"We are not done with this, Officer Michaels." I grabbed the cart and started to walk away. Connor followed me to the register, shifting uncomfortably behind me as we waited in line.

"He fucking ignored me, Jenny. He was trying to get you back, and I was *standing right there!*"

"So, he isn't very observant. He's always been an idiot, and I think it's worse now. You didn't have to scare him."

"All I did was send him a subtle message," he muttered.

I snorted. "Subtle? Dragging him out back and beating him with your nightstick would have been more subtle."

He leaned forward, his lips ghosting my ear. "The only person I want to take out my 'nightstick' for is you, Jenny."

"Stop it," I said with a hiss. "I'm mad at you."

"Damn it! I should have taken a swing at him. It would've served him right."

"Why would you say that?" I gasped.

"Fucker just cost me some hot sexing with my girlfriend," he grumbled, his soft lips pouting the way I liked. Every time he pouted like that, I wanted to kiss him—hard.

He looked at me, winked, and deliberately pouted, lowering his face in a silent invitation. I felt a smile tug on my lips, knowing I had spoken out loud again as well as loving the pleading, hopeful expression on his face. Leaning up, I kissed his pouty lips, unable to refuse him.

"Jaywalking, Connor? Your fellow officers have nothing better to do than watch for him to jaywalk?"

He chuckled. "He makes it too easy on them." He pressed his lips to mine. "Don't be angry. I hate it when you're angry."

I glared at him. I was still pissed, although somewhat amused. I was also turned on by the way he stood up for me. I still wanted to get him home and naked. Maybe even punish him a little.

A delighted grin broke out on his face. He leaned forward, dragging my face to his.

"Go with it, Jenny." He kissed me hard. "I'll take it."

Internal dialogue. Damn it.

CHAPTER 5

CONNOR

"Oh God ... *Baby*... Please..." I begged, pulling on the handcuffs restraining me. I lifted my head, desperately trying to figure out where Jenny had gone. I couldn't see because the little vixen had slipped a mask over my eyes, plunging me into darkness, then she disappeared.

Where was she?

Jenny's voice was far away. "Please what, Connor?"

I loved it when she let her slightly kinky side come out to play. When we got back to my apartment, she'd tackled me on the bed, kissing and licking her way up and down my chest, before she surprised me by snapping on the handcuffs and the mask.

Punishment time.

I was good with that. Really good.

Except, I was lying on my bed, naked and aching for her, and she was gone. I yanked on the cuffs again, raising my head. "Jenny, come back."

"Maybe I should just leave you here, all tied up, nowhere to go..." Her voice teased from the foot of the bed. "I could go home and have a good night's sleep."

Fuck no. I didn't deserve that kind of suffering. That would be a real punishment, and I much preferred Jenny's form of torture. It was far more satisfying.

I lowered my voice to the deep tone I knew she loved. "Come back, baby. Let me show you how sorry I am."

Her hand drifted over my foot, caressing and stroking, rubbing my ankle in a long, slow drag. I blinked under the mask as I realized she had just tied it to the foot of the bed. That was a new move. She repeated the gesture with the other foot, and I heard a long, contented sigh escape her throat.

I was truly at her mercy, and I swallowed in anticipation.

"See something you like, Jenny?" I murmured huskily, playfully arching my hips.

"Isn't that a lovely sight," she whispered. Her hands were once again on my legs, slowly drifting up and down, each time edging closer to where I wanted them the most. I groaned in eagerness then frustration as her hands disappeared.

The mattress dipped, and she straddled my waist. I could feel her warm skin sliding against my abdomen, and then her mouth covered mine. I strained my head up, my tongue searching and sucking as we kissed, both of us moaning. She pulled away, leaning back, her hands now splayed across my chest. "You were very...*naughty* in the store, weren't you, Connor?"

"Yes. Give me your mouth back, Jenny. Please, baby."

She ignored me.

"All the dirty talk that you know turns me on—is that what you want-ed?" She pressed down against me, her center hot and wet against my skin. "Can you feel what you do to me?"

"*God, yes.*"

I felt a soft flicker dance across my chest, and I groaned. I knew that feeling. Jenny had a feather in her hand, and if she had a feather, that meant she had the jar of honey dust as well. It was her favorite torture toy. She loved sprinkling it on my chest and stomach, driving me mad with the feather before licking it off.

The licking was my favorite part.

She moved off me, and sure enough, I felt the downy sensation of the sweet dust settle across my chest, followed by the trailing of the feather as it ghosted over my skin. But it didn't stop at my chest. Soon, I was nothing but a blaze of sensation as Jenny's honey dust settled over my entire body. Her feather swirled and teased, moving and touching every inch of my skin, only to slip to a new place, drawing yet another groan from my lips. Her feather trailed over my torso, teasing my taut nipples, up and down my legs and arms, soft and light as it went, leaving me panting, aching, and wanting. Like a whisper of air, I felt the sensation float over my throbbing cock, and I hissed and arched into the sensation. I wanted more. I wanted her mouth on me.

My voice was low and rough as I pleaded with her. "Jenny, *please…*"

Seconds later, I was lost in a fog of need as her tongue met my skin. Swirling and dancing, it drifted and tormented, her mouth licked and stroked, nipped and teased. I bent and twisted, wanting free of my cuffs, begging her for release. When I felt her move between my legs, my voice was wild as my arms and legs pulled on my restraints.

"Jenny… Please, baby, put your mouth on me. *Now,* God, please…"

Her low laughter caused a breath of warm air to drift across my cock, and finally, I felt her tongue run a soft trail over my length before the heat of her lips closed around me. I growled and shuddered as I arched into her wet mouth. The way her tongue swirled around the head had me bowing upward, desperate to be closer to the source of pleasure as I moaned and writhed. Her hands cupped and stroked my balls as she sucked and licked, humming around my cock as I begged and groaned, thrusting and yearning.

I wanted more. I always wanted more of her.

"I need to be inside you."

One last long lick and she moved up, straddling me again. Her wet, slick heat engulfed me, and I cursed as she started to move. She pushed and pulled, rocking into me, her hands braced on my thighs as she whimpered and undulated above me. "You feel so good, Connor. So good. I love how you feel inside me."

I continued with my pleading. "Let me see you—now, Wren. *Now.*"

Light poured into my eyes, and I blinked and focused on the beautiful woman riding me. Her face was a study of emotions, and I knew she was close. Her eyes were wide and wild as she looked down at me, her entire frame trembling with passion. She was so stunning in her need, and I knew what she wanted, what *we* wanted.

"Unlock me, baby."

Jenny leaned back, first releasing my feet before she moved forward and snapped open the cuffs restraining my wrists. I watched her body curve as she moved, my desire only raging higher as I glimpsed her fluidness. I sat up, drawing up my legs and enclosing her in my arms, both of us gasping at the new angle. This was her favorite position—me buried deep inside her, my arms holding her close, anchoring her to me as she fell apart. She loved the intimacy, and I loved sensing her body shudder and clench, feeling her orgasm ripple through her. My mouth covered hers, sharing deep, bruising, unrestrained kisses before she stilled, gasping my name. I buried my head in her neck, thrusting into her heat until I was spent, groaning in ecstasy.

The room was quiet except for our heavy breathing. Gradually, I leaned back, taking her with me, keeping her pressed into my chest. Reaching down, I gently helped her straighten her legs, drawing the blanket around us. For a while we were silent, just relaxing into each other. When she shifted, I rolled us onto our sides, keeping her close. I didn't want to let her go. Her eyes were wide and soft as she gazed at me, and I leaned down to kiss her. They were slow, indulgent, sweet kisses this time. Teasing and gentle, my lips lingered on hers.

She sighed and snuggled into my chest. "Learned your lesson?"

I chuckled. "Which one, Wren? Not to tease you in the grocery store or not to flash my badge?"

"Both?"

"I can't promise not to tease you, especially when you're so sexy and adorable." I sighed. "I'll try to hold off on the flashing, though."

"Get them to back off harassing John. It's over and done."

I pulled her closer, my voice betraying my sudden nervousness. "Jenny…"

She frowned and pushed herself up on her elbow. "What is it?"

"Tonight, did you ever consider—?" I couldn't even finish my thought.

Her eyes widened, and she cupped my face, holding it tight. "Why would you ask that?"

I shrugged. "John could give you things I can't, Jenny. He is a successful businessman. I'm just an underpaid cop and about to be an even poorer one once I go back to school. I can't offer you the same things he could."

She exhaled. "All he gave me was a lot of lonely nights and the promise of being second best—if that. I don't care about material stuff. I never did. So, the answer is no. Never. John is my past and not even a good part of it. You're my present…and my future."

"Jenny?"

She smiled, a heartwarming, lovely expression on her face. "I love you, Connor Michaels."

My heart hammered in my chest. I had told her how much I loved her many times over the past weeks we'd been together, but she had never said the words back to me. Every caring gesture, every sweet smile, each time we made love, I felt it, but I knew she wasn't ready to say it yet. I had been waiting for the moment since our first day together.

My breath caught in my throat.

"Don't ever doubt what you mean to me. I knew you were going to change my life, I just didn't know how much. You're my everything."

I pulled her to me and kissed her until we were breathless. "I adore you, Jenny Reynolds. I love how you ramble when you're tipsy and make me want you all the time." I teased her, but my voice was serious when I continued. "I love how you take care of me. I love you so much. And it just keeps getting stronger." My fingers danced over her soft skin. "I want to wake up beside you in the morning and fall asleep beside you every night. Promise me I can."

Her eyes glowed. "Every day, Connor."

"Then, Jenny Wren, I have all I could ever want."

~

CONNOR

"Does my hand feel good? Is it what you want?" Jenny's voice hummed low in my ear.

I groaned. "No, baby, I want your mouth."

"All you can have is my hand. Use it, Connor."

I growled as the movement picked up. I pressed my head against the pillows, the soft plush rising around my face. My hips arched off the bed.

"Harder, Connor. More," Jenny's voice rasped.

My hand sped up. "Are you close, Wren? Come with me," I begged.

"Now," she whimpered. "Now."

I shouted out her name, panting and heaving, coming and coming before I was satisfied. My hand slowed and finally stopped as my body became boneless.

Jenny's voice was warm and distant in my ear. "Connor? You with me, baby?"

I sighed as I found the phone. "Fuck, Jenny. That was amazing." I blew out a big breath. "One hell of a wake-up call."

She laughed softly. "I aim to please."

I chuckled. "Please you did. How much have you had to drink tonight?"

"One glass of wine."

I laughed. "More than one, I think. You wouldn't be making dirty-talking, let's-have-phone-sex calls on one glass of wine, my girl. Not that I'm complaining."

Her voice lowered as if she were telling me a secret. "Okay—maybe two or three. Got you going, though."

I looked down at the mess I had made. "You certainly did, and like I said, I'm not complaining—although I would rather have you here."

The tone of her voice suddenly turned serious. "I miss you, Connor."

I sat up in bed. "I miss you. But it's only another seven days, and you're home."

She sighed. "This trip came at a bad time."

She and Jackey were at a convention, then Jenny was going to see another friend that lived in the area. As pharmaceutical reps, they'd had the trip planned long before Jenny and I got together. As much as I missed her, I wanted her to have a good time and enjoy herself. She worked hard and deserved it. I knew she was looking forward to spending a few days with her old friend.

"It's fine. While I would've rather spent it with you, school is whipping my ass and I'm looking forward to the weekend, even though I'll be hitting the books the whole time."

"Is that what you're gonna do all weekend? Study?"

"Well, I've got someone looking at my car tomorrow. And I have a bunch of errands to do, and then, yeah, I'll be studying."

"Connor—"

"Jenny, we discussed this. I have to sell it. I have to get rid of as much overhead as possible for the time being."

"You love that car."

"I'll buy another when I'm done school and working again." Wanting to make her smile, I tried teasing her. "You'll have to be my chauffeur for a while. Be at my beck and call."

Her voice lightened. "I'll happily be your beck-and-call girl."

"Excellent."

I walked back into the apartment building, frowning. The offer the guy made on my car was low. Way lower than I had hoped. It would barely cover what I still owed on the loan. Maybe Jenny was right and I should keep it, except I would still have to insure it and pay for gas. I felt like banging my head against the wall.

While it was the right move for me, giving up a full-time job and going back to school was a scary and expensive proposition. Even more than I had realized, once I found out I didn't qualify for some of the financial aid I'd thought I could get. I had thought I would work part-time, but I quickly realized that was not going to happen. I had to devote myself fully to the endeavor, which meant I had to make some changes I hadn't planned. Jenny had been so supportive, even offering to loan me money, but I couldn't take her offer. I had to do this on my own.

I stepped into the elevator and pressed the button for my floor, hating the thought that kept floating through my head. A last resort, but one that, in the end, might be the only choice I had.

Move.

I could get a less expensive apartment and save money that way. If I sold my car and found a cheaper apartment, things would be tight, but manageable. I would have to stick to a strict budget, which didn't bother me. What bothered me was the thought of not living next door to Jenny, but I could still see her.

Just not as easily.

"Hold the door!" a familiar voice shouted.

I grabbed the door and was almost run down by a fast-moving pile of cardboard that barely missed slamming into me. "Hey!" I laughed when I saw Luc's face behind the pile.

"Shit. Sorry, Connor."

"What's going on, man?"

"I'm moving."

"Since when?"

He grinned behind the boxes. "Since I got a great job offer in Vancouver. The only drawback is I gotta be there this week."

"Well, congrats. That's great for you."

"It was all great until about an hour ago. I had a sublet for the apartment all set up, but it fell through. Joe's girlfriend dumped him, and he decided he didn't need a two-bedroom place. He wants a smaller one. So, I have to figure that out. I doubt I can find another person to sublet on such short notice. I may end up paying rent in two places for a while. But what am I gonna do?"

I nodded in sympathy as the doors opened. Luc walked ahead of me, down the hall, balancing his boxes. I stopped at my door, and it hit me. I hurried down the hall after him.

"Hey, Luc... Can I see your place?"

CHAPTER 6

CONNOR

An hour later, I looked down at the papers in my hand. I checked and rechecked the math. This could work.

Luc's rent was only three hundred more than I paid now. If Jenny and I moved in to the larger two-bedroom together, we'd both save money every month, since she paid the same rent as I currently did. The new place overlooked the back garden, which she had mentioned before she liked, had two good-sized bedrooms, so we could use one as an office, and overall, it was bigger and more open. I also knew Jenny would love the kitchen. Luc had even had the place painted not long ago, so it was in great shape. We both liked the building and the people we knew in it, so we could stay there and have more space. With what I saved in rent and shared utilities, I could even keep my car. I wouldn't have to move, and we'd be together. The guy who had looked at Luc's place agreed to come and look at mine, and if he liked it, he could take over the lease. I knew there was a waiting list for one-bedroom places in the building, so management should easily find someone for Jenny's apartment.

We were almost living together anyway. We rarely spent a night apart, and Jenny was hardly ever at her place. I was sure she'd stuffed most of her clothes into my closet and drawers. Her favorite reading chair even had a spot in my living room.

Moving us would be simple. It was only down the hall. Luc planned to be gone in forty-eight hours. With the help of my friends, I could move all my stuff over in short order—probably Jenny's as well. I could have it all done by the time she got home. She wouldn't even have to think about it.

She'd be thrilled. We'd be together, and all she'd have to do would be to add her own touches and settle in. With me.

She'd love it.

I only had to convince her of that fact.

Quickly.

I dialed her number, my hand shaking.

Was she ready for what I was about to propose? Would she want to live with me, officially? I knew I wanted to be with her all the time. But I also knew I had been one step ahead of her our whole relationship. I wanted this…more than anything.

She answered immediately, and I could hear the background noise. "Hey, Wren."

"Connor? Are you okay?"

"Can you find a quiet corner and we could do a video chat?"

"Give me five minutes."

"Okay."

I hung up and paced the room.

~

I looked at her shocked face on my screen.

"You want us to move in together?"

"Yes."

"Take over Luc's lease?"

"Yes."

"And you want me to decide—right now."

My fingers clutched my hair "I know it's fast, Jenny, but it works so well. It all lines up."

"So, we'd save money, you wouldn't have to sell your car, and you'd stay in the building?"

"Yes." I nodded emphatically.

She'd been shocked when I'd told her my original plan once I knew I couldn't get as much for my car as I'd hoped. I could see she disliked the idea of me moving as much as I did. I also knew she was surprised at the solution I offered. I hated doing it over the phone, but Luc had to have an answer soon. If I told him no, he needed to find someone else.

I didn't want to tell him no.

"So, this is a convenience, Connor? We'd be roomies?"

I gaped at her.

That was what she thought?

Fuck's sake, of course she did. I'd called her up unexpectedly, told her I had a great apartment we could share, then expounded on the fact of all the money we would save. I made it sound like a budgeting thing. Not one word about the fact that even if I still had to sell my car and take a part-time job for it to happen, I wanted to live with her.

I sat back and smiled into the screen.

"Jenny Wren, listen to me. Listen well. Do you know why moving in together would be such a great thing?"

"You can keep your car?"

"No. I don't care about the damned car. It's so great because it means I don't have to leave you. The thought of being far away from you was killing me." I ran a hand over my face, scrubbing my cheeks roughly. "It means that every morning I can wake up with you. The last thing I will see every night is your sweet face. When I get home, I know you'll be there. I want that. More than anything."

"Really?"

"Yes. And while getting to keep my car is a bonus, getting you—living with you, is my dream." I paused and closed my eyes for a moment. "I love you, Jenny. And I want this for us."

"It's so fast."

I sighed. "I know, and if you don't want it—one hundred percent want it—I understand. I still love you, and I hope one day I get my dream."

"Yeah?"

"Yeah. I'll wait, Jenny. I'll wait for you." Then I winked at her, so she knew it was okay. I was asking too much of her, expecting an answer immediately to a decision so large. "You'll just have to get used to being at my beck and call." I chuckled. "Or the bus."

I could see the tears on her cheeks. I wanted to kiss them away.

"Connor?"

I traced the screen with my finger, wishing she were in front of me for real. "Yeah, Wren?"

"I want it, too."

≈

I paced around, constantly glancing at my watch. Jenny would be home soon.

Our home.

I had done it. I took over Luc's lease, Joe had taken my apartment, and, within a day, management had a new tenant for Jenny's place, one who would move in next week. With the help of my fellow officers and some firefighter friends, we had moved both apartments in the span of two evenings. Nothing was packed; we simply carried everything from the old apartments into the new one, in one long conga line. I put the furniture in the right rooms but knew Jenny would rearrange things once she arrived. She would make the space a home for us. For now, our dishes, pans, and linens were mingled together in the various cupboards, and I grinned every time I opened a door and saw them.

Jenny had no idea the entire move had happened. She thought we would be doing it when she got home, and I kept that information to myself. However, she wouldn't have to do a thing except settle into her new place—our new place.

I had dinner in the oven and plenty of bottles of wine in the refrigerator. I fully expected lots of tipsy comments and hot sex as we celebrated and broke in every new room this weekend. Sex with Jenny was always hot.

I was looking forward to that.

My phone buzzed.

Downstairs the screen read.

I smiled at Jackey's message. She was in on the surprise.

The biggest grin split my face as I went down the hall to meet Jenny at the elevator. I had missed her.

And I was excited she was home.

God, her mouth was back on mine, her hands in my hair, tugging and pulling me close as I kissed her deeply. I had missed her so damn much. Missed *us*. With a groan, I crushed her to my chest, kissing her with everything I had in me. When I finally released her, it was only to bury my face into her neck and breathe her in.

"I missed you so much," she whispered.

"I missed you too, Wren."

She giggled, the sweet sound filling my ears. "You must have. You barely let the elevator doors open."

I grinned. I hadn't. As soon as I saw her, I had reached in and pulled her into my arms. Two weeks was two weeks too long without her.

My mouth covered hers again, my tongue greedy for more of her taste. I lifted her, groaning as she wrapped her legs around my waist. I barely had enough sense left to grab her suitcase with one hand while I held her tightly against me with the other. I stumbled down the hall, refusing to move my mouth off hers or let her down.

She pulled back, gasping for breath. "Connor! You missed your door!"

I laughed and kissed her again. I kept walking until I stopped in front of the door at the end of the hall. I set her back on her feet, pushed open the door, then with a huge grin, scooped her up bridal style, chuckling at her gasp.

"What are you doing?"

I kissed her once more and carried her inside. "This is the door now, Jenny. *Our* door."

~

JENNY

I ran my fingers ran over the shiny surface of the stainless-steel appliances in the kitchen. They were so pretty—such nice appliances in this apartment.

I giggled. My new apartment. I giggled again.

The apartment I now lived in with Connor.

Connor.

My Connor.

He was so pretty, too. So excited as he had handed me a large glass of wine and shown me around the new place, pointing out all the things he knew I would like. He surprised me by having all our things already moved in, living together in cupboards and on shelves. Just waiting for me to come back and join them.

Join him.

I took another sip of wine, my hand on the cool surface of the granite. I liked these counters. Connor liked them too.

I bet he'd like to fuck me on these counters.

I'd like that.

I should go find him and ask.

His arms encircled my waist. His warm breath drifted over my cheek as his lips pulled at my lobe. "No need to look, Wren. I'm right here." His warm tongue ran up my neck. "I'll fuck you anywhere, anytime. Name the place, and we are so on."

I groaned as my head fell back on his shoulder.

How much had I had to drink?

He chuckled. "Enough." He wrapped his hand around my hair, pulling back my head. "My favorite Jenny is here." Then his mouth covered mine possessively, his hands sliding under my shirt, up and over my breasts, fondling and pinching my nipples that were hard and aching for his touch. I pressed myself back against him, groaning as his mouth left mine and trailed over to my ear, licking and nipping at the sensitive skin behind it. I could feel him hard and straining against me, and I moaned with desire.

God, I wanted him. Now. On the counter, the floor, against the fridge, and anywhere else we could find in the room.

He spun me around. "That'll do for starters," he growled in my ear.

I grinned against his lips.

He knew exactly how to get me to open up, in more ways than one.

His hand found the zipper on my jeans. "Damn right, I do. Open for me. Show me how well I know you."

I whimpered. I wanted him. I wanted him buried inside me. Oh God, I was aching for him.

"I'll ease the ache, baby. Promise."

My shirt disappeared, my jeans pulled down and discarded. A few flicks of his wrists and I was bare for him—throbbing and wet, wanting him. His mouth was possessive and hot as his tongue twisted with mine, his bare chest warm against my body. I gripped his shoulders as he lifted me up onto the edge of the countertop, opening my legs, and in one quick, deep thrust, plunged into me. He started moving, his pace fast, hips swiveling as he pounded me. His arms were like a vise holding me, his head dropping to my shoulder as he panted and whispered in my ear.

Fuck...baby...yes...Jenny...mine...missed you... Fuck...there...like that...yes... your legs...up...tighter, Jenny... Fuck!

I wrapped my legs higher, clinging tightly as I shuddered and shattered around him, my release burning and tearing through me. I gasped his name as he stilled, his entire body locking down, and he gripped me hard, murmuring my name, his voice tender and loving.

We stayed locked together as we gradually returned to reality. I stroked the hair on the back of his head as he nuzzled the damp skin on my neck, his hands gentle and soft. Slowly, he pulled back, his warm blue eyes blinking at me. "Round one." He grinned.

I cupped his cheek, my fingers tracing the rough stubble on his chin. "Planning round two in here, Connor?"

He leaned forward, his lips brushing mine. "We have an entire apartment to break in. Lots of rounds to go."

"Our apartment. Ours," I murmured against his lips.

He smiled. The smile he used only for me. One of love and warmth.

"Ours. Welcome home, Jenny."

CHAPTER 7

CONNOR

Jenny's grip on my hand was tight, her nervousness showing through. I squeezed her palm. "Relax, Wren. It's gonna be fine."

She turned her head, meeting my gaze. "What if they don't like me?"

I laughed. "How could they not like you? You've spoken with my mother a hundred times, spent hours on the phone with my sister, and even got my dad emailing you on a regular basis. They already love you."

"That's social and fun. This is me in their home, the woman sleeping with their son."

I frowned. "We live together, Jenny. In a committed relationship. We're not just fucking around. They know that and are thrilled. They are going to love you even harder in person."

"What if I'm not what they expect in real life? I mean, I know I'm entertaining and all, but…" She trailed off.

"You just be you. Jenny. They'll love you even more."

The plane taxied to its stop by the terminal. Jenny peeked out the window at the small airport. "Wow."

I chuckled. "I told you this was going to be a culture shock."

My parents lived in a small town in New Brunswick. We had moved there from Ontario when I was fifteen and my sister fourteen. She loved it —I was restless. It was a good place to spend my teens, mostly free from crime and trouble. As soon as I could, though, I returned to Toronto—

only to discover I didn't like big-city living either, which was how I ended up in the smaller town of Grimsby. It was a good compromise between the two environments, and my best decision ever—it led me to Jenny.

I was finally able to find the time to bring her home to meet my parents and sister. I had never once brought a girl home—even in my teens. They knew I was serious about Jenny. They had known it the first time I mentioned her name, and when we finally got together, they had been thrilled for me. They even supported our living together, although I knew they were more old-fashioned and would prefer us getting married.

I was working on that plan, and this was step one.

I waited until most of the passengers disembarked, then stood and grabbed our bags from the overhead bin. I held out my hand. "Ready?"

She slipped her hand into mine. "Yes."

We walked down the steps, Jenny still in culture shock. "I had no idea planes just unloaded people on the tarmac."

I chuckled. "The terminal is too small for big planes, and there are no gates per se. Just one going in and one going out."

I could see my parents and my sister Carly, waiting, excited and anxious. "Brace yourself," I warned Jenny. "The hugs are about to start."

"Duly noted," she said.

~

I was right, and they adored her. I sat in the front seat with my dad on the drive back from the airport, and Jenny was sandwiched in the back between my mom and my sister, who talked her ear off.

It was the same when we got to the house. They monopolized her. Pictures, stories, and chatting went on all day. I practically had to drag her upstairs to bed to get her alone.

She collapsed on the bed, laughing. "I love your family."

I settled beside her, laying my head on her chest. She ran her fingers through my hair in long, tender strokes. "They love you very much, you know," she whispered.

"I know. Judging from the number of pictures and embarrassing stories, they love me a great deal," I grumped, even though I wasn't at all angry—or surprised.

"I want that," she said quietly.

I lifted my head, meeting her eyes. "Want what, Jenny Wren?"

"Books full of pictures. Memories to share. Stores to tell. Growing up with divorced parents who never really wanted you, I had none of that. I have a small box of pictures my dad had, but my mom was always too busy to bother with stuff like that."

I heard her hurt. Saw the pain in her eyes. I hated knowing how lonely and insecure she had been growing up. I vowed she would never feel that way again in her lifetime. I cupped the back of her neck, bringing her mouth to mine. "You'll have it—all of it. We're going to build a great life together. I promise."

She sighed, her breath washing over me. I kissed her, slanting my mouth over hers and sliding my tongue into her sweet mouth. I kissed her until she forgot her sadness. Forgot where we were, except that I was there with her. I pulled her under me, pressing her into the mattress, covering her with my body, and keeping her in that moment with me.

She pulled away, her cheeks flushed, her mouth swollen. "Do you plan on having sex with me in your parents' house?" she whisper-yelled.

"As often as I can," I responded. "Every story they tell, every picture they show, I'm keeping track. This is me getting even."

She blinked. Then grinned. "Just asking."

I waggled my eyebrows. "Do you know how often I fantasized about having a girl in my bedroom? You have a lot to live up to."

She slid her hand between us, cupping my erection. "I think I'm up for the challenge."

"I'm counting on it."

The weekend went too fast for all of us. For the first time since I moved, my parents decided it was time to come for a visit. Carly had come to see me a couple of times, but they had never made the trip back to Ontario. Now, apparently, a trip was needed. I was thrilled, and I knew it was because of Jenny—and I was good with that.

Goodbyes were tearful, and Jenny sniffled into a tissue on the plane. I wrapped my arm around her shoulder and pulled her close.

"We'll go back next year, Wren. They're going to come visit in the spring."

"That's so far away."

I chuckled. "I've waited a long time for that visit. It's only a few months. I guarantee you Carly will be calling you with flight times for a visit much sooner."

That brightened her up. She and my sister had gotten along well.

"Good." She wiped her eyes. "Your family is great."

"Yeah," I agreed. "They are pretty cool." I met her gaze. "They're your family now too, you know."

Her eyes lit, bright and happy. "Then I'm the luckiest girl in the world."

I kissed her. "I'm feeling pretty damn lucky myself."

CONNOR

Thank God it was Friday. In the weeks since we'd returned from my parents', the days had been long, the nights and weekends too short, and time had flown by as I studied hard. Now, I was off until after the Christmas holidays, and I was looking forward to the break and spending some quality time with Jenny—and inside her.

It didn't matter how often we made out like teenagers, fucked like rabbits, or made love—it wasn't enough. I'd never get enough of her. I knew from the day she first smiled at me and let me take her hand, she was it for me. I waited, and when I finally could show her, tell her how I felt, my life changed and only for the better.

My hand closed around the small box in my pocket.

Tonight, I planned to show her exactly how much she had changed it.

I sighed in contentment. My head rested on Jenny's lap, her hand rhythmically stroking through my hair as we sat in the darkness, the only light in the room the soft glow of the Christmas tree in the corner. I loved those quiet moments with her when it was just the two of us alone. Her eyes were unfocused as she gazed at the tree, a soft smile on her lips while she played with my hair. She sipped her wine, glancing down at me.

"Hey," she teased, "I thought you were asleep."

I stroked her cheek with my thumb. "I was watching you, Wren." I smiled up at her. "You are so pretty, my girl."

I felt the heat under my hand and grinned. She never failed to react to my words.

"Stop it," she admonished, setting down her glass.

I pulled her face down, meeting her partway, nuzzling her lips with mine. She tasted of wine, the chocolate she was nibbling, and Jenny. Perfect. Lazily, our tongues met as her fingers buried themselves in my hair, and she whimpered quietly as the kiss deepened. She told me once kissing me was her favorite thing in the world. It was my job to make her happy, so who was I to deny Jenny her favorite thing? Besides, it was my favorite thing as well. Slowly and thoroughly I explored her, savoring her sweetness. Finally, I tempered the kiss, softening my mouth to gentle, indulgent sweeps of my lips before pulling back and smiling at her.

Now this, *this* was my favorite look for Jenny. Her cheeks lightly flushed, lips swollen, hair mussed up from my hands—and the look in her eyes. Love, want, and desire, and she directed them all at me—always for me. I knew mine reflected the same back at her. She was it for me.

Abruptly, I sat up and pulled Jenny onto my lap, cupping her face. "I love you."

Her hand covered mine. "I love you too." She frowned at the expression on my face. "Connor, what is it? What's wrong?"

I shook my head. "Nothing is wrong. Everything is right. You make everything right, Wren." I kissed her. "You always make everything so right."

Her expression was soft as she gazed at me.

I drew in a deep breath. "I want you to make it right…" I swallowed. "For the rest of our lives."

"Connor…" she breathed.

"I know we've only been together a short time and living together for a few months. But, baby, you're it for me. I know it. I *feel* it. I don't ever want to be without you."

"You won't be."

"I'm not rich, but I promise to give you everything you didn't have growing up. You'll never be alone. You'll never feel unwanted or wishing for a home and security. You'll have that. You'll have me."

I lifted her hand and kissed the palm, pressing the small box into it. "Marry me, Jenny. Make me the happiest man on earth and say yes."

A tiny sound escaped her mouth as she stared in shock at the box. Her tear-filled eyes met mine.

"Please," I murmured. "I need to know I have you forever. I want to wake up to you every morning and know you're here, at the end of the day, waiting for me." I kissed her. "I want your smiles and laughter. I want all those thoughts you can't keep inside your head. I want to be there for you when you need me. I want a life, children, with you." I paused and cupped her face. "Please be mine."

"Yes," she whispered.

I took the box and opened it for her, removing the ring from its velvet bed. "It was my grandmother's," I explained as I slipped it on her finger. "My mom gave it to me to give to you."

The simple solitaire set in filigreed white gold twinkled in the light. "It's so beautiful."

"So are you."

I wiped the tears from her cheek and sealed our engagement with a kiss to her ring then to her lips. She wound her arms around my neck, and I pulled her against me. Standing, I lifted her and carried her to our room. Laying her on the bed, I smiled at her as I tucked a stray curl behind her ear.

"I love you, Wren."

She opened her arms, pulling me down to her. "I love you, Connor."

I kissed her with all I had and held her close.

I would be eternally grateful for the day she mistook my door for hers.

Her bad day changed my life for the better.

Because she became mine, forever.

EPILOGUE

CONNOR

THREE YEARS LATER

I stood on the sidewalk, admiring the small Cape Cod-style house. Flowers lined the sidewalk, making it bright and cheery. A porch swing sat to the right, piled with pillows, beckoning you to sit and have a cold drink, rest a spell and relax. The creamy white paint was fresh, and the shutters and trim painted a cheerful blue.

The color of my eyes, Jenny said.

I was still struck every time I saw it. That it was ours. That inside, waiting, was my family.

My Jenny Wren, and as of two and half months ago, my little Robyn.

I hurried up the steps, anxious to see my girls. Inside, music was playing, the soft beat echoing off the walls. I could hear Jenny singing, and I followed the sound to the kitchen. I stopped in the doorway, leaning on the frame, taking in the sight before me.

Jenny was leaning against the counter, singing to our daughter. My little girl, tiny and perfect, was in her carrier, staring up at her mommy, transfixed. She always did when Jenny sang. I crossed my arms, grinning. It was one of Jenny's made-up songs. A frog in a log jumping high to the sky —funny little lines that made no sense but rhymed and made my daughter happy.

"I know you're there," Jenny sang, peeking over her shoulder. "I can feel your stare."

I stepped forward, wrapping my arms around her waist and leaning on her shoulder. I smiled down at Robyn, her blue eyes, so like mine, staring up at us. "How are my girls?" I murmured.

Jenny turned her head and kissed my cheek. "Good now you're home."

"Home for four days," I murmured happily. "Four days of us time."

"Yay!" Jenny cooed, bending close to Robyn. "Four days Mommy can sleep in!"

I laughed, knowing Jenny was teasing, although I planned on making sure she did get in some extra sleep time.

I nipped her neck then reached into the carrier, lifting Robyn out and cuddling her to my chest as Jenny stirred something on the stove.

"Something smells good."

"I made a pot of potato soup, and I baked some muffins earlier. Robyn and I had a good day. We went for a walk, sat in the park and had coffee with Jackey, and I even got a nap."

"Wow. You did have a good day."

The first month after Robyn was born was a huge adjustment for us. She was a good baby, but she apparently felt the nights were made for playtime and cuddles, not sleeping. Both Jenny and I looked like the walking dead by week three, and I was worried about returning to work and how Jenny was going to be able to cope with a baby and only a nap or two during the day to get by. Then my mom came for a visit, and somehow, by the end of the week she spent with us, Robyn's schedule had changed, and she was sleeping for almost six hours every night. The difference in Jenny was remarkable. As soon as Robyn was down for the night, so was Jenny. And when our daughter would nap, Jenny did too, and slowly a new routine evolved.

Jenny met my eyes, hers warm and happy. "She slept for seven hours last night. Seven hours of uninterrupted sleep. Then after I fed her, she went back to sleep for two more hours. And a whole hour nap today—twice. I had a nap this afternoon, and this morning I had a shower, sat on the sofa, actually read a little of my book, and drank a cup of coffee—while it was hot, Connor. Hot coffee. Has it always tasted that good?"

I laughed, nuzzling Robyn's head. "You've been a good girl for Mommy."

Jenny laughed and leaned up, pressing a kiss to my mouth, then one to

Robyn's head. "Maybe you'll have a good night." She winked lewdly. "If Daddy works his magic, you never know what will happen."

I grinned. Robyn liked her baths, and I liked being the one to give them to her. My mom had shown me the trick of some lavender in the water to soothe and relax her, and then I gave her a little baby massage, talking quietly with the lights dim, followed by her last feeding, and hopefully, sleep.

And tonight, maybe, some alone time with Mommy. My body tightened at the thought.

It had been a while since that happened. We'd gotten the green light a few weeks ago, but Jenny was so tired and stressed, sex was the last thing on her mind. I had missed her, missed us, and if she was feeling better, I was happy to accommodate.

More than happy.

We had dinner, Robyn in her carrier, happy to gaze around, gurgling and kicking her feet. I told Jenny about the new schedule I had been given today at the lab. "Revolving days off. Three on and four off as usual. But every month, the day we start changes, which means, even as low man on the ladder, I'll get weekends eventually." Right now, all my days off were Tuesday to Friday. My days were long—twelve-hour shifts, six a.m. to six p.m., but then I had four days with my family, which I loved.

She grinned. "That is awesome."

I returned her smile. "It is."

I stood, taking Robyn. "You go relax. I'll take care of the munchkin." I bent and kissed Jenny, and she slid her hand around my neck, holding me close, kissing me back with ardor. I eased back, my breath short.

"Hold that thought."

"I'll meet you in our room," she replied.

I walked out of the kitchen a little faster than I needed to.

I'd bathed Robyn, given her a massage, a final feeding, and a fresh diaper, then rocked her to sleep. I tucked her in, peaceful and happy, and stood, looking down at her. She was perfect and precious, and I loved our nighttime routine. It was our chance to connect after a day apart, and I enjoyed every minute of it.

But tonight, my wife was waiting.

I padded down the hall after a hot shower, a towel draped around my waist. My body was tight with anticipation, my erection already kicking up and ready.

I slipped into our room and stopped.

Jenny was draped across our bed, wearing only one of my T-shirts, her hair down, looking sexy and alluring.

And sound asleep.

So asleep, she was snoring.

My lust dissipated as I watched her slumber, tenderness and love replacing the burning desire. She'd been so amazing, running on next to no sleep so I could get a few hours before heading to work. She needed to catch up.

I dropped the towel and slid in beside her. I wrapped my arm around her, tugging her to my chest. She roused slightly, nuzzling into my chest.

"Ready to go, big man?" she slurred out, lifting her hand to caress my face and missing it completely. "Give me two minutes—I'm right with you."

I tried not to laugh as she began to snore again.

I kissed her forehead. "Later, Jenny Wren. Sleep."

The monitor blinked beside me, and Robyn gurgled in her sleep. My wife's sounds were louder, but somehow just as comforting and endearing.

My family was safe and content.

Tomorrow, I would spend the day with them and make sure Jenny got lots of extra sleep. After dinner, we would re-establish our connection. By then, Jenny would be raring to go and eager.

Maybe I would make another house arrest.

It worked out rather well last time.

With that thought in my head, I joined my family in sleep.

ACKNOWLEDGMENTS

As usual, a few thanks.

As always, Lisa, thank you I learned something new, but I cannot guarantee I will retain it—just saying.

Melissa, Deb and Barbara—thank you for your feedback and support.
Your comments make the story better—always.

Karen, I love you. Simple and true. Thank you.

To all the bloggers, readers, and my promo team. Thank you for everything you do. Shouting your love of books—of my work, posting, sharing—your recommendations keep my TBR list full, and the support you have shown me is deeply appreciated.

Many thanks to the organizers of the anthologies these stories were once part of before they grew for this book. Skye Warren, Jennifer & Morgan Locklear, and Amy Marie—I was honored to work with you.

My reader group, Melanie's Minions—love you all.

ALSO BY MELANIE MORELAND

Vested Interest Series

BAM - The Beginning (Prequel)

Bentley (Vested Interest #1)

Aiden (Vested Interest #2)

Maddox (Vested Interest #3)

Reid (Vested Interest #4)

Van (Vested Interest #5)

Halton (Vested Interest #6)

Sandy (Vested Interest #7)

Insta-Spark Collection

It Started with a Kiss

Christmas Sugar

An Instant Connection

An Unexpected Gift

The Contract Series

The Contract (The Contract #1)

The Baby Clause (The Contract #2)

The Amendment (The Contract #3)

Mission Cove

The Summer of Us Book 1

Standalones

Into the Storm

Beneath the Scars

Over the Fence

My Image of You (Random House/Loveswept)

Revved to the Maxx

Happily Ever After Collection

ABOUT THE AUTHOR

NYT/WSJ/USAT international bestselling author Melanie Moreland, lives a happy and content life in a quiet area of Ontario with her beloved husband of thirty-plus years and their rescue cat, Amber. Nothing means more to her than her friends and family, and she cherishes every moment spent with them.

While seriously addicted to coffee, and highly challenged with all things computer-related and technical, she relishes baking, cooking, and trying new recipes for people to sample. She loves to throw dinner parties, and enjoys traveling, here and abroad, but finds coming home is always the best part of any trip.

Melanie loves stories, especially paired with a good wine, and enjoys skydiving (free falling over a fleck of dust) extreme snowboarding (falling down stairs) and piloting her own helicopter (tripping over her own feet.) She's learned happily ever afters, even bumpy ones, are all in how you tell the story.

Melanie is represented by Flavia Viotti at Bookcase Literary Agency. For any questions regarding subsidiary or translation rights please contact her at flavia@bookcaseagency.com

Connect with Melanie

Like reader groups? Lots of fun and giveaways! Check it out Melanie Moreland's Minions

Join my newsletter for up-to-date news, sales, book announcements and excerpts (no spam). Click here to sign up Melanie Moreland's newsletter

or visit https://bit.ly/MMorelandNewsletter

Visit my website www.melaniemoreland.com

facebook.com/authormoreland

twitter.com/morelandmelanie

instagram.com/morelandmelanie

Made in the USA
Monee, IL
08 August 2020